THE WORLD TURNED
UPSIDE DOWN

The World Turned Upside Down

EMMA L. PATTERSON

LONGMANS, GREEN AND CO.

NEW YORK · LONDON · TORONTO

1953

LONGMANS, GREEN AND CO., INC.
55 FIFTH AVENUE, NEW YORK 3

LONGMANS, GREEN AND CO., LTD.
6 & 7 CLIFFORD STREET, LONDON W 1

LONGMANS, GREEN AND CO.
215 VICTORIA STREET, TORONTO 1

THE WORLD TURNED UPSIDE DOWN

FIRST EDITION

LIBRARY OF CONGRESS CATALOG CARD NUMBER 52-12699

Printed in the United States of America

THE WORLD TURNED
UPSIDE DOWN

☆ 1 ☆

"HEAR YE! HEAR YE!" BAWLED THE TOWN CRIER, STRIDING along the street of Peekskill. "News from the Continental Congress! The colonies have declared their independence. A copy of this declaration will be read before the tavern directly."

The crier's hand bell resumed its clangor as he passed down the street. Housewives, shopkeepers, and children emerged from their doorways and began trooping toward the tavern with an excited babble.

Dirk Hollenbeck stood beside an ox team looking on. He was a tall young man of eighteen with a big muscular frame. His broad face was serious, with a shallow cleft in the square-cut chin and well-set eyes of an intense blue. His thick yellow hair was drawn back into a tight pigtail. He wore a stout smock dyed butternut brown and a pair of leathern breeches.

When the town crier passed, Dirk and the ox team had just emerged from a lane that led to Stroup's grist mill. In the oxcart lay a dozen bags of flour newly ground and atop the load rode his younger brother, Peter, a chubby towhead of three.

"What say you, Peter?" asked Dirk, looking back. "Shall we go to the tavern and hear what all this shouting is about?"

Peter replied by smiling cherubically, as he usually did whenever Dirk looked in his direction, so it scarcely constituted an answer to the question. Dirk took it for an affirmative, however. With a loud "Gee!" he turned the oxen up the street.

In the inn yard about a score of people had gathered. Dirk halted the oxen on the outskirts of the group. Elias Phinn was standing before the tavern entrance with the sticks poised over his snare drum. When a leather-booted stranger appeared in the doorway wiping his mouth, Elias began to beat his drum. The noise rolled out in long rattling waves. It seemed to be winding a spring inside Dirk's body. Tighter and tighter it was drawn until Dirk felt that he must do something violent at once. Then, just when the tension had become almost unendurable, the noise reached a crescendo and stopped abruptly. In the stunning silence, Dirk let out his breath.

With an air of importance, the stranger drew forth a cylinder of foolscap from his knapsack and unrolled it.

"In Congress, July 4, 1776," he read. "The unanimous Declaration of the thirteen united States of America."

He paused to harrumph impressively. Dirk's mind was slowly turning over those last words — United States of America. They sounded right. He liked them. Then the courier's strident voice launched into the body of the declaration.

"When in the Course of human events, it becomes necessary for one people to dissolve the political bands which have connected them with another — "

From the oxcart, Peter began to pipe noisily that he could not see the "talker." Dirk swept him up hastily to a perch of vantage on his shoulder.

The messenger was now reading: "We hold these truths to be self-evident, that all men are created equal, that they are endowed by their Creator with certain unalienable Rights, that among these are Life, Liberty and the pursuit of Happiness."

The strident voice went on, but Dirk's attention reverted to one clause — "that all men are created equal." What a false and ridiculous statement! Why, the world was full of proof that it was wrong. But he must not dwell upon this point and miss all the rest of the matter.

He focused his thoughts once more upon the reading. The argument now, as nearly as he could comprehend it, ran thus: that it was the business of government to guarantee to people these "unalienable rights" but that the King of Great Britain had not done this; that he had, on the contrary, sought to establish an absolute tyranny over the colonies. There followed a long list of accusations against him to establish this point.

Here the attention of the listeners began to waver. They shifted their feet in the gravel of the yard and exchanged low-voiced remarks. Dirk strained his ears in a vain effort to hear. At length the courier paused, cleared his throat, and spat over the foot scraper on the doorstep. It was evident from his manner that he had reached a climax in the document. The chattering stopped. He resumed in a more impressive tone.

"We, therefore, the Representatives of the United States of America, in General Congress, Assembled, appealing to the Supreme Judge of the world for the rectitude of our intentions, do, in the Name, and by the Authority of the good People of these Colonies, solemnly publish and declare, That these United Colonies are, and of Right ought to be, Free and Independent States."

Some abortive cheers broke out from the listeners, obscuring the reader's voice. By the time they had been silenced, he had reached the last sentence.

"And for the support of this Declaration, with a firm reliance on the protection of divine Providence, we mutually pledge to each other our Lives, our Fortunes and our sacred Honor."

The cheers broke out now, unrestrained. A foxskin cap was tossed into the air. Several felt hats followed. Someone fired a musket.

"This calls fer drinks," an old man chirped in a cracked voice.

Henry Mandeville, the innkeeper, appeared at the tavern door. "One round on the house," he shouted.

This announcement received a far greater ovation than had the declaration itself. With a roar of delight, most of the men began trooping into the inn. The women called to their children and drifted homeward. Dirk noticed that most of them wore a troubled expression.

"They don't understand this any better than I do," he said to himself.

A few people lingered to watch the courier tack up the declaration on the wall beside the inn door. Some stepped close and read phrases aloud, proud to display their learning. An old man with a cane tottered away muttering to himself and shaking his head dolefully.

"Well, young sir, what say you? Shall we go?" asked Dirk playfully of the boy on his shoulder.

Receiving a grunt of assent, he tossed the child back upon the flour sacks and shouted at the oxen. They began to proceed slowly southward, back through the town, toward home. The cart trundled along on its two solid wooden wheels, its customary rattles muted by the soft weight of the grain. The little boy soon fell asleep, lying sprawled upon his back with one arm flung above his head. Dirk took his accustomed position slightly in advance of the team and modified his pace to their slow stolid gait. There were four miles to go, and they would take two hours for it.

It did not occur to Dirk to feel impatience at this tiresome journey. The nature of oxen was to be slow, and one accepted it. Besides, on this particular occasion, he rather welcomed the opportunity to think over what he had just heard.

Of course, the whole argument had been the most arrant nonsense. Take that first statement again — that all men were created equal. Why, by such reasoning, Dirk could call himself equal to the lord of the manor on which he was a farm hand — equal to Mr. Roderick Stone, no less. Obviously, nothing could be farther from the fact.

Not that Dirk resented Mr. Stone's being his master. Quite the contrary. He felt for him only the deepest gratitude and loyalty, for had not Mr. Stone supported Dirk and his brother and sister during the two years since their father had died? It was true that their father had been killed while in Roderick Stone's employ, gored by a bull on the Stone estate, Riverbrink, and for that reason Mr. Stone had said that he felt an obligation toward the dead man's family. But this, after all, only proved his real kindness of heart. He was not bound by law to help them.

It was true also that Dirk was now doing a man's work on the estate, that if Mr. Stone had lost money on the Hollenbecks for a few years, he was gaining it back now. Of course, Dirk could not yet fill his father's place as manager of the manor farm. But that, too, might come. Mr. Stone had hinted as much.

Two miles below Peekskill, a road branched westward, and a crude signboard stated that this led to the King's Ferry. Here the oxen turned of their own accord and quickened their pace. It was as if they knew that they were now on their master's property. Though narrow, the road was well-traveled, for it led to the most important ferry crossing on the Hudson. It was a pleasant road, overhung with great trees and bordered by small farms, all occupied by tenants of the manor.

The King's Ferry crossed the river between Verplanck's Point on the east bank and Stony Point on the west. The road Dirk was following emerged rather abruptly on the eastern terminal, which was not (as one might have expected) at the extreme end of the Point nearest the opposite shore, but was, instead, in a cove on the southern side of the Point where the ferry could make a sheltered landing even when the river was rough. Here the highway ended in a wooden platform that sloped down into the water. Opposite the landing stood the ferryman's house.

The oxen continued without pause past the ferry terminal and into a graveled lane that led up a hill northwestward across the Point toward the manor house. Dirk lingered a moment, gazing out over the inlet and across the river. The sun had dropped behind the hills of the opposite shore. A few clouds overhead were beginning to take on a pink tinge. There would be a nice sunset. The river was glassy except where some cross current gave its surface a contrasting texture. No craft was in sight except the ferry, just rounding the end of the Point, a scow propelled by two men with long oars. Dirk took a deep breath of the cool river air before he turned away.

The oxcart was out of sight. He quickened his step and overtook it beyond the crest of the hill. They continued along the lane, which sloped upward again between neatly cut hayfields for nearly a quarter of a mile until they reached the grounds of the manor house. At the entrance stood the cottage where the Hollenbecks lived. This was a low-eaved, one-room structure that served both as tenant house and gate-house for the estate. Dirk halted the team and lifted the sleeping child from the cart.

As he approached the cottage with his burden, his fourteen-year-old sister, Christina, looked out of the top half of the Dutch door. She had heavy flaxen hair like her brother's. It was plaited in two braids. And her eyes were the same vivid blue. But there was more gaiety in her expression, and indeed her mood was a merry one. This Dirk could never understand, for the girl had known little but sorrow, toil, and loneliness since her mother's death at the time Peter was born three years before. A year later, their father had also died. Dirk had tried to take all the burden of grief and responsibility upon himself, to make Christina feel loved and secure always. He liked to think that this had been at least partly the cause of her gaiety. But probably she simply had a sunny nature.

Now she looked with pretended curiosity upon Dirk's armload and inquired playfully, "What is this that you have brought from town, kind sir?"

"A juicy little pig for roasting," Dirk answered, handing Peter to his sister through the top part of the door.

"It looks to be already roasted," she remarked, pressing her lips against the child's flushed cheek.

"Most likely," Dirk agreed. "It needs basting with a little soapy water."

They both laughed at this and the child stirred sleepily, nuzzling his face against Christina's shoulder.

8

"Any news from town?" she asked.

"The greatest. But I've no time to tell you properly now. Wait until I come for supper."

Dirk ran after the oxen and caught up with them as they were attempting to draw the cart into the narrow stable door. He maneuvered the team up onto the threshing floor where he left the cart to be unloaded in the morning. Then he hurried down to the cow stable. Jedediah Pike had already started milking. He rolled a reproving eye at Dirk from his perch beneath a cow's belly.

"Got hanging around the tavern, I s'pose," he remarked with an attempt at irony.

"Yes, I did," Dirk admitted, picking up a wooden pail and stool.

"You did!" Pike raised up in astonishment and stared over the back of a cow. He was a tall, stooped man of middle age with a lantern jaw. In his mouth he carried a straw on which he sucked perpetually.

Dirk sat down and began milking before he explained briefly what had happened at the tavern.

Pike was silent a moment. "All this cheerin' and hurrahin'," he said. "You didn't join in with it?"

"No."

"That's right. You just lay low. Wait and see how the cat's goin' t' jump. Them that cheer today may find a halter 'round their necks tomorrow."

There was much more in the same vein. Dirk thought it was probably very shrewd advice, but, with the phrases of that declaration ringing in his ears, he found this attitude niggardly and unworthy. Did he want his own life to be like Jedediah Pike's? he wondered. Did he want always to choose what was safe rather than what was right? Was there no cause in life for which a man, a real man, would take a bold risk? The signers of that declaration had thought so.

It was dark in the stable when they had finished milking, but outside the sky was still bright. Jedediah carried two buckets of milk to put in the springhouse behind the great house. Dirk had a wooden pitcherful to take to his own cottage. They separated and Pike moved off across the vegetable garden, his lank, stooped figure outlined against the red sky. He lived a short way along the King's Ferry Road and would have to walk home after delivering the milk to the manor house.

At the cottage, Christina had dragged the trestle table up near the doorway so that they could eat their supper without a candle. Three bowls of mush were set out in a row and Peter was already seated on the bench flourishing a little wooden spoon and kicking his legs under his long nightgown. While Dirk washed, Christina poured some of the milk he had brought into the bowls. Then they all fell to eating and for a time there was no sound but the busy click of wooden spoons against wooden bowls.

As he ate, Dirk glanced occasionally out of the door where the grounds of Riverbrink lay spread before him. Between the cottage and the back of the great house was a large flower garden, riotous with color all season. To the right of the cottage lay the farm buildings. They had been constructed where the land fell sharply away so that the second floors, consisting of the hayloft and coach house, were level with and facing on the garden, while the stable floors beneath faced outward away from the manor house and grounds. The great house itself stood on a bluff looking northwestward over the river. Dirk's eyes dwelt on its tall chimneys outlined against the evening sky.

Before Peter was quite finished with his supper, his head began to nod. Without ceremony, Christina shoved the last spoonfuls into his mouth and packed him into the big bed in the corner.

"Now for the news," she reminded Dirk as she replenished his bowl.

"Well, the Continental Congress has announced that the colonies are independent of England."

"Oh, is that all?" Christina's face fell. "I thought it would be real news — about somebody I knew."

Dirk laughed. "The news isn't big enough, eh?"

"I guess I don't understand it," Christina confessed. "What does it mean?"

Dirk paused to consider. "I'm not sure I know myself," he admitted. "It means war, I suppose."

"But there is war already, isn't there?" Christina demanded. "At Boston."

"Yes, but this means that all the other colonies will stand behind Boston."

"And the war will come right here?" Alarm leaped to

Christina's eyes. She slid along the bench until her shoulder touched Dirk's arm.

"No, no, of course the war won't come here," he assured her, sliding his arm protectively across her shoulders.

He looked around at the familiar darkening room, then through the door at the silhouette of the manor house. It seemed indeed an absurd girlish fantasy that war could touch this peaceful scene. He chuckled and, after a moment, Christina joined in rather shakily.

"No, Tina dear, war doesn't come rampaging into people's houses and chase little girls under the bed, you know," he explained with mock condescension. "War comes only to men who go out looking for it."

"Ah, but that's what you'll do!" cried Christina. "You'll go out to the war and that will be just as bad."

Dirk's head came up sharply as he was gripped by a sudden memory of Elias Phinn's drum. To march to that sound! To march away with a gun over his shoulder! To see far-off places and to have a part in great events!

He was recalled by a tug at his arm. "Promise me you won't do that."

Dirk looked down into Christina's anxious face and smiled reassuringly. What a foolish dream! Honor might compel other men to go to war, but it would keep him tamely at home supporting his family.

"Never fear, Tina," he said. "I'll not go out to war. Why, there isn't the least danger of it. I don't even know which side to join."

Across their laughter, they caught the sound of a raucous blast blown on a ram's horn. It was the signal that someone from the cottage was wanted at the great house. At this time of day, it usually meant that Aunt Lina, the cook, had some tidbit to give them from the Stone's dinner table. She had started this practice when the Hollenbeck family first lost their mother, giving them then at least one full meal a day. As Christina had grown older, however, she had gradually been able to take over more and more of the cooking until now there was only an occasional gift from the manor-house kitchen.

"I'll go!" cried Christina, springing up. "Oh, I do hope it's huckleberry muffins." And she scurried out.

But in a moment she returned empty-handed.

"Mr. Stone wants you to go over and tell him about the news you heard this afternoon," she panted. "And no muffins in sight."

Dirk slung his legs over the bench. "I can't go in this dirty smock," he said. Stripping it off, he began to rummage in an oak chest.

"Your clean smocks are up in the loft," Christina reminded him.

"I thought I'd put on a coat — that good one of Pa's," said Dirk. "My own is threadbare."

Christina found it for him, a brown homespun smelling strongly of camphor. It was much too tight across Dirk's shoulders and too short in the arms.

"You need a shirt under it," advised Christina.

13

"There's no room for a shirt," Dirk objected. "But my bare neck does look odd. If we had a stock — "

Christina knelt again beside the chest and fumbled about, at length producing a white stock yellowed with age.

"It will appear well enough by candlelight," she assured him as she wound it around his neck. "Now you look just like the gentry."

There was a lovely gloaming light on the garden as Dirk followed the footpath across it. But he could not pause to enjoy it, for his mind was consumed by thoughts of the coming encounter. Here was an unexpected chance to meet Miss Ellen! That was the reason for the coat and stock, though Christina had not guessed it. How should she, indeed, he thought bitterly. How should anyone guess that a farm hand would be so bold and so foolish as to raise his eyes to the very mistress of the manor, the daughter of the lord himself? He hitched his shoulders in the tight coat and hurried on.

Aunt Lina sat beside the kitchen door, her feet in a tub of water. With a word of greeting, Dirk circled around her dark bulk and stepped into the kitchen. It was hot, although the fire in the huge fireplace was nearly out. At the trestle table, two girls were washing dishes.

"Where's Mr. Stone?" asked Dirk.

When they turned and looked at him, he knew for sure that the coat and stock were a mistake. Molly stared and Thirza burst into laughter.

"Look what we have here!" she chortled. "One of the

master's dinner guests, no doubt! You're too late, *sir*. They're having their wine."

Even Caleb, the young Negro butler, grinned when he looked at Dirk.

Feeling his face redden, Dirk walked self-consciously across the room and through a door into the front hallway. Here he paused and fingered his stock nervously, then moved forward, his thick-soled shoes clumping across the polished floor. Candles burned in sconces around the white-paneled wall. The great central chandelier had not been lighted so that the stairs curved upward into deepening gloom. Dirk stepped to the open front doors and stood looking out into the fragrant night. Before his eyes could adjust to the darkness and see the river sparkling far below, Mr. Stone's voice called him from the dining room.

"Come here, boy."

Dirk moved to the dining room and bobbed his head in a clumsy, perfunctory bow. There were three people seated at the table — Mr. Roderick Stone, his daughter Ellen, and a suitor of hers named Gerit Van Wyck from a distant manor. Glasses of wine stood on the table before them. Mr. Stone was a smallish man with a narrow, high-bred face. His expression was chronically stern and worried. He fixed Dirk with a frowning glance.

"I am displeased, boy, that you did not come at once to me with this news. I had to learn of it from a maid, who was told by the cook, who heard it, I believe, from the farmer."

"I'm sorry, sir. I meant no disrespect. I thought you might not be especially interested."

"Not interested!" Roderick Stone gripped the arms of his chair.

Miss Ellen laid her hand quietly upon his. "Now, Father, you know what happens when you get angry after a meal," she remonstrated.

Dirk let himself look at her. She was turned away from him in speaking to her father, and he could get only a rapid impression of a shining golden gown with her shoulders rising smoothly above it and into the soft curve of her neck. Her hair was a dusky cloud drawn back from her face to the crown of her head and falling in a cascade of curls to her nape.

"Well, well," said Roderick Stone, controlling himself with an evident effort, "we'll overlook all that. Tell me about this document that was read. What exactly was it?"

"They called it a declaration of independence, sir. It was gotten out by the representatives in the Continental Congress."

"Representatives!" Mr. Stone seized upon the word. "That rabble of blackguards doesn't represent me."

"Nor me either, sir."

It was Gerit Van Wyck speaking. He was a handsome young man, Dirk had to admit to himself. The total impression he gave was one of compactness, self-sufficiency. He had a smallish head and features so regular as to be almost pretty. His hair was a close-set helmet of chestnut curls, his tiny ears laid neatly back. He wore a claret-colored coat with lace cuffs falling well over the backs of his hands. At sight of them, Dirk swung his own arms behind him, clasping one exposed wrist with the other hand.

Mr. Stone had resumed his comments. "No, that body in Philadelphia does not at all represent the great bulk of the propertied class in these colonies."

It crossed Dirk's mind that no one had considered for an instant whether he himself was represented in the Continental Congress. Of course he did not deserve to be; he had no property. But then, had not the declaration said . . . ?

Suddenly he found himself speaking without having been addressed. "Sir, there was one statement in this declaration that — that I remember. It said, 'All men are created equal.'"

Young Van Wyck laughed. He looked straight at Dirk and laughed as though it were insupportably funny that this farm hand before him should be called his equal. Dirk's face grew hot. The stock began to choke him.

"Well!" exclaimed Mr. Stone. "Upon my soul!" He did not look amused, only indignant. "Here, by heaven, you have a clear example of how these men appeal to the lower classes, telling them they are our equals indeed!"

"A palpably absurd statement," Van Wyck agreed.

"And yet," continued Stone, "it may have its effect. It is a very dangerous doctrine. If it actually arouses the peasantry, we shall have a civil war on our hands. It will take all the resources of the mother country to help us put down our own servants."

17

Dirk had never felt so thoroughly uncomfortable in his life as these words made him. A servant, in a sense, he might be, though he had always thought of himself as a tenant farmer. But "lower classes" and "peasantry" — these were terms that he resented bitterly. And as for that curly-headed young turkey cock who had the insolence to laugh in his face, he would show him where to find his equal, yes, his better, in a fight. Dirk swung his clenched hands before him and took a step toward where Van Wyck was sitting.

Then he thought of Miss Ellen and paused. She was looking at him. The expression in her dark eyes was reserved, but kindly. If she had been laughing too! Dirk dropped his fists and drew back.

"Father, you sent for Dirk to ask him about that document," she said gently, "but now that he is here, you launch into a political speech and give him no chance to tell you."

"What? Oh, yes, yes." Roderick Stone cleared his throat nervously and took a sip of wine. "The boy can well profit from what I have said." He fixed a frowning gaze upon Dirk. "Are you persuaded, boy, from hearing this declaration read, that all men *are* equal?"

"No, sir. It looks to me as though it's just the contrary," Dirk replied.

"Quite right, boy. Men are not equal, and shouting from the housetops that they are will not make them so. As a practical man, I tell you. Disregard the mouthings of these rebels. Your interests are the same as mine. If the men of wealth and property in this country are ruined, the — uh — the working

18

people will go down with them. The whole fabric of society will be destroyed. Do you see that this is true?"

Dirk stood a moment with lowered head before he replied. "Sir, I know nothing of politics. It may all be as you say. What I do know is that I — and my family — owe you a debt that I cannot repay in a lifetime of service. Whatever I may be persuaded are my rights, I could never lift a hand against you, sir."

There was a small silence.

"I stand rebuked," confessed Stone with a wry smile, reaching out to twist the stem of his wine glass. "While I prate of material advantage like a petty tradesman, you speak of honor like a gentleman."

Van Wyck stirred impatiently. "Perhaps, sir, we are making too much of this matter," he suggested. "Your servant here has no very clear idea of what it is about. Should we not suspend judgment until we have an opportunity to study the document for ourselves?"

"It is posted beside the inn door," offered Dirk.

"So? That is excellent. Perhaps we could all take a canter up to the village tomorrow morning and see it." Van Wyck looked inquiringly toward the two others.

"Not I," Stone declared at once. "I'll not be seen acknowledging the existence of that document. You two may go if you wish."

Van Wyck looked toward Miss Ellen and made a graceful inclination of the body which asked her pleasure.

"It would be amusing," she agreed.

"We'll not need you further, then, Dirk," said Mr. Stone. "Thank you for coming."

At last Dirk was out in the cool dark night again, running across the garden and jerking at his throat to remove the stock. At first it tightened with a strangling tension. Then suddenly the rotten fabric gave way and he was holding the two strands. He stripped off the coat and conquered an impulse to fling them both away. Never again would he try to play the fine gentleman.

The cottage was dark and quiet. Christina had gone to bed. Dirk tiptoed across the floor and climbed to the loft. The air here was close and warm. He dragged his straw pallet to the window in the south gable where a light breeze was blowing in. But he was too excited for sleep.

"We hold these truths to be self-evident, that all men are created equal."

Dirk considered this again. He ought now to dismiss it from his mind. Mr. Stone had told him — what he himself knew — that it was nonsense. And yet — and yet — something within him responded to it, told him it had a profound meaning. It was the same "something," no doubt, that made him resent being called a peasant and made him feel that his manhood was the equal of Gerit Van Wyck's, gentleman though the latter might be. As for Miss Ellen, well, he didn't feel equal to her but he wanted to. If he believed for one instant that these so-called fanatics in Philadelphia could make true their contention about equality by winning the war, he would join them gladly.

But wait! He could not do that. Had he not assured Mr. Stone that he would never take arms against him? Surely he could not prove himself the equal of the Stones by showing such ingratitude and disloyalty.

Dirk tossed upon the pallet. It would be best to forget the whole hopeless business. He closed his eyes. His big body slowly relaxed, drifting toward slumber. The face of Ellen Stone, dark-eyed, smiling, swam before his half-conscious mind. Impatiently he roused himself to dismiss the vision. Perhaps he could concentrate on that declaration instead. How did the words go? He could not remember the beginning at all. Take the end. Those words had impressed him. He pushed back slumber until he recalled them.

"And for the support of this Declaration, with a firm reliance on the protection of divine Providence, we mutually pledge to each other our Lives, our Fortunes and our sacred Honor."

☆ 2 ☆

Miss Ellen and Van Wyck made their trip to town the next day and came back greatly reassured. The document, they said, was obviously the product of impractical fanatics. It was addressed to no one in particular and was so defiant of the King that it must incite him to make a maximum effort against the colonial forces. This could only end in an early defeat for the rebels.

So they reasoned and continued their accustomed ways. Van Wyck finished his visit in a few days and returned to his own manor in North Castle. It was rumored that he and Miss Ellen were betrothed. This news, although quite the expected thing, filled Dirk with a great heaviness of spirit. Not that he had ever for an instant believed that she could belong to him. But he dreaded the time when she would no longer live at Riverbrink, when he could not at least catch a glimpse of her every day and at most accompany her on a horseback ride.

The days droned past at Riverbrink, full of work and summer heat and monotony. July drifted into August and Dirk, immersed in farm work, almost forgot that there was a war.

His chief reminder was a neighbor youth named Samuel Higgins. The war was Sam's consuming interest and he was determined to join up in some capacity. As he was sixteen years old, this would not have been difficult except that his father was sternly opposed. In the local militia himself, Sam's father felt that he was thereby fulfilling the military obligations of the family. He would not even let Sam attend the drilling of the militia in Peekskill. Sam's only recourse was to go to the village as often as possible and glean all the news of the war. Then he would hurry to Riverbrink to talk it over with Dirk.

Throughout the summer, news was scarce, consisting mostly of rumor and local Whig-Tory differences. Then, in the last days of August, came exciting tidings. The British had arrived in New York Harbor. There had been a battle on Long Island and the Americans had saved themselves from annihilation only by a precipitate retreat to New York. When Sam heard this, he was in despair. He sought out Dirk, who was picking apples in the north orchard.

"The whole war will be over before I can join up," he grumbled. "Why can't our Colonials hold on a while till a fellow can get there?"

Sam's dark, thin face was tense with excitement. He seized an apple out of the barrel that Dirk was filling and cracked out a large bite.

"If the Colonials are to be beaten so quickly, I should think you'd be glad you weren't mixed up with them," remarked Dirk with quiet reasonableness.

He began climbing back up the ladder into an apple tree.

"But don't you see? If enough men like me went into it now, we could stop those redcoats."

Dirk smiled quietly at Sam's calling himself a man. The boy was small for his age, yet he had the tough, resilient frame and combative spirit that made the best kind of soldier. Dirk did not doubt that enough "men" like Sam Higgins might stop the British army, but he hoped there would not be enough. Better to end this futile struggle before hundreds more became involved.

He said something to this effect, but Sam retorted indignantly, "You're talking just like Old Tory Stone."

"What do you know of Mr. Stone's opinions?" Dirk demanded.

Holding the apple in his teeth, Sam scrambled up the tree and perched himself on a limb opposite to where Dirk was picking.

"Only what the whole town knows. He talks very freely up at the tavern, he and Dr. Huggerford."

"A man has a right to think as he pleases," Dirk declared.

"If he thinks like Old Tory Stone, he'd better keep still about it," remarked Sam. "Some day Old Stone's going to find himself straddle of a rail."

Dirk was considerably disturbed. He felt that he ought to warn Mr. Stone, yet he dreaded to. It would seem presumptuous for him to advise the lord of the manor. Besides, Dirk was sure a warning would do no good. Mr. Stone was not a man to be frightened by threats.

24

Then, too, Dirk was concerned for himself. If he should remain loyal to Mr. Stone, he must expect to suffer the same fate. This he felt he would be willing to do if he could be quite sure that Mr. Stone's beliefs were the right ones. A hundred times he reasoned the matter through and every time his common sense told him Mr. Stone's arguments were sound. Yet something deeper than reason argued silently within Dirk's heart that the rebel cause was his cause.

For several days, Dirk debated speaking to Mr. Stone. Then he was spared the necessity, at least temporarily, by the departure of the master and Miss Ellen for their ancestral estate, Stonehaven, in the central part of the county. This trip was an annual affair. They usually stayed there a month or two, visiting Mr. Stone's mother.

This year there had been some question about the advisability of Miss Ellen's going, since there was no knowing how far north the war might range. The British had occupied New York City and the Continental army was hovering around the northern end of York Island. Mr. Stone was quite sure the war would come no farther north.

"Those rebels have got themselves into another trap," he asserted, "the same as they did on Long Island. And Howe will see to it that they don't make another lucky escape. He'll surround them and annihilate them right there."

Having reached this conclusion, Roderick Stone decided that it was safe to take his daughter with him. So, in the latter part of September, they left in the family coach with Jedediah Pike driving. Two days later Pike returned on horseback, reporting that the countryside was quiet.

For a fortnight there was little news. Then returning militiamen and civilian refugees reported that the American forces were withdrawing hastily into the southern part of Westchester County. Again they had slipped out of their trap but the British were in close pursuit. Dirk began to worry a little about Miss Ellen's safety. How near were the armies to Stonehaven?

One afternoon late in October, Dirk and Jedediah Pike were behind the barn dressing a couple of beeves they had butchered the day before. The weather was cold and cloudy with a threat of rain. Suddenly Christina appeared, a gray shawl over her head, and announced that the ferryman's little girl had come up with a message left for delivery to Riverbrink by a man who had just taken the ferry. It was from Mr. Stone and requested that Pike ride to Stonehaven at once with an extra horse to take Miss Ellen back home.

"I'm not going," Jedediah stated flatly. "It's too dangerous. Why, I hear tell there's a battle on right now at White Plains, and — "

"I'll go," said Dirk quietly. He tried to keep from showing his elation at the prospect.

"Oh, Dirk, if it's dangerous — " Christina began.

"Not at all," he assured her. "The truth is that Mr. Pike objects to such a long horseback ride."

Taking his cue from Dirk, Jedediah corroborated this statement.

Dirk would have liked to leave at once and ride all night,

but as he did not know the way, he might become lost after dark. Besides, Christina and Jedediah would both wonder at such eagerness. So instead, that evening, he made his preparations for the trip.

He considered taking his father's musket, which he used for small game, but it would be awkward to carry, especially on the way down with two fractious horses to manage. Besides, if it should rain, the powder would get wet, making the gun useless. He finally decided upon a sword and got one of Mr. Stone's from the great house. It was a gentleman's weapon and he did not know how to use it, but it would look impressive.

The next morning he awoke to the sound of a torrential downpour thundering upon the roof. Christina was already up and had a fire snapping in the grate. For breakfast, besides the usual bread and milk, she fried some sausage and wrapped what was left in a napkin with some bread and two apples for Dirk to eat en route. He packed this luncheon into a saddlebag along with a leather jerkin.

During all their preparations, Christina's eyes dwelt lingeringly upon Dirk, but she did not urge him to stay home nor cling to him unduly when he kissed her good-by. Peter, who had slept until Dirk was on the point of departure, sat up in the great bed and howled at being left behind.

The horses, at the outset of the journey, were all but unmanageable. Neither had been exercised sufficiently since the departure of the master and mistress so that they were full of high spirits. Besides this, the deluge of rain confused

27

and frightened them. Dirk rode Mr. Stone's black gelding named Prince and led Miss Ellen's mare, Star, a handsome bay. He had strapped a blanket over Miss Ellen's side saddle to protect it from the storm, but the effort was futile.

The rain pelted down in a cold lashing fury. It streamed into Dirk's eyes and down his neck. His thick, rusty great-coat was a long time wetting through but it grew heavier and heavier with all the water it absorbed. On top of it was the unaccustomed weight of the sword. Dirk had not been out in the downpour an hour before he was soaked to the skin with runnels of icy water coursing down his chest and back.

For the first few miles the horses were skittish, but the rain soon dampened their spirits in a very literal sense. They re-signed themselves to slogging along, trying to find a safe footing in the slippery ruts and puddles. At the post road, Dirk turned north and traveled into Peekskill where he swung eastward to Crompond. This was not the most direct route but it avoided a ferry crossing over the Croton River. From Crompond he turned south and crossed the Croton by Pine's Bridge.

So far, the roads had been deserted. But below Pine's Bridge, Dirk began to meet occasional small groups of riders, whom he judged to be militiamen or soldiers of the Continental army. Most of them paid little attention to him. Farther southward foot soldiers began to appear, straggling along the road. They looked upon Dirk's extra horse with covetous eyes. Once Dirk pulled off to a side lane to let a troop of infantrymen come through. One bedraggled fellow with his feet bound in rags spied Star although Dirk had drawn her up on the opposite side of Prince.

"Look, Lieutenant," he called back to a mounted man at the rear. "Here's a party that's got an extra horse. How about commandeering it?"

The officer pulled up beside Dirk. His face was scarcely visible between a hat pulled low and the folds of a military cape. "Where are you going with this mare?" he demanded.

Dirk drew himself up tall and looked out over the officer's head. "I have my orders," he said with a quiet finality.

"I'm asking what your orders are," the lieutenant insisted, raising his voice.

Two or three men paused in the mud to listen. Water dripped from the lieutenant's tricorn hat as he waited.

"I'm sorry, sir," said Dirk at length, "but I cannot tell you my orders. As you can see, I am going toward the army and taking an extra horse. Would you prevent re-enforcements from reaching the troops?"

A husky crow of laughter broke out. "He's got the right of it," said an infantryman. "We're the ones going in the wrong direction."

The lieutenant turned from Dirk and brandished his riding crop at the speaker. "Get on with you," he roared. "You've had no orders to halt."

Without another word to Dirk, he reined his horse back into the road and began bellowing at a few stragglers. In a moment the entire troop had sloshed past. Dirk let his breath out in a whistling sigh as he continued on his way.

29

In this drenched sunless world there were no means of telling the time of day, but Dirk's stomach gave him notice when the lunch hour came around. The rain had not abated, however, and he pressed on until he came to a deserted farm. The windows of the house gaped emptily and the barn door hung ajar on one hinge. Dirk guided his horses along a grass-grown track and into the barn. The sudden cessation of rain pelting upon his body gave him an odd feeling of buoyancy. The barn seemed so dry, so quiet, with its wide threshing floor and empty haymows stretching to either side.

Dirk dismounted stiffly and interchanged the two saddles, thinking as he did so how fortunate it was that he had strapped a blanket over Miss Ellen's. The lieutenant might well have questioned the Colonial army's need of a side saddle.

While finishing his bait of sausage and bread, Dirk saw through the crack of the door two men trudging along the grassy track toward the barn. Both carried guns. Dirk sprang across the floor and untied the horses from one of the pillars of the haymow. When the men entered, he was approaching them leading the horses. They paused in astonishment.

"We-ell!" exclaimed the foremost, a thin chap with a red muffler wound about his neck. "Looka here, Abe. Dummed if we ain't caught a horse thief red-handed!"

"Shore enough," agreed the other delightedly, slatting the water out of his eyes.

"Get out of my way," growled Dirk.

"Looks like he's a-goin' to resist," said the man with the muffler. "You take the horses, Abe. I'll stand him off."

And drawing back a step, he leveled his musket upon Dirk. Though Dirk was reasonably sure that the gun was too wet to fire, still the sight of that muzzle trained upon him sent a prickly sensation across his neck. Shifting both sets of reins to his left hand, he seized the musket by the barrel and flung it squarely at its owner's face. The man caught the blow on a upraised arm and toppled backward.

Meanwhile the other one had edged around Dirk and was setting his toe into Star's stirrup. With a hoarse exclamation, Dirk advanced upon him, fumbling for his sword. He drew it and brandished it awkwardly. The man's eyes goggled at the gleaming blade. He scrambled down from the horse, making little whimpering noises in his throat.

Dirk dragged the horses through the door and mounted Star. The mufflered man looked out of the door but made no move to follow him. Back on the highway, he struggled to get the sword into its sheath. Then he was plodding along once again under the beat of the cold rain. If he were not mounted on Star instead of Prince, he might have thought the violent interlude in the barn had been an illusion, although there was a quivering along his muscles that told of the tension they had been under.

It was shortly before nightfall when Dirk reached Stonehaven. He recognized it at once from Pike's description — a big house with a gambrel roof standing near a crossroad. A row of sunflowers against the weathered shingles of the wall drooped in sodden arcs. The building was much older than the house at Riverbrink and a contrast in architecture to that classic pillared mansion.

As Dirk and his two weary horses slogged into the driveway of Stonehaven, a boy with a square of canvas thrown over his head hurried out from a side door. Under one arm he carried a musket.

Accosting Dirk, he demanded, "What's your business here?"

"Why, I've come for Miss Ellen," said Dirk, surprised and offended by this welcome.

"Oh, very well. The stable's on beyond."

The boy ran back toward the house and Dirk continued along the driveway to the stable. It was dark inside. He stood at the heads of the two horses, mopping the water from his face. A man appeared from another room and eyed Dirk sharply. Again, as with the boy, Dirk was aware of fear and hostility in the man's bearing.

"I came for Miss Ellen," he explained. "My name is Dirk Hollenbeck."

"Ah, yes, of course. We were looking for Mr. Pike."

The man appeared friendly enough now. He advanced and took Prince's leading strap from Dirk. He was middle-aged, of average height, heavily muscled, with a mane of coarse gray hair worn loose that flowed back on his head in perfect waves. His features were somewhat too rugged to be handsome but they gave an effect of nobility. Dirk decided this must be Matthew East, overseer of the Stonehaven estate.

"What is the reason, sir, for this suspicion of me?" asked Dirk. "I was met at the gate by a boy with a gun."

East's jaw set in a stern line. "We have learned by hard experience to suspect everyone we don't know," he replied. "A week ago the Colonials stole all our horses but one. That is why Mr. Stone sent for you to bring down a horse for Miss Ellen."

"You mean the Continental army raided your stables?"

"Oh, they had a fancy name for what they were doing. 'Commandeered' the beasts, they said. What are the odds? Theft is theft. Next time they come, they are going to have to risk their lives for whatever they get."

Dirk swung the saddlebags from Star's back and began to unsaddle her. The clumsy topcoat hampered him. He took off the sword and tried vainly to peel the sodden coat from his arms.

East sprang to help him. "Good lack, boy, you're soaked to the skin!" he exclaimed. "You must go to my cottage and put on dry clothes."

"I'll rub down the horses first," said Dirk.

"No, I'll take care of them. Get along with you. You can see the cottage from in front of the barn."

East's cottage was in a secluded part of the grounds beyond the manor house, hidden from the road by a grove of trees. Mrs. East, in crisp white apron and mob cap, opened the door to Dirk's knock.

"I'm from Riverbrink," he began to explain, but after one glance at his drenched figure, she drew him inside.

"You poor boy! Come right in here by the fire and take off those wet clothes. I'll bring you some of Matthew's to put on."

For the first time Dirk became aware that he was shivering violently. He stumbled to the fire and began tugging off his wet clothing. Mrs. East came back with some garments on her arm and a rough towel. Then she left him before the fire. He stripped and rubbed his skin with the towel until he was warmly atingle. The dry clothes were a ridiculous fit but he donned them gratefully. The shoes, however, were hopelessly small. When Mrs. East returned, he was trying to crowd his feet back into his own wet ones.

"Let your shoes dry at the fire," she said. "You won't need them until you go out again."

"I must go back to the stable," Dirk muttered, continuing to tug at the shoes. "Must see to the horses, grease the leather before it gets stiff."

"Matthew will tend to all that," said Mrs. East soothingly. "You are to roll in a blanket and lie on the bed until you are thoroughly warm."

Dirk tried to protest that there was no time for this, but a lassitude had begun to steal over him.

"You must keep up your strength for the trip back," she urged.

At this reminder, he let her lead him to the bedroom. An instant later he had fallen into soft, warm oblivion.

34

☆ 3 ☆

EARLIER IN THE AFTERNOON OF THAT DAY, ELLEN STONE stood at the living-room window and watched the rain lash in long slanting streaks across the lawn and driveway outside. Sometimes a gust of wind would fling a mass of water against the small square panes, making her draw back instinctively. As soon as the glass cleared, she would step back and gaze out once more, her vivid lips pursed in annoyance. She stood very straight, proudly carrying her dark head with its smooth coiffure. Her flowered chintz gown, looped over a yellow quilted petticoat, made a bright note in the shadowy room.

"Is it raining, Ellen?" demanded her grandmother's quavering voice.

The girl faced into the room where the fireplace made a reddish glow. Here sat the old woman in her high-backed chair. She wore a voluminous black alpaca dress in which the contours of her shriveled little body were entirely lost. A white fichu was drawn about her shoulders and a little lace bonnet was tied under her chin.

Ellen crossed to the old lady's side. "Yes, Grandmother, it's raining very hard," she shouted. Then to her father, she added in a normal tone, "Mr. Pike will never venture out in this weather."

Roderick Stone was half-reclining in the depths of a wing chair, his feet propped on a hassock. He was suffering from one of his periodic attacks of severe pain in the stomach. He sat with eyes closed, his face gray and drawn.

"No, Pike won't come today," he agreed. "Perhaps it is as well. I begin to wonder if you would not be safer here than on the road. The King's troops may move in soon and then you need not leave at all."

"Perhaps Gerit is among them!" exclaimed Ellen with a sudden thought. "Do you think he is in the King's army by now?"

"Let's see. He left a fortnight ago. Yes, he may well be a commissioned officer by this time but I doubt that he is in battle yet. More likely he's in the city trying to recruit a company."

Ellen paused to imagine Gerit in the gaudy red uniform of the British officer with a cockaded hat and a sword. Such an outfit would become him.

She became aware that her father was speaking. " — a highly suitable young man, of your own social rank, with considerable property. I am sorry you couldn't find it in your heart to give Van Wyck a little more encouragement."

"Well, I didn't exactly discourage him, Father. I like him, really, very much. It's just that I don't feel I know him well enough to — to marry him."

Roderick Stone laid a thin, dry hand upon his daughter's.

36

"No doubt you acted wisely in putting the boy off," he said. "Pay no heed to what I say when I'm ill like this. It is only that I worry over who would look after you should I be taken away."

Ellen perched on the arm of her father's chair. "Is the pain so very bad now?" she asked, drawing her hand gently along his cheek.

"Quite," he admitted. "Perhaps if I could have a good bloodletting, it might be relieved."

"You're the one who should go back to Riverbrink," Ellen declared with sudden conviction, "back to your own doctor."

"No, I must stay with your grandmother."

"Eh? What's that?" cried the old lady who, deaf though she was, had an uncanny knack of hearing any reference to herself.

"I was saying, Mother, that I would not go back to River-brink," shouted Stone.

"Riverbrink!" exclaimed Mrs. Stone. "Of course I'll not go there. No one must go. We'd be scalped in our beds, likely."

For the old lady, the existing conflict was a mere continuation of the French and Indian War. And Riverbrink she considered an outpost deep in the wilderness.

"I can't see why you're moping to get back there anyhow, Ellen. There's plenty to do here. Why don't you read something? Read to me. I'd like to hear some Shakespeare."

Ellen looked toward her father who seconded the suggestion.

"Which play shall it be?" she asked, stepping to the bookcase.

"*The Tempest* would be most appropriate," Mr. Stone answered. "And you might as well sit near a window where you can see. Your grandmother won't be able to hear you anyhow."

"I can hear every word!" snapped the old lady.

Ellen took a chair beside a window and began to read in a low-pitched, pleasant voice, glancing up occasionally at the torrent outside. The shipwreck scene passed rapidly. In the next, Prospero and Miranda came forth to gaze upon the storm at sea. Ellen read Miranda's first words.

> *"If by your art, my dearest father, you have*
> *Put the wild waters in this roar, allay them."*

She turned to smile at her father over the aptness of these lines. But he sat with closed eyes, his thin lips drawn downward.

Ellen soon became absorbed in the drama. Miranda had her first sight of a young man from the world of mortals and fell in love with him at once. In vain did her father try to convince her that, as mortals went, this man was ordinary.

> *"My affections*
> *Are then most humble: I have no ambition*
> *To see a goodlier man."*

As Ellen read Miranda's lines, some movement out of doors caught her eye and she looked up. A tall man was riding past in the driveway, his bare yellow head bent to the storm. He wore a sword buckled to his waist and led a black

38

horse by a strap. All this Ellen noted before she realized who it was.

"Why, Father!" she exclaimed, springing to her feet. "It's Dirk Hollenbeck. He's come to take me back to Riverbrink."

"That boy, instead of Pike! Well — you'll not go back to Riverbrink with him."

"But, Father, Dirk is much stronger than Pike, yes, and more courageous, too. Oh, please don't say I can't go. At least, don't make a decision now."

"Very well. It will be best to rest the horses tomorrow anyhow."

That evening Mr. Stone sent for Dirk. Ellen was not present at this interview, but her father told her the boy had reported his only trouble had been in keeping possession of the extra horse. Mr. Stone thought this not too serious a matter. His greatest concern was over what turn the battle at White Plains might have taken. All seemed quiet now to the south. The sound of cannonading had ceased. It appeared as favorable a time for traveling as they were likely to get. Ellen would be safer at Riverbrink once she arrived, and the risks on the road did not seem great. He decided to let her go.

The second day after Dirk's arrival, Ellen and he prepared to return. It was a dull, warmish day. Since the roads would be a welter of mire, Ellen was obliged to wear a rain cape over her handsome maroon riding habit. She stepped forth from the house on her father's arm.

Dirk, standing on the driveway with the two horses, smiled up eagerly at Ellen. He wore a leather jerkin over his woolen shirt. The greatcoat was strapped to his saddlebag. It crossed Ellen's mind that Dirk was a striking figure of a man.

Roderick Stone kissed his daughter and helped her into the saddle. Then he stepped to Dirk's side and handed him a silver-mounted pistol.

"Try to keep out of trouble," he said, "but use this if you get into it."

"Thank you, sir. I've got this sword. Shall I leave it?"

"No. Take them both. If it would insure her safety, I'd hang a whole arsenal on you. Remember, boy," — Stone tapped on Dirk's arm for emphasis — "take no unnecessary risks. Your one job is to get Miss Ellen home safely. I'm depending on you."

Dirk's wide-set eyes returned Stone's glance with a level intensity. "I'll do my best, sir," he promised.

Stone stepped back. "Very well, then. Go," he said.

Dirk handed Ellen her reins and then swung onto Prince's back. The two horses sprang forward. Ellen turned to smile and wave at her father. He raised an arm in response, but for as long as she could see his face, it remained grave and brooding.

Out on the road, Star broke at once into a canter. Ellen let her run, for her own mood was one of release, release from an atmosphere of old age and sickness. She had not been aware how much her spirits had been depressed until now that they could break free.

Dirk came up with her. "Better hold Star in, ma'am," he cautioned. "She could throw herself in one of these mudholes."

Ellen pulled her horse up, but she was irked by the advice. This solemn Dutchman was going to be a tiresome companion now that her father had so impressed him with the need for caution. She stole a glance at him. That sword was ridiculous. One could tell just from the awkward way he wore it that he would not know how to use it.

Ellen recalled the line she had been reading just as Dirk arrived, that she "had no ambition to see a goodlier man." How odd that she should have been saying this at just that time! But of course it was not in the least true. Her heart was set upon a far goodlier man, one who could wear a sword with an air, yes, and use it with skill. If only it were Gerit with her now, what a gay adventure they would make of this. Then Ellen remembered her situation and had the grace to be ashamed of her thoughts, for had not Dirk braved the most forbidding weather to come after her? And here she was feeling peevish because his company was rather dull.

As they neared the main road, they noticed a party of horsemen approaching from the south.

"We'd best wait for them to pass," Dirk decided, and they pulled up their horses.

"Do you think they're rebel soldiers?" asked Ellen.

41

"No doubt of it, ma'am."

"Then they're retreating! They've lost the battle."

"It may be." Dirk's narrowed eyes studied the little group. "But they're in no hurry. If the British were behind them, they'd be pushing their horses faster, I think."

Before this party was quite out of sight, another group appeared in the road to the southward. These men were slogging along on foot.

"We'd best get ahead of them," Dirk decided.

Ellen thought all these precautions to avoid people a little foolish, but she said nothing. To her it was inconceivable that this shabby little army in flight should concern itself with the affairs of a lady and her servant.

They pushed out to the main road and turned north. Around the first bend, they overtook another group of foot soldiers. On their approach, the group separated, leaving a passage through. Most of the men dragged forward with heads down, but one boy, his arm in a grimy sling, looked up at Ellen.

"Well, blast my eyes, it's a lady!" he exclaimed in astonishment. "Say, ain't she a beauty!"

At this, every eye was turned upon Ellen and there was a general outcry of delight.

"Ma'am, got room fer me up there?"

"Treat you to a drink at the next tavern, lady."

"Give us a ride on your horse, ma'am? It's muddy down here."

With flaming cheeks and gaze set rigidly ahead, Ellen

urged her horse forward and soon had drawn away from the soldiers. After a moment Dirk rode up beside her.

"It looks as if their whole army's on the move," he said uneasily. "Maybe we'd best turn back."

"Are you afraid?" she challenged.

"No, ma'am, but I want to do what's safest for you. Your father, I think, would want us to turn back."

"If he were here, he would never have let those men say such things to me," said Ellen abruptly.

They rode some distance before Dirk spoke. "What would you have had me do, ma'am?" he asked gently. "If I had tried to fight that whole squad, I would have got beaten up or taken prisoner. That would have left you without any protection."

Dirk's broad face was flushed, his eyes fixed upon her with a troubled, appealing expression.

"Besides, Miss Ellen, they didn't really mean any offence. It was just their way of admiring you."

"You're right, of course. I'm sorry I spoke as I did."

"But this or worse may happen again, ma'am," Dirk warned, "and I do think your father would want us to return."

"I'm not going to," Ellen declared. "I want to go home and a parcel of rude soldiers isn't going to prevent me."

They rode a long way, then, in silence. Ellen found herself even more disturbed than she had at first realized. She was all aquiver inside. She told herself impatiently that nothing much had happened. A few men had shouted at her rudely. That was all. Why, to a servant girl such remarks would have meant nothing. Such a person might even have taken them as compliments. But this thought did not console her. She had thought that a lady like herself was innately superior and entitled to respect as a matter of course. Now it appeared that a lady was merely an accident of circumstance.

It was Ellen, thereafter, more than Dirk who wished to avoid encountering people on the road, but it was impossible to do so. There were hundreds of men plodding northward, most of them in rags. Some wore no shoes, their bare feet caked with mud. Others of the shoeless had their feet wrapped in filthy rags. Many wore tattered blankets over their shoulders. Their weapons were equally nondescript, ranging from a few long-barreled rifles through muskets, pistols, and swords to blunderbusses and even pitchforks. Sometimes a party of mounted men, presumably officers, would whirl past with a great thumping and splashing of hoofs. When this occurred, everyone, including Ellen and Dirk, hustled for the ditches. These officers were better dressed than the foot soldiers but many of them were in civilian clothes.

As Ellen and Dirk rode through a dark wood, they came up with a string of wagons carrying wounded soldiers. The men were laid in rows on the wagon boxes, some groaning, others lying as though dead. Over the whole area in which this train moved there hung a nauseating odor of decay. Even after they had advanced far ahead, Ellen could not get the smell out of her nostrils nor the sight of those miserable men out of her mind.

At noontime they reached The Golden Pheasant, a tavern where the Stones had always stopped for rest and refreshment on their journeys between the two manors. Dirk dismounted and was handing Ellen down when a red-headed youth wearing a greasy apron popped forth from the inn.

"Ain't no room here," he announced abruptly. "Full of army officers."

"But tell Mr. Barlow it's Miss Stone," protested Ellen.

"He seen you," the young man replied brusquely. "He says to tell you the tavern's full."

On the road once more, Ellen could scarcely keep back her anger. This rebuff on top of her hunger and weariness was almost too much. Memories of previous visits to The Golden Pheasant flooded her mind. Mr. Barlow with a profusion of bows and smiles, handing her out of the coach. Mrs. Barlow, with rheumatic curtsies, showing her from room to room so that she might have her choice. And now they did not so much as come to the door to turn her away.

"At the next place," she said to Dirk, "you will go in first and ask whether it will please them to admit me."

They found accommodations at last in a shabby little house run by the Widow Plummer. She prepared and served the meal in the one main room of the cottage, setting up two places at the end of a long table. It was evident that she expected Dirk and Ellen to dine together, and such was

Ellen's disturbed state of mind that she accepted this arrangement without protest. In the past few hours, Dirk had come to seem someone more important than a servant, more of a guardian. When he returned from the stable, he paused in the doorway, his great shoulders nearly filling its frame. At a glance he noted the situation.

"I believe I'd like to eat from the mantel shelf," he said. "I've been in the saddle so long it would be a relief to stand up for a while."

The Widow Plummer looked mildly surprised, but ordered her daughter, Hannah, to transfer his dishes. The girl, a skinny, unattractive creature, was so obviously put in a flutter by the presence of Dirk that she gave only half her attention to the duty of serving the vegetable soup and omelette. To Ellen, this was just another surprising incident in a most upsetting day, for she herself was accustomed to being the center of attraction, and, having removed her rain cape, she sat resplendent in her maroon riding habit and plumed hat, only to be outshone by her servant wearing a leather jerkin too short in the sleeves.

Ellen picked up her wooden spoon and dipped it into her wooden bowl of soup. Never before had she eaten with such crude utensils. They were clumsy, but she soon adapted herself to their use; she was hungry.

Meanwhile Dirk was inquiring of the Widow Plummer what she knew about the outcome of the battle at White Plains. Like everyone else, she said, she had heard widely varying stories, but the night before, some soldiers who had

46

slept in her barn had reported that the battle had been inconclusive and that both armies were withdrawing from the field.

"Where are these Colonial troops going?" Dirk asked.

"They don't seem to know," was the widow's reply. "Some think to Peekskill. Some think they're going up to cross at the King's Ferry."

Dirk looked across the room at Ellen.

"It seems we're out of the frying pan into the fire," she remarked.

"Do you want to go back?" Dirk asked.

"Gracious, no!" she replied. "At least, this way we're going with the current."

When they plunged once more into the stream of travelers, it seemed to Ellen that they had been forging along like this for days. She was somewhat accustomed now to the astonished stares and even to the rude remarks. These things had become more endurable because now she understood the men better. As Dirk had tried to tell her, they did not mean any malice or even disrespect. They were only expressing, though crudely, their admiration. And she pitied them for their miserable condition.

It was just falling dusk when they turned off the King's Ferry Road and wound up the driveway with the chimneys and gables of Riverbrink looming into the red-stained sky ahead. Never had the sight been so welcome to Ellen's eyes. The horses, though tired, broke into a canter and they pulled up before the white-pillared porch with a flourish. Dirk gave a shout to announce their arrival, then dismounted and handed Ellen down to the horse block.

An instant later, the great double doors were burst open and servants were hurrying down the steps to welcome their mistress. The sight of the curtsies and the bustling attendant upon her arrival went far to restore Ellen's spirits. She was swept into the house and placed before the fire while Aunt Lina came in to ask her instructions for dinner. Here, at least, Ellen thought, she was still mistress of a great manor, obeyed, respected and cherished by all. She began to feel like her old self and wondered at the misgivings she had experienced during the day. In this restored mood, she went to bed and lay cozily watching the play of firelight on the ceiling. All around stood the familiar details of her own room and overhead the blue tester of her bed arched in protection. She was at home, utterly safe, and everything was as it had always been.

But when she closed her eyes, at once she was on the road again, passing, passing, endlessly passing lines of plodding men. Repeatedly, they would fall behind only to reappear up forward, be overtaken, and fall behind once more. It was as if she and Star were on a treadmill. Once she glimpsed, as though down a long, long vista, her father's upraised arm and grave face. Had it been only that morning that he had kissed her and put her on her horse? It seemed years ago and worlds away. She could never go back to that time again.

What had happened? Nothing and everything. She had had a glimpse of the real world. Intuitively she knew that it was real and the world she had been living in was artificial and, now it seemed, unstable. This real world was vast and bleak, full of people in tatters who stared rudely at her, not seeming to realize that a lady should command their respect. It was as though they considered themselves her equal. Suddenly her body went rigid in the bed as some lines from that rebel document flashed into her mind.

"We hold these truths to be self-evident [*self-evident,* no less] that all men are created equal."

Yes, they believed that. It was their creed. It did not even, in their opinion, need to be proved. And now they were ready to suffer anything in defense of this belief — to go in tatters, hungry, homeless, wounded, to risk death.

For the first time, a terrifying premonition entered her mind. Was it possible that the royal army would be defeated? They had superior armaments. But these rebels had a stupendous conviction. Did the King's forces cherish any beliefs to correspond with that? She thought of the royal soldier that she knew best. Was there any belief under heaven for which Gerit Van Wyck would be willing to go in tatters? She doubted it.

Nervous tremors began to tug at her. This was all foolishness, she told herself, letting her thoughts run away with her like this. Why, tomorrow in daylight she could laugh at such fears. In fact, right now she had only to open her eyes and the sight of her familiar surroundings would restore her sense of balance.

She opened her eyes upon total darkness; the fire had gone

49

out. As soon as she closed them, she was on the road once more, her body swaying to the motion of the horse, and again the plodding men filed along beside her, gradually falling behind and inevitably reappearing up ahead.

☆ 4 ☆

For nearly a fortnight after Dirk had returned home with Miss Ellen the American army continued to straggle past on the highway and cross the river by the King's Ferry. General Washington was taking them to New Jersey for the winter. Rowboats, galleys, barges, and scows were assembled to transport them. It was a stupendous task. Dirk watched from the edge of the Riverbrink property. There were about ten thousand men to be carried, besides their horses, artillery, and supplies. Day and night the boats plied back and forth amid a confusion of hoarsely shouted commands.

Every night a large number of men still awaiting transportation were obliged to camp on the eastern shore. This troubled Dirk as there was always the danger that some of them would walk the quarter mile up to Riverbrink. He patrolled the grounds until late at night carrying his father's gun. It was a great relief when the last of this ragged army had been ferried over the river and life went back to normal again. Dirk was expressing this relief to Sam Higgins a day or so afterward when the latter interrupted him.

51

"You're not rid of soldiers around these parts, though, Dirk. They're thick up to Peekskill. Settling in for the winter, too. You just ought to see them."

Dirk remarked that he wouldn't care if he never saw another soldier. As it happened, however, only a few days later, he had to take some broken harness to the village for mending and Sam went along. The two boys struck off across the fields, Sam carrying the harness and Dirk with Peter mounted upon his shoulder. It was a crisp sunny day in mid-November.

The village was indeed an armed camp. Sam hurried eagerly a few steps in advance, pointing out "our barracks," "our powder magazine," "our general's headquarters," and "our parade ground." Scores of soldiers lounged about the street and dragoons clattered past on horseback.

One freckled youth with a bright red cockade in his hat called out to Dirk, "Hey, there, Dutchman, come on and join up. We need a few your size."

Dirk looked around, too startled to reply.

But Sam was equal to the occasion, "Ah, what's your hurry?" he tossed back. "Can't you wait till the boy gets his growth?"

Dirk felt no desire to join up. The men he found here were, for the most part, the same scarecrows he had seen on the road and at the ferry. Even the permanent camp they were making on Oak Hill was a jerry-built affair of tents, mud huts, and a few log shelters. All of this made a soldier's life seem to him one of discomfort and futility.

Yet there was one instant when he felt different about it. They were in Peekskill village and Sam was pointing out the general's headquarters. Suddenly from behind the building swept a squad of horsemen in smart blue-gray uniforms with shiny black leather boots and plumed helmets. At the corner they wheeled with one impulse like a flock of birds and thundered southward. Peter drummed his feet against Dirk's chest and squealed with delight. Sam stood looking down the road long after the dragoons had disappeared.

"What wouldn't I give!" he murmured wistfully. "What wouldn't I give!"

Dirk did not have to ask Sam what he meant. At that moment he knew very well.

On leaving the harness shop, they separated, Sam to go to the tavern for war news, Dirk and Peter to return home. The two had reached the lower end of town and were just about to cut across the fields, when a yellow coach rumbled up. The door swung open, and seated inside was Roderick Stone.

"Get in, boy," he commanded, not unkindly.

He motioned Dirk to the seat opposite his. Dirk lifted Peter inside. The child perched stiffly with legs outthrust and one hand gripping Dirk's sleeve.

"Is all well at Riverbrink?" Mr. Stone demanded at once.

"Yes, sir," Dirk replied.

"Good! Good! I have been well-nigh out of my mind with worry ever since I learned that I had let my daughter go out into the very midst of the rebel army."

53

"She was not harmed, sir," Dirk assured him.

"Ah, thank God! You did well to bring her through that villainous rabble in safety, boy."

Dirk was pleased at this praise but found himself resenting such a reference to the American army. A rabble, perhaps, they had been, but surely not villainous.

He changed the subject. "I would gladly have gone down for you, sir."

"It was not necessary. A gentleman who lives on a neighboring manor had sent his family up to Fishkill, for safety during the battle at the White Plains. Now that the danger is over, he is sending his coach up to take them back home and has allowed me to ride up in it. We will keep it overnight at Riverbrink."

"Then it is safe down there now, sir?"

"Oh, utterly quiet. The dangerous ground now is up here. I came back to protect my daughter and to consult my doctor."

Mr. Stone did look ill, Dirk thought. His face was gray and drawn.

"Shall I go and get the doctor at once, sir?" Dirk offered.

"No. He will bleed me, no doubt, and that is temporarily weakening. I am well-nigh exhausted now with this bone-racking ride. I'll rest tonight and send for him later on."

Dirk thought that the coach did seem most uncomfortable. He had never ridden inside one before but had always thought them luxurious with their cushioned seats and handsomely lined interiors. Now he found that this one at least

54

seemed stuffy with a slightly musty smell. Besides that, it swayed, pitched, and jolted. He would have preferred to be out in the fresh air on horseback. He wondered whether the gentry were so enviable after all.

"Did you encounter any trouble on your way back the other day?" asked Mr. Stone.

Dirk hesitated only an instant. "No, sir, nothing very serious," he replied.

His big hands gripped his knees as the memory of that homeward journey flowed over him. He could never forget his feeling of helpless rage when those men had started making rude remarks to Miss Ellen. How he had longed to strike out at them with his fists, to show them — yes, and Miss Ellen, too — that he was prepared to protect her against all comers. Thank heaven, he had had sense enough to restrain himself. They would have overpowered him if it took the whole squad to do it. Instead of showing her how brave and strong he was, the first thing he would have shown would have been that he was no fit escort for a lady.

Dirk hoped that Mr. Stone would not ask for any details of that trip home. There seemed little danger of his doing so, for he appeared to have lost interest in the conversation. He sat with one hand pressed against his midriff and his face bore a withdrawn and unhappy expression.

"Are you suffering now, sir?" asked Dirk timidly.

"I have pain nearly all the time of late," said Mr. Stone, "except for an hour or two after meals — a nagging, gnawing pain. I believe I shall send you for the doctor in the morning."

When he set out the next day, riding Prince, Dirk did not go directly to the doctor's house east of Peekskill. First he rode through the village, looking at each hitching post for the familiar dappled gray mare that the old physician always rode. Sure enough, there it was tied before Mandeville's Tavern.

Dirk looped Prince's bridle to the rail and walked around to the rear of the building. Here Mrs. Mandeville and one of her servant girls, Hannah Higgins, were seated on the back steps picking chickens. Between them stood a bucket of scalding water in which they occasionally immersed the fowls. On the steam that arose into the crisp morning air was the flat odor of wet feathers.

Hannah was Sam Higgins' sister, a strong, buxom girl of twenty with a plain but healthy-looking face.

"Well, Dirk Hollenbeck, what brings you to the tavern so early in the day?" she inquired with heavy playfulness. "None but gentlemen can afford to tipple at this hour."

When Dirk explained his errand, Mrs. Mandeville replied, "Ay, the doctor's in there right enough, hobnobbing with one of his Tory friends."

"Why does Mr. Mandeville let him come here, madam?" asked Hannah. "People don't like it. Some say they won't come here themselves if he's allowed."

"Well, my husband doesn't like to put the old gentleman out. He's been respected for years."

"There'll be trouble, though, ma'am, if he keeps on coming. He'll anger some of the army officers and they'll arrest him — or worse."

"It's the business of the Committee of Safety to make all arrests of civilians," said Mrs. Mandeville.

"The Committee of Safety?" Dirk repeated. "I never heard of them."

"You will, never fear," remarked Hannah in a knowing manner. "They're out to get all Tories and either send them packing or put them in jail."

The girl's glance challenged Dirk to declare his own allegiance. He shifted his feet uncomfortably and averted his eyes.

"Colonel Van Cortlandt is head of the Committee," said Mrs. Mandeville.

"Who needs a doctor at Riverbrink?" asked Hannah abruptly.

"Mr. Stone."

Hannah sniffed. "He's another one will hear from the Committee of Safety." Suddenly Hannah's face assumed an expression of violent anger. "Yes, and what's more, Dirk Hollenbeck, if you stay with Old Tory Stone and keep a tight mouth as you're doing, next thing, they'll be saying you're a Tory too."

Dirk stood completely taken aback. "Why, Hannah," he said, "why, you know I couldn't leave Mr. Stone."

"Nobody's asking you to," snapped Hannah. She began picking her chicken with vicious jerks. Her face was very red.

"You came to see the doctor. Why don't you go on in and see him?"

As he made his way to the taproom, Dirk puzzled over Hannah's behavior. Girls were queer, it seemed. Now he had always thought she rather liked him and yet today she acted as if she hated the sight of him. Hannah was on his mind as much as a minute before he caught sight of Dr. Huggerford and walked over to his table.

As soon as Dirk had explained his errand, the old physician was ready to accompany him. They mounted their horses and started riding southward through the village. The doctor sat stooped in the saddle looking up from under drooping eyelids. He seemed to Dirk weary and sad.

"It is kind of you to come so promptly," said Dirk. "I was afraid you might be too busy."

"Oh, I'm not very busy nowadays," the doctor remarked. "A lot of people had rather die than have a 'Tory' make them well. And some of them have died, too. But then, some have gotten better." He gave a sharp, mirthless laugh. "Take Amos Waters. He was in bed for years and I bled him regularly. Now, since he's dismissed me, he's up and around real chipper."

As they rode down through the village, Dirk noticed that most people did not speak to them.

"And to think," commented the doctor dispassionately, "that a scant year ago everybody in town spoke to me. It was 'Dr. Huggerford this' and 'Dr. Huggerford that' on every side. And the strange part is that I haven't changed. I say

58

now as I said then, 'God save the King!' But they have all changed and that puts me in the wrong."

"I guess they haven't anything against you, sir," Dirk ventured. "It's just that they favor independence and you don't."

"Yes, I know." The doctor drew a long breath. "Independence," he mused. "They don't understand what they're talking about. It's just a fine-sounding word to them." He shook his head. "To talk of independence from England is nonsense. Why, England is home. We owe her everything. All I know of medicine I learned there."

The doctor paused and regarded Dirk out of faded blue eyes. "But you couldn't be expected to understand my point of view," he said with a gentle smile. "After all, what is England to you — a native American of Dutch extraction?"

"I can understand, sir," said Dirk. He paused, then added thoughtfully, "And I think I understand somewhat of the way it looks to the rebels, too."

"God help you, lad!" exclaimed the doctor feelingly. "If you can understand both sides of this insane controversy, you're headed for plenty of trouble."

Before the great house at Riverbrink, Dirk held the dappled gray while the doctor alighted. He was leading the two mounts away when he was hailed from the door.

"Mr. Stone wants you should come in and help the doctor," called Molly, one of the servant girls.

Dirk was puzzled at this summons as Caleb had always done this duty.

59

When he arrived in the parlor, the doctor was taking instruments out of his saddlebag and laying them on a stand. Mr. Stone was questioning Molly, and Miss Ellen stood by, listening.

"Where has Caleb gone?" demanded Mr. Stone, fixing Molly with a stern glance that would ordinarily have reduced her to sniveling.

But now she faced up to him with boldness. "I don't know. All I know is he ran away."

"You know something of his whereabouts," Mr. Stone insisted. "Come now. A slave has run away. It is your duty to help recover him."

"Oh, you won't get him back," retorted Molly, and her satisfaction at this was unmistakable.

Mr. Stone seized her wrist. "See here, my wench, you tell me what you know about Caleb. *Where is he?*"

His eyes blazed down upon Molly. She flinched slightly under the pressure of his lean fingers.

"I've *heard tell* Caleb joined the army," she said.

"The rebel army?"

"The *American* army."

"Get out of my sight, you saucy chit," Mr. Stone shouted.

Molly walked away with head held high.

Mr. Stone paced dramatically across the room. "As Heaven is my witness, a man was never more put upon than I!" he groaned. "Illness, war, and now this. Well, at least this is something I can deal with. I'll go direct to their head-

60

quarters, if they have such a thing, and demand that they turn the slave over to me."

"You'd better not do that, Roderick," remarked the doctor mildly. "The less you call yourself to their attention, the better off you'll be."

Mr. Stone gave an impatient snort. "I'm not the man to sit idle and let them steal a slave right from under my nose," he asserted. "Why, Caleb is *my* property, *my personal property.*" He paused to pound on a table that was conveniently at hand.

"Now, Roderick, you know we'll both be very fortunate indeed if we come through this conflict with no more loss than a slave or two," Dr. Huggerford put in quietly. "We stand to lose every stick of property we possess."

"I'd like to see them try to take mine away from me!" Mr. Stone's face was flushed darkly.

"What's to prevent them, Roderick?"

"Fear of constituted authority! Fear of the King's army! That's what will prevent them."

Miss Ellen, who had been watching her father's mounting excitement with troubled eyes, now ran across the room and clasped his arm.

"Father, please, please try to be calm," she begged. "You know you'll be dreadfully ill if you let yourself get so worked up. The war, our property — they don't matter. Nothing is important but your health."

"The girl is right, Roderick," agreed the doctor. "You aggravate your condition by these fits of temper. As I have

61

told you countless times, the passions have great influence upon the bodily humors — "

"Very well, doctor! Very well! I'll try to behave. But I'm blamed if I can act as cool as you at the prospect of losing all my possessions."

"Don't misunderstand me," protested the doctor. "I have complete confidence in the ultimate victory of the King's forces. We will be reinstated. But we must bear this intervening time with patience."

"Well, you bear it your way and I'll bear it mine," retorted Mr. Stone curtly. "And now let's get on with this bloodletting." He took off his coat and began folding back his left sleeve. "Ellen, you had better leave."

"Oh, Father, may I stay? I'll sit on the hassock here beside your chair and won't make a bit of trouble."

"Well, I don't know, pet." Mr. Stone patted his daughter's hand. "What do you think, doctor?"

"Eh? Oh, good thing! Good thing! A woman should see procedures like this. No telling when her acquaintance with it might be useful."

The doctor slipped a tourniquet over Mr. Stone's arm and attached it loosely until it should be time to check the flow of blood. He drew a thin-bladed scalpel from a leather sheath and tested it gingerly against his thumb. At his instruction, Dirk held a shallow earthenware basin under Mr. Stone's extended arm. The doctor poised his scalpel and made a small neat incision in the arm. The blood welled up and trickled in a crimson path across the white skin. It began running into the bowl with a small patter.

There was a rustling sound and a thud. Beyond the couch, Miss Ellen lay on the floor, her face chalky, one arm flung above her head. The dish of blood was jostled as Mr. Stone, with an exclamation, tried to rise.

"Lie still!" cried the doctor sharply. "There's no occasion for alarm. The girl has simply fainted. We'll attend to her in a moment."

The doctor's calm voice steadied Dirk whose first impulse had been to rush to Miss Ellen's aid. The doctor tightened the tourniquet, showed Dirk how to hold it and began bandaging the incision.

"Molly!" cried Mr. Stone in a surprisingly weak tone. "Call a servant, doctor."

"All in good time, Roderick," replied the doctor. "We want no more swooning women on our hands." He tied off the bandage with a firm knot. "Now, Dirk, I can manage here. You carry the girl up to her room. I'll be along directly."

Dirk stepped around the couch and dropped to one knee beside Miss Ellen. His heart was thumping in a violent rhythm. He gathered her up, supporting her head against his shoulder, and walked across the room. In the hall he deliberately slowed his pace to prolong his journey upstairs. A flower scent drifted to his nostrils. He had noticed it before, more faintly, when he had been helping her mount Star. He turned his head and let his eyes dwell on the lovely face so close to his own — the gentle curve of the cheek, the dark sweep of eyelashes, the soft cloud of dusky hair.

He had only to lower his head by a small degree and his lips would be in contact with her face, her mouth. Why shouldn't he? Never in all of his life would he have such another opportunity. It would do her no harm, surely, and she would never know of it. But, even while thinking all this, he restrained himself. It would not be honorable, he felt, to do a thing, however harmless, to which she would most certainly object if she were conscious. He would be ashamed to face her the next time they met.

In the bedroom he laid her down reluctantly on the four-poster. One of her hands dangled over the side of the bed. It was cold and he chafed it lightly. At least, he thought, even a farm boy was privileged to kiss a lady's hand. That would be taking no undue liberty. He turned her hand over and set his lips in the palm.

At the sound of feet clattering on the stairs, he drew away and walked into the hall. Molly was approaching with a bottle of smelling salts. After her came another housemaid, Thirza, carrying a bed warmer. And on the stairs Dirk met Dr. Huggerford.

In the living room Mr. Stone was lying back with closed eyes, his face almost as pale as his daughter's. Dirk tiptoed in and picked up his blue knitted cap from a chair.

Back in the hall, he stood at the foot of the stairs listening to the tread of feet above, the occasional muttered orders of the doctor. At length came the sound for which he had been

64

waiting, the low but unmistakable murmur of Miss Ellen's voice.

Dirk let himself out of the front door and, standing beside a tall white pillar, looked out over the river. It lay placid without a ripple, the hills, dusted with snow, rising tranquil beyond. Dirk gazed long, letting the peace of this prospect wash over his turbulent spirit. He drew deep breaths of the crisp air.

At length he started down the steps. Prince must be stabled and a morning's work lay ahead, interrupted by this journey for the doctor.

☆ 5 ☆

THE WINTER WAS A COLD ONE. THE RIVER FROZE SOLID
from shore to shore so that the ferry stopped running and
people could walk or ride at will from one side to the other.
Military travel continued on the King's Ferry Road.

Dirk's life went on in its accustomed rhythm like a familiar monotonous tune with the war playing it a dissonant
obbligato. Everything was the same and yet different because
no one knew how long it would be the same.

Dirk and Jedediah Pike began their winter's chore of cutting logs in a nearby wood lot and hauling them to the house
with oxen. Sometimes Peter went along. One cold day the
two men were chopping in an alternating rhythm, their
breath puffing out in cloudy spurts. Peter watched them,
then turned away. Suddenly he began piping excitedly. The
men paused. He was pointing a red-mittened hand toward
the cottage where the smoke rose from the chimney in a white
plume.

"House breathing!" he cried.

Dirk smiled, Pike grunted, and they went on with their
work. But that evening after supper, when Dirk happened to

66

remember the incident and told Christina, she laughed out-right, hugging Peter against her side. Then the child, in his elation at having amused his sister, cavorted about the room squealing until Christina had to become stern and threaten to put him to bed before they popped the corn.

Finally, the little household quieted down. Dirk sat in the one armchair, his stockinged feet propped on an andiron. Christina knelt on the hearth shaking a covered skillet of popcorn over a heap of coals that had been raked aside from the fire. And Peter sat on his own little hassock, his round blue eyes riveted on the skillet, visibly restraining himself from squealing.

"They sent for me over at the great house today," said Christina. "Molly has left. She was very pert about it, too. Said she wouldn't work any longer for a dirty Tory."

"Dirty Tory," repeated Peter, but no one seemed to notice.

Dirk shook his head. "I've been expecting it."

"And Thirza will be next," Christina continued. "She acts dreadful. Lazes around and sasses Aunt Lina. Miss Ellen says she'd send her packing only she's afraid she couldn't find anybody else."

"You talked to Miss Ellen?"

"Yes. She wants me to take Molly's place."

"I don't know where you've got any time to work at the great house," protested Dirk. "You keep pretty busy around here."

"That's what I told her, but her idea is for us to move in

over at the great house. Then Aunt Lina could get meals for us all."

Dirk's feet dropped from the andiron as he sat up to consider this startling idea. To be under the same roof with Miss Ellen! The thought made him draw in a quick breath. Yet there was something that almost canceled out his pleasure in it — this business of living in the servants' quarters. Here in their own home, though he worked for Mr. Stone, it seemed different. There in the great house, they would be nothing more than servants.

"Would you like that, Tina?" he asked.

A fury of explosions broke out in the skillet. Simultaneously, one squeal escaped from Peter's mouth before he could clamp both hands over it. Christina began shaking the skillet with redoubled vigor.

"Fetch the yellow bowl, Peter!" she cried.

He carried it carefully from the other side of the hearth where it had been warming and Christina poured in the skilletful of puffy white kernels. A belated pop exploded a dozen fluffy balls about the floor. Peter scrambled after them. Then Christina stirred in some salt and melted butter and began popping another skilletful while Peter and Dirk fell to eating the corn.

As he ate, Dirk looked about him at the familiar room. His first glance was for the carved oak chest, the family's dearest treasure, which had been brought from Holland. His eye ranged on, pausing at the trestle table that his father had hewn and planed out of a log, at the oval rug that Christina had braided, at the three-legged stool that he himself had made for Peter. A cozy little home they had created.

Then he thought of the great house with its barn of a kitchen, its drafty corridors, and cold rooms in the servants' wing. He did not relish the exchange. But if Miss Ellen wanted Christina's help, surely he should not put his own pride and comfort ahead of her needs.

Dirk had just reached this difficult point in his meditations when there was a knock at the door and Sam Higgins stamped in. His head and neck were swathed in a long black muffler from which emerged only his nose, bright red with the cold. By the time he had "unwound himself" and warmed his hands at the fire, Christina had popped another batch of corn and they all fell to eating from the yellow bowl.

"Out with it, Sam!" exclaimed Dirk. "You've got some big piece of news to tell. It's written all over your face."

"Yes, Sam," chimed in Christina. "Has the enemy surrendered?"

"Next thing to it," replied Sam with a grin. "*I'm* to get into the fighting."

Both Dirk and Christina showed a gratifying degree of astonishment.

"Has your father let you join the army?" asked Christina.

"No, but for this job I don't have to. You see, our general, Heath, has taken to sending raiding parties down against the enemy outposts in the Bronx. It's quite a journey and these soldiers at the camps don't know their way. So our general has taken to sending some local men along as guides. That's what I'm going to do."

"Let's see. You Higginses came from the Bronx, didn't you?" asked Dirk.

"Sure, I know all that country like my own hand."

There was something about Sam's manner tonight that Dirk had never noticed before and it puzzled him — a self-consciousness, an excitement, and a certain constraint. The excitement he could lay to this news. But what of the other qualities? Then he noticed something else, that whoever asked Sam a question, the answer was directed at Christina. Painfully he arrived at the inevitable conclusion: Sam Higgins was "sweet on" his sister. Furthermore, Christina was thoroughly aware of her effect upon Sam. Not that she was arch or coy. But there was an assurance in her manner and a twinkle in her eye that told she was conscious of having made a conquest.

Dirk emerged from the stupefaction into which these discoveries had plunged him to hear Sam saying, "Of course these raids the army makes aren't on helpless private families. They're against enemy-held outposts and they're dangerous. A guide doesn't have to take part in the fighting, but I expect to if I get a chance. I'll wager I'll skewer my share of Lobster-backs."

Dirk looked away disgusted. Sam was bragging like a fool. It was unbelievable what nonsense a boy would indulge in to impress a girl. Much as he liked Sam, Dirk was really glad when the poor fellow wrapped that mawkish expression back up in the muffler and left.

After tucking Peter in bed, Christina sat down before the fire with a basket of mending.

"About this work at the great house," Dirk began heavily, "wouldn't it be too much for you to do?"

"I don't mind that," said Christina, "but I'm not sure it would be good for Peter. He'd be lost over there. A little boy like him really needs a nice snug home."

"That settles it," Dirk declared. "We aren't to move. You help Miss Ellen what you can but we'll live right here."

So it was arranged. In the ensuing weeks, Dirk sometimes thought guiltily that the problem had been neatly solved so as to work no hardship on anyone but Christina. She did not complain, however. Every morning she went to the great house to "help out," usually bringing back the main dish for their family dinner. As she had prophesied, Thirza soon left, making them more short-handed than ever. Then Christina began to report that Miss Ellen herself was helping with the work, that she tidied her own room and sometimes actually came out to the kitchen and took a hand with the cooking.

Dirk did not see much of Miss Ellen that winter. Mr. Stone became well enough to escort her on her daily rides. That gentleman's health had mended almost immediately upon his return to Riverbrink. He attributed the improvement to the bleedings he received, but to Dirk it seemed more likely that the reason was Mr. Stone's greater ease of mind.

71

Through these winter months war activities were at a standstill. And Mr. Stone was confident that in the spring, when the ice went out of the river, the British fleet would come sailing up in force and make short work of rebel resistance.

The rebels themselves, meanwhile, undertook to rid the vicinity of British sympathizers. Dirk first saw their methods in operation on a windy afternoon early in March. He was in the carpenter shop trying to carve a new whiffletree for the plow out of a maple stick he had laid aside for the purpose during woodcutting, when Sam Higgins burst in.

"Come on up to the village," he shouted. "They're arrestin' Tories."

"You want me to go up and stop them?" asked Dirk with his slow grin. "I'd rather not try."

But Sam dragged him along. On the post road, they found the first evidence of rebel activity. In the dooryard of Mr. Jeremiah Travis' house about a hundred men were drawn up in ragged lines.

"Continental soldiers?" asked Dirk.

"Nah. Connecticut militia," Sam replied with some disgust.

Two men with cockades in their hats were pounding on the door of the house and shouting, "Open up!" Dirk recognized one as Jacob Stroup, the local miller. After a brief wait, Stroup backed off and rammed his gun butt through a panel of the door. A moment later they had burst into the house, followed by a score or more of armed men.

"What's going on?" Dirk demanded.

"They're searching the house for weapons," explained Sam.

Thumps, trampling, and shouted orders could be heard from within. At length an upstairs window was flung open and a man leaned out, holding a tooled leather box. Another broke ranks and, running forward, caught the box as it was tossed down.

"Funny-looking weapon," remarked Dirk acidly.

"Well, you can't expect perfect discipline with militiamen," Sam retorted, looking embarrassed.

More windows popped open and more "weapons" rained down. Men scrambled on the ground retrieving them. Two fell into a fist fight over a bundle of clothes. Another walked away with the bundle. By the time Stroup emerged from the door, the group had lost all semblance of military formation. He walked pompously to a cart and placed on it the one real firearm that had been found — an old blunderbuss. There was a bawling of commands, a scramble for position and the ragged column swung up the road. The two boys joined some stragglers in the rear.

"I don't like this," Dirk declared.

"Nor I either," Sam agreed unexpectedly. "We Yorkers could handle our own Tories. No need for a crowd of Yankees to butt in and do it for us and carry a lot of loot back to Connecticut."

"That isn't what I mean," said Dirk. "I mean this whole business of searching houses and arresting men."

Sam stopped in the road. "What would you do," he de-

73

manded, "let these Tories stay behind our lines? This is war. If enemy troops should invade, these Tories wouldn't hesitate to harbor them, yes, and turn their own weapons against us. Old Tory Stone would do that, wouldn't he?"

"I suppose he would," Dirk admitted.

"Well, then, can't you see we've got to get rid of such people?"

Dirk walked on. "Just the same I don't like it," he repeated stubbornly.

In Peekskill village the militiamen met a similarly constituted group moving southward. This unit had a prisoner in custody whom Dirk recognized as Mr. Nathaniel Merrit. The gentleman was mounted on horseback, his face, very pale, set stonily ahead. He wore no coat but only a flowered waistcoat and the full sleeves of his white linen shirt billowed in the March wind. There were shouted greetings between the militiamen of the two parties before the other group swung off on the road to Crompond.

"Where are they taking him?" Dirk asked.

"Before the Committee of Safety," Sam replied. "He'll have to swear an oath of allegiance to the Continental Congress."

"And if he refuses?"

"Then they'll either take him back to Connecticut with them and keep him on parole or else they'll turn him loose on the road to New York where he can join the enemy."

Dirk's set face indicated his disapproval.

Stroup led the militiamen to the yard of Mandeville's

74

Tavern. Dirk had thought this might simply be a halt for refreshment until he caught sight of a dappled gray mare at the hitching bar. Then he went rigid, gripped by a terrible apprehension. Again Stroup and his henchmen walked inside. When they reappeared in the doorway, they had Dr. Huggerford grasped between two of them. His wig had been knocked askew, revealing a few strands of yellowish gray hair. He was struggling weakly.

"Unhand me. I'll come quietly," he was saying.

But the two big men on either side hauled him along without any regard for his request.

Dirk was not aware that his fists were clenched until the fingernails bit into the palms.

"Stop, Dirk! Are you crazy?" Sam hissed, dragging back on his arm. "You can't help the doctor. You'll only get yourself arrested."

Dirk paused and stood panting. "I'm going home," he said and strode abruptly away.

He pursued a blind course down the street, plunging along with eyes set unseeingly upon the distance. At the lower end of town, he met another outfit of militia with two prisoners. As he was letting them pass, the sudden conviction swept over him that a similar posse was visiting Riverbrink in his absence. He broke into a stumbling run.

When at last he topped the rise of ground that brought Riverbrink into view, all seemed as usual and he slowed his step. A horseman was approaching. It was Colonel Pierre Van Cortlandt, one of the leading patriots of the colony and lord of the large manor of which Riverbrink had once been a part. Through marrige to a Van Cortlandt, Roderick Stone had acquired this estate. The colonel was dressed all in black as usual, save for a white stock. He was an elderly man with a broad, benign countenance. At sight of Dirk, he lifted his tricorn hat.

"Good afternoon, Mr. Hollenbeck," he said courteously.

Dirk clawed off his knitted cap and muttered a reply. Then he stood staring as the older man rode on. *Mr.* Hollenbeck! No one had ever called him that before. He liked it. He lifted his head and squared his shoulders. It crossed his mind that Mr. Van Cortlandt might have spoken ironically, but he thought not. The colonel wasn't that sort of man. He had said it simply and sincerely, just as he would have done to another person of his class. And he had lifted his hat!

Why — it came to Dirk in a dazzling flash — perhaps Mr. Van Cortlandt actually believed their Declaration of Independence, that all men were created equal. If a person in the colonel's position could believe it, there must be some truth to it. Dirk felt he would like to have a talk with him. Perhaps he could explain exactly what the words meant, how they could be true. Mr. Stone had given him a thorough explanation of why they could *not* be true. He'd like to hear those two get together and discuss the question.

But they had been together. What had they talked about? Why had Van Cortlandt come? Again Dirk broke into a run, up the road and across the garden toward the great house. Why hadn't he realized at once that the colonel's visit

76

meant trouble? The two families had not exchanged social calls since the war started.

Dirk flung himself into the kitchen of the great house. Aunt Lina was standing beside the half-opened door to the hall in an attitude of listening. She turned to Dirk with tears pouring down her face.

"Something dreadful has happened!" she exclaimed in a low, trembling voice. "Colonel Van Cortlandt was just here and he says we have got to leave right away or Mr. Stone will be arrested. Colonel says he can't hold the militia off any longer. And Mr. Stone is carrying on dreadful. Listen!"

She drew Dirk into the doorway where Stone's voice was clearly audible, harsh with fury.

"I'll not stir an inch. Van Cortlandt is only trying to frighten me off from this property. He has wanted it back ever since I acquired it and he thinks this is his chance. Well, he'll find I don't frighten."

"But, Father, the colonel has done us a kindness by this warning." Miss Ellen's voice was shaking with emotion. "He was only trying to save you from the disgrace of being arrested."

"Arrested, pah! They wouldn't dare arrest me. They know that when the King's peace is restored, they would hang for it. This is my property and here I'll stay."

Dirk brushed past Aunt Lina's bulky figure and strode across the hall. In the doorway of the parlor he paused. Mr. Stone was pacing the floor, his face a gray-white except for a spot of red on each cheekbone. Miss Ellen stood opposite the

77

door, very erect as always, her hands clasped tightly together and her dark eyes glistening with tears.

"Sir, they've just arrested Dr. Huggerford," said Dirk. "I saw them do it."

Mr. Stone turned upon Dirk and for an instant a fierce resentment burned in his eyes as though he blamed the boy for the news he brought. Then suddenly the man seemed to crumple. His face went slack. He collapsed into a chair, his head in his hands. Miss Ellen ran and sank to her knees beside him.

"We must go, Father. You see? We must go at once," she said brokenly and, leaning her forehead against his arm, she began to sob.

After a moment Mr. Stone raised his head. "Very well, let the rebels come," he said in a quieter tone. "I'll stay here and fight them singlehanded. If they kill me, well, I'd as soon be dead as living under this mob rule."

"Then what would become of Miss Ellen?" asked Dirk.

Stone pulled himself upright and slid an arm about his daughter's shoulders. "Ah, boy, I am ashamed that you must needs remind me of my first duty," he said. "I must take my daughter to a place of safety. I'll take her back to Stonehaven." He looked up at Dirk. "I shall leave Riverbrink in your charge. You will guard it from the rebels."

"I, sir!" exclaimed Dirk, completely taken aback. "But what could I do? They'd know I was keeping it for you."

"Pretend to become a rebel," Stone suggested. "Then

78

you'd have as good a right to it as anybody in their eyes. Ha! You might even get it away from Van Cortlandt. That would really please me."

"Oh, I couldn't do that, sir, any of it," protested Dirk. "Perhaps Mr. Pike would — "

"Pah, Pike! I don't trust him. But you would never play me false, boy."

"That I wouldn't," asserted Dirk stoutly. "But I couldn't play anyone else false, either. And that's what you're asking of me, isn't it?"

Miss Ellen had raised her head and was looking at Dirk searchingly, almost as if she really saw him for the first time.

"Well, how can we work this matter out? Let me see." Mr. Stone seemed to have recovered somewhat of his usual presence. He helped Miss Ellen to her feet and resumed his pacing. "How can we protect Riverbrink?"

"Perhaps, sir," Dirk suggested, "they will not harm this manor if you are gone."

Mr. Stone halted his pacing. "That is possible, entirely possible. It will be a short time anyhow that you will have this responsibility. In a few weeks at most His Majesty's fleet will come up the river, crushing this damnable rebellion as it advances. Then we will come back and turn the tables on these blackguards."

"But surely, Father," said Miss Ellen, "you don't expect Dirk to risk his own life defending Riverbrink?"

"No, of course not, my dear." Mr. Stone turned back to

79

Dirk. "It will only be a question of your guarding the place against prowlers, boy. If a mob comes, the worst thing you could do would be to resist."

"Yes, sir. I saw the truth of that today."

"Tell us about Dr. Huggerford's arrest," said Miss Ellen.

Dirk related all the incidents of the afternoon, sparing no offensive details so that Mr. Stone would be convinced of the necessity for flight. When he had finished, his audience was silent.

At length Mr. Stone drew a long breath. "We must go," he declared. "No question of it. We'll leave tomorrow for Stonehaven. Let's see. The coach is already down there. That's awkward. Well, get the two saddle horses ready for us, boy, and Pike will follow with our baggage on the ox-cart."

"Oh, sir, can't I take the baggage down?" urged Dirk. "Mr. Pike doesn't like to — "

"You will stay right here and guard the house," broke in Mr. Stone brusquely. "And now if we are to take flight (which I never thought I would do) we had best be about our preparations. We'll make ready tonight and start early in the morning. Boy, fetch the wagon to the back door so that you can load it."

The remainder of the day passed in a flurry of preparations. Dirk had little time to ponder on what this great change in his life would mean. He was aware only of an almost intolerable heaviness of spirit as he worked, carrying baggage, packing the wagon, grooming the horses.

He took every opportunity to gaze upon Miss Ellen, trying to fix in his memory every trait and gesture — the proud way she walked, the curve of her cheek when her face was turned aside, the modulations of her voice, for there was no knowing when, if ever, he would see her again. From Stonehaven she might go to New York and never return to Riverbrink. The war might drag on for years, and even if it didn't, there was always Gerit Van Wyck waiting to carry her off in marriage.

The next morning Dirk was determined to be on hand early so that he might help Miss Ellen into the saddle. So directly after breakfast he arrived in front of the great house with Prince and Star ready. The saddlebags had been set out on the porch. As he mounted the steps to get them, Miss Ellen came out of the door. She was wearing the maroon riding habit that brought out the rich beauty of her coloring, and the gray plume on her hat swept in a graceful arc down over her dusky hair. Her sudden appearance was so exactly what he had been longing for that his foolish heart started to race and he could only stand stupidly gazing up at her.

"Oh, good morning, Dirk!" she exclaimed. "I nearly forgot my comb and brush. Will you put them into my saddlebags?"

She handed them to him and, while he fumbled at the straps of a bag, walked across the porch to stand looking out over the river.

"It is so beautiful here! I shall miss it," she declared. "But we must go for my father's sake."

"Perhaps you can come back soon, ma'am," said Dirk. "I most certainly hope so."

"Yes, I know. You hate being responsible for the house, don't you?" she asked, misconstruing his meaning.

He wanted to cry out that it was the separation he hated but he knew such words would not be seemly.

So he was thoughtful for a moment and then said, "Not so much that, ma'am. But I'm not settled in my own mind about this business of Tories and rebels."

"You mean that you might become a rebel?" Miss Ellen's tone was incredulous.

"It hardly seems so, ma'am, 'specially after what I saw yesterday. I guess I'd just like to feel I could if I did want to."

"I see. And this duty of guarding the house commits you to the loyalists."

"Understand, though, ma'am, I'm glad to do it for Mr. Stone. I owe it to him, and a great deal more."

Dirk finished restrapping the saddlebag. He stood up, dangling it from his hand. Miss Ellen was looking at him, her dark eyes level and intent.

"I understand your feeling," she said thoughtfully. "No matter how much you may consider yourself beholden to my father, you're not obligated to think the way he does." She turned her gaze over the river once more. "I think, however, that if you should ever decide to join the rebels, you ought to come and tell my father."

"That I give you my promise to do, Miss Ellen," Dirk

agreed promptly, "though it's not likely I shall ever come with such news."

Then Mr. Stone strode out of the house in a frenzy to be gone, and their conversation was ended. Dirk had the opportunity he had craved, to put Miss Ellen into the saddle. It was soon over — a brief clasp of her gray glove, the quick pressure of her other hand upon his shoulder, and then she was riding away.

At the turn of the driveway, she looked back and Dirk swung his cap in farewell. But she did not respond. Then he realized that she had been looking at the house, not at him. For her, he had probably ceased to exist.

☆ 6 ☆

DIRK FOUND HIMSELF OVERNIGHT THE MANAGER AND SOLE laborer on a large manor farm. Into the work he put all of his energies and most of his thoughts, determined that Mr. Stone's estimate of his abilities should be more than justified. Aside from his feeling of responsibility, however, he found himself enjoying the sense of mastery which his new position gave him. He liked regulating his own life, making decisions about the work and planning for the coming season.

He soon came to realize that he would never again be content to serve as a mere farm hand, or even as an overseer. He wanted a farm of his own. He would stand in the cow stable and look about on the score of angular rumps, thinking what it would be like to own that herd of cattle. A firm determination formed in his mind that one day he would own a farm. He would have to start with just a few head of cattle, perhaps only one cow. With one cow and one ox a man could make a beginning.

On Sunday afternoons, dressed in his "good" clothes, Dirk would stroll over the manor farm inspecting the property. He would make note of all needed repairs and plan his crops for the spring planting. Often his little family would trail along after him.

"I'll put this field to buckwheat," Dirk would say, standing with legs widespread.

"This field to queet," echoed Peter, his stubby limbs at exactly the same angle.

And Christina regarded them both with twinkling eyes.

When Jedediah Pike returned with the ox team, it was at once evident that he would be of little help on the farm. Dirk guessed that Mr. Stone had told Pike who was to be in authority at Riverbrink and Pike, not unnaturally, resented it. But there was no indication of this resentment in his bearing toward Dirk. He merely said that he did not care to continue working for a confessed Tory.

" 'Course any time you get real short-handed, I'd be willing to help out," he added, "just to oblige *you*."

Thus he provided a loophole by which he might reinstate himself at Riverbrink whenever that should seem desirable. Dirk heard through Sam that Pike was claiming he had himself been offered the position of overseer at Riverbrink by Mr. Stone but had refused on patriotic grounds.

"Do people really believe that?" Dirk asked Sam.

"Oh, everybody knows old Jedediah," Sam replied. "He trims his sails to every breeze."

"What do they say of me?" Dirk demanded suddenly.

"You? Oh, I tell them you'll wake up after a while. They'll wait."

"And suppose I don't 'wake up' as you call it?"

85

"You will." Sam's manner was one of quiet assurance. "You're a dummed slow Dutchman, but you're one of us. Some time you'll discover it."

And meanwhile, Dirk realized, Sam was answering for him to the rest of the rebels, shielding him from their mistrust and hostility. Dirk was touched. He knew that he had a real friend.

So, he was let alone that spring and summer to run the Riverbrink farm as best he could. During the planting season and again at haying time, Jedediah Pike helped him. By tacit agreement, Pike always worked in a field out of sight from the public road. Thus he could maintain the fiction among his neighbors that he scorned the employ of a Tory. Dirk kept careful reckoning of Pike's days of labor so that he could pay him in crops at harvest time.

Farm produce was bringing good prices that summer, but payment was in state money, of unreliable value. Dirk preferred barter. Many farmers were selling their crops to the army camps at good rates. Dirk did not do so as he thought Mr. Stone would not approve.

The army had its share of Riverbrink produce nonetheless. One day in early July an empty forage wagon rattled up the driveway, its four occupants carrying pitchforks. A man hopped off and accosted Dirk.

"Sergeant McDermott at your service," he announced. "Army requires a load of hay from your farm. How about that cock over in the field?"

"One is as good as another," said Dirk.

86

So they drove the forage wagon through a break in the stone wall and in a short time had transferred the hay to the wagon. Then, without any further notice of Dirk, they rattled away again. Dirk walked into the lot and kicked at a few wisps of hay left among the stubble. He resented this high-handed appropriation, not from any profound political conviction, but simply because he had been made to feel a helpless victim. He realized, however, that the army must need many tons of grain for men and beasts and that they had no other recourse to obtain it. Army horses were raising a perpetual dust in the King's Ferry Road. And Sam told many tales of the numbers of regiments stationed about Peekskill.

Sam enjoyed his work of guide. He gave Dirk long accounts of the raiding parties that he conducted to the enemy outposts. After one of his first expeditions, he dropped a remark that troubled Dirk. The two boys were perched on a fence rail at the Point watching the distant ferry.

"It isn't just when we get to the enemy lines that we're in danger," said Sam with a touch of boastfulness. "We're in danger right straight acrost the Neutral Ground."

"The Neutral Ground? What's that?"

"Why, it's all the territory below the Croton River. They call it neutral because it doesn't belong to us and it doesn't belong to the British either. Men from both sides have to be alert when they're on it."

"Is Stonehaven in the Neutral Ground?"

"Certain it is."

"Well, but then it's not safe for the Stones."

"Ah, that old Tory is as safe as he deserves to be."

"But Miss Ellen!"

"Oh, yes, Miss Ellen." Sam shot a keen glance at Dirk. "Why, I tell you. I don't think you need to worry about her. She's got two good men to protect her."

"But it is dangerous there for a woman, isn't it?"

"There's some danger, yes. But tell me this, Dirk Hollenbeck. Where is a woman truly safe in these times? Look at your own sister, Christina."

"Well, what about her? She's safe enough."

"You think so? Suppose the British fleet should come sailing up the river. First thing they'd do would be to raid some of these big manor houses. Then how safe would Christina be?"

"Why, I — I guess I hadn't thought much about that."

"Well, I have, I'll tell you. I've thought about it a good deal, and — " Sam halted, reddening.

But Dirk was paying him little heed. "Maybe I ought to send her inland somewhere, or farther north," he muttered.

"There, now, no need of that," Sam protested. "I was only showing you nobody is safe anywhere."

After this conversation, Dirk worried about his sister as well as Miss Ellen. But Christina, happily unaware of his concern, worked hard that summer, keeping the house, caring for Peter, and cultivating the kitchen garden.

The Hollenbecks now were the only residents of River-brink. Aunt Lina had gone to live with a brother in Fishkill and the great house was closed. The place seemed hauntingly lonely. No one except Sam Higgins ever stopped in to see them. There was no doubt of the reason for this; people considered them Tories. They needed no better reflection of public opinion than Jedediah Pike's attitude. So long as he was afraid to be seen there, they were under public disapproval. And he did not come near them from haying time until after the harvest season. Then one day in the latter part of September, he appeared.

Dirk was cutting down cornstalks on a back field of the manor and Peter was playing nearby with a bow and arrow Dirk had made for him. Dirk had also arranged one shock of corn with a hollow center so that the little boy could crawl in and out, pretending it was a wigwam.

Pike approached across the fields. "Pretty good corn crop you've got this year," he remarked, perching his lank form on a fence rail.

Dirk remained stooped over, hacking the cornstalks with his sickle. "Tolerable," he agreed.

"Good potato crop, too," Pike added.

Dirk conceded this also.

"Got more than your folks can use, ain't you?"

Dirk thought he knew what Pike was driving at. He raised up. "You'll get your share, never fear," he said coldly.

Pike shifted the piece of straw between his teeth. "Nah, it ain't that. I was only thinking if you could sell some of this —"

"For paper money? There's no profit in that."

Pike let a moment's impressive silence intervene before he said, "For hard money."

"And where, pray, can a man trade for hard money?"

Dirk set the stalks upright and began binding them with intertwined leaves of the corn.

"You have only to carry your produce down the post road a bit to Teller's Point." Pike lowered his voice. "A ship stands off from there on a certain night in the week. It'll send a boat ashore if you flash a signal. They'll take your produce and pay you coin of the realm."

"A ship? Then it must be British."

" 'Course it's British. Does that matter to you?"

Dirk shook his head. "I wouldn't do that," he said. And moving away, he began to wield his sickle again.

Pike followed him. "Why not? You don't favor the rebels, do you?"

"I don't know as I do, but as long as I'm living in their territory, I'll abide by their laws."

"It's Mr. Stone's property you're dealing with. He'd want you to do it."

"As to that, I don't know. But I made him no promise except to take care of the place, and that's all I'll do."

"You've no need to be afeared about it, for there's very little danger. The patrols are busy watching Pine's Bridge and the ferry crossing. They don't try to keep track of the whole length of shore line."

"Well, safe or no, I'll not deal with the British unless I decide to join them, so there's an end of it."

Dirk straightened and began binding another shock.

Frowning, Pike spat out the straw. Then abruptly, he shrugged. "Dunno but what you're right," he remarked carelessly. "Just thought I'd better tell you what I'd heard. Here, let me hold that shock for you."

Pike remained to help Dirk the rest of the afternoon. There was no further mention of the subject he had introduced. He seemed to accept Dirk's decision in perfect good nature. When the job was done, he offered to help the next day.

So for nearly a week thereafter Pike came regularly, doing his tasks with unusual affability and slipping home after dark through back lots. Dirk realized afterward that he should have suspected from Pike's oily manner that something was in the wind, but he did not. So what happened a few days later came as a complete shock.

He had just arisen that October morning, slipped into his breeches and stepped to the window in the loft to look at the weather, when he saw three horsemen approaching on the driveway. Hastily catching up his woolen smock, he scrambled down the ladder and tiptoed past the bed where Christina and Peter lay asleep. Hauling his smock over his head, he stepped out of the door.

The horsemen were dismounting before the cottage. It was a group of minutemen — Jacob Stroup, the captain, and Brom Kronkheit and Amos Hart. They led an extra horse.

"Come on, Hollenbeck, get on this nag," Stroup ordered. "You're going back to town with us."

"You mean you're arresting me?" asked Dirk. "Why?"

"You know why well enough. Hurry up, now. You've kept us up all night as it is."

"Look here, I don't know what you're talking about." Dirk found himself more angry than frightened.

"You mean to deny you were trying to smuggle a load of food to the enemy last night?"

"Of course I deny it. I was asleep in bed."

"Then I presume your oxen are in their stalls?"

"Most certainly they are."

"Let's see them."

The four men trooped to the stable, Dirk striding in the lead. He flung open the door. The oxen were gone. He turned back in bewilderment.

"See here! Where are those oxen?" he demanded. "If you took them —" His fists came up.

"Certain we took them," Stroup retorted. "They're in my stable right now."

Dirk lowered his fists. "Exactly what happened?" he asked more quietly.

"Don't tell him, Jake," cautioned Hart. "He's only trying to find how much we know."

Stroup's narrowed eyes did not leave Dirk's face. "I'll tell him. I know every move he made last night. He can't make up a story that will clear him."

"Let's hear it," Dirk challenged.

"Well, Hollenbeck, you filled up your cart with stuff off your farm — potatoes, shell beans, apples, rolls of butter with the Riverbrink print on. *That* was a mistake, Hollenbeck."

"Go on," said Dirk grimly.

"You hitched your oxen to the cart. That off one with the twisted horn I'd know anywhere for Stone's. Soon as I saw it, I said —"

"Then what?" Dirk broke in.

"Why, you drove down the post road and had got way below the American lines when a patrol caught up with you. Before they could seize you, you skinned over the tailboard of the cart and lit out across lots."

"If these were army patrols, what have you to do with this?" Dirk demanded.

"The patrols came to me. The army won't try a private citizen. It'll be a case for the Committee of Safety."

"Hey, but, Jake," cried Hart. "The Committee don't meet for three days. What'll we do with him till then?"

"Tell you what. Colonel Van Cortlandt is at his daughter's house now," said Kronkheit. "We could take him there."

" 'Twould be easiest," Stroup conceded. "Well, come along now, Hollenbeck."

"I'll have to tell my sister," said Dirk.

Stroup entered the cottage with him. They found Christina up and dressed. Dirk told her briefly what had happened.

"You'll have to do the milking this morning," he said, "but I'll be back to tend to it by night."

"Don't you worry about Peter and me," she said stoutly. "We'll make out."

93

She ran to fetch his leather jerkin and managed a tremulous smile as he left. Peter had not awakened.

There was no noise in all the pale world except the rhythmic clop of horses' hoofs on the road and no movement but their bobbing heads. Dirk's three captors were stooped in their saddles, nearly asleep. It had all happened so suddenly; he could scarcely realize, even now, that he was a prisoner. A flood of worries swept through his mind, chief of which was what would become of Christina and Peter.

Of course Dirk did not need to puzzle over who had been driving the ox team. It had to be Jedediah Pike. As they rode past his farm, Dirk debated telling these men his suspicions, demanding that they ride in and arrest Pike also. But he knew they would not believe him. And what proof would he have? He would only be made to look more foolish.

When they passed the Higgins farm, Dirk had an impulse to whistle the shrill signal call that would bring Sam to the door. But he refrained. Sam had compromised himself enough already in championing Dirk without getting involved in this predicament. The best thing Sam could do would be to help Christina. And that, Dirk realized, he would not fail to do. With this assurance Dirk felt much relieved.

The house where Colonel Van Cortlandt was staying was about a mile above the village, a new building of yellow brick set back from the road. The horsemen clattered around to the rear and dismounted. As they waited on a brick-flagged terrace, a fat genial Negress told them the colonel was having his breakfast. Just then the gentleman himself appeared. His hair, a beautiful silvery white, was combed smoothly back and fell to his collar. He gazed quietly upon the little group of men until Stroup took a step forward.

"This here's a man we arrested for smuggling a load of farm stuff to the enemy," Stroup blurted out.

Colonel Van Cortlandt bent a searching glance upon Dirk. "I'll talk to him," he said. "Meanwhile, if you gentlemen care to step into the kitchen, Belinda can provide you with some coffee."

The men acted upon this suggestion with alacrity while the colonel led Dirk into the dining room. Here he seated himself once more at the table.

"Mr. Hollenbeck, I am gravely disappointed in you," he said sternly. "I took you for an honest man if perhaps a wrong-headed one."

"But I didn't do it, sir," protested Dirk. "It must have been the Riverbrink ox team but I wasn't driving them. I knew nothing about it."

For a long moment the colonel studied Dirk's face. "I believe you," he said at length. "Do you know who did do it?"

"I have a strong suspicion, sir, but no proof."

"Sit down and tell me about it. I'll have Belinda bring some breakfast for you."

So it was that Dirk found himself breakfasting at the same table with the lord of a great manor and telling him in halting words about his suspicion of Jedediah Pike. He ate heartily, too, though in the excitement he had been unaware of his

95

hunger. There were coffee, scrambled eggs, bacon, and a raised biscuit dripping with butter. Belinda chuckled at his appetite and plied him with more helpings.

"Them men out in the kitchen is eating scandalous, too," she announced gleefully.

After Dirk had finished his account, the colonel sat in thought. Then he said, "I think we had better not arrest this Jedediah Pike. It would be his word against yours, and just now people would not be disposed to believe you. He wouldn't try it again anyhow, would he?"

"I'm sure he wouldn't."

"Well, then, my thought would be to hush this all up so that other smugglers wouldn't be warned away. We know now about the British ship coming to Teller's Point and we know the night it comes is Wednesday. Next Wednesday, then, we could lay a trap and perhaps catch a number of these smugglers."

"Meanwhile, sir, what happens to me and my family?"

The colonel considered this question. "You may take your oxen and go home," he decided.

A great warmth of relief flooded over Dirk at these words. "Oh, thank you, sir!" he exclaimed.

"Now understand, young man, this is only a temporary measure. It is all I have the authority to do. I must report your case to the other members of the Committee of Safety and they will no doubt summon you to appear before them. I'll suggest, however, that they wait a week before doing so."

"You mean so that you can catch the smugglers?"

96

"Yes, and also, Mr. Hollenbeck, so that you can make up your mind which side you'll support in this war. You can't continue any longer as you're doing. Surely you can see that. The local patriots won't stand for it, particularly after what has happened now."

"Yes, I do see that."

"May I ask which side you favor?"

"Well, sir, if I must make a choice, I'm afraid it will have to be for the King."

"Why?"

"Well, you see, sir, Mr. Stone — "

"Ah, Mr. Stone, eh? He has persuaded you that the British cause is the just one?"

"Not so much that, but — Why, I just couldn't go against him, Colonel. I owe him, my family owes him, everything."

Van Cortlandt leaned back in his chair. "Your feeling of gratitude and loyalty do you great credit, Mr. Hollenbeck," he said, "even though they may not be fully warranted."

"What do you mean by that, sir?" Dirk demanded with an edge of sharpness in his voice.

"Simply that Roderick Stone treated your family as any intelligent businessman would treat a good investment. Your father gave him invaluable service for years as overseer. When he was killed, you were a young lad who gave every promise of growing up to be as valuable a man as your father. It was in Mr. Stone's best interests to tide you over a few years so as to have first claim upon your services."

Dirk's back stiffened. "Sir, I am sure you misjudge Mr.

Stone. He did what he did for us in a true spirit of kindness, not thinking of himself, but of us."

The colonel smiled. "It may be so," he agreed. "I have no wish to belittle Mr. Stone in your eyes. I am only trying to make you see that you have no such immense obligation toward him as you seem to think. If the accounts between you should be closed as of this hour, he would have received full value on his investment."

"Do you know, sir, Miss Ellen told me the same as you are saying — that I should not feel obliged to take the same politics as her father."

"Did she indeed? A true Van Cortlandt, sir! A true Van Cortlandt! Apparently she realizes what I am trying to tell you — that this decision you must make goes beyond all personal relationships. It is a matter of one's philosophy, one's principles."

"Principles!" Dirk spat out the word. "I fail to see anything very noble about the principles of the rebels around here — yourself excepted, sir. They loot and plunder like ordinary criminals."

Van Cortlandt leaned back and lowered his eyes. "That is all too true, I fear," he agreed with a sigh. "But such things are bound to happen in any war, on both sides. They bear no relation to the essential worth of the cause for which we are fighting."

"Could you tell me, sir, exactly what that cause is?"

"A large order, Mr. Hollenbeck, and one which I am poorly qualified to fill." He leaned forward and his eyes held

Dirk's. "But this much I will attempt. It is freedom from Britain, yes, but more than that. It is the rights of free men everywhere that we are fighting for, the right of every man to govern himself, to stand on an equal footing with every other man."

"Is that what it means, sir, in the Declaration of Independence where it says all men are created equal? I puzzled over that, sir, and could make little of it. It seems to me that men are far from being equal."

"In superficial ways, yes. They are unequal in wealth, in physical power, in mental capacity. But before God all men are equal. You believe that, don't you?"

"Yes, of course, sir."

"In short, men are *created* equal. No man is born either a peasant or a nobleman. That is a designation that society imposes upon him. Now, in this new nation we are striving to build, society will not impose that designation. Every man will have an equal right to attain what rank he can. The government will protect him in that right and he himself will create and maintain that government."

A great surging response welled up in Dirk at these words. Here indeed was a cause that a man could work for and fight for with a will. The impulse was strong in him to rise up at that moment and pledge himself to the patriots. But an innate caution held him back.

"Thank you, sir, for explaining it to me," he said at length. "I understand it better than I did. But I must think more about it."

"Ah, well, I suppose I must have patience," remarked Van Cortlandt with a smile. "We Dutch are slow to make up our minds. But once we do, man or Satan cannot shake us."

Then the colonel led the way back to the terrace where the three men were waiting. He instructed Stroup to restore Dirk's oxen and cart and to release him to return home until the Committee should summon him. Stroup listened respectfully, but once they were on the road again, he began to grumble.

"Colonel's too easy! We ketch a Tory red-handed and then he makes us let him go."

"Only till the Committee summons him," Hart put in.

"Oh, certain! And where'll the villain be by then? He'll have sneaked away to the Neutral Ground."

Dirk's temper, which had been rising slowly all morning, suddenly boiled. He pulled up his horse.

"I'm here now," he said with quiet rage. "Whatever you'd like to do to me, come ahead and try it." And he began to dismount.

"Now, ain't you the big brave bucko," sneered Stroup. "I'd be right scairt if I didn't have a pistol in my belt."

"You're afraid to settle it with fists," Dirk challenged.

"I'd admire to, but trouble is — you're still in my custody. If you attacked me, I'd be obliged to shoot you." Stroup suddenly drew his weapon and said in a menacing tone, "Get back in that saddle."

There was nothing for Dirk to do but comply and he rode on sullenly.

"Say, Jake!" exclaimed Kronkheit. "Colonel didn't tell us what to do with the stuff in that cart. Do we give that back to Hollenbeck?"

"Well, now." Stroup pretended to ponder the question with broad winks at his two henchmen. "I'd say colonel must have meant us to use our judgment. What'd you fellers say?"

"*I'd* say that side of beef in the cart 'd be reasonable pay for my night's work," Kronkheit remarked.

"I'll take the ham," Hart put in eagerly.

"Here now, I'm fresh out of ham myself," Stroup protested.

When they reached Stroup's barn, they all fell upon the cart and piled its contents into three heaps on the floor. As soon as the cart was empty, Dirk turned the oxen around and was halfway out of the door before anyone noticed him.

Then Stroup roared out, "That's right. Get on with you and be damned. Here, keep this nest egg for your next load and when we catch you with it, we'll string you up."

Dirk felt a stinging blow on his shoulder and an onion tumbled onto the floor of the cart. It rolled and bumped about as the oxen started toward home. In all his unhurried existence Dirk had never been so irked by the pace of the oxen as he was that morning. He must constantly fight an impulse to run ahead of them, to get back to Christina and tell her he was safe.

Yet surely the time spent in the journey would be none too long to ponder the great problem he must settle. Now, to consider the opposite side from the one the colonel had presented. What would Mr. Stone say to these arguments? It was not hard to imagine. He would say that it was foolish twaddle, that all down the ages some men had been masters while others were servants and so it would always be. He would claim that this sort of talk was just a trick played by the leaders of the revolution to lure ambitious boys like Dirk to their side. Then Dirk thought of Colonel Van Cortlandt's kindly open countenance and knew that he, at least, had been sincere.

So he swayed alternately from one side to the other until his mind was hopelessly confused. If only this necessity of immediate choice had not come upon him! And who was to blame that it had come? No other than Jedediah Pike. Gradually, as he inched his way along the King's Ferry Road, all the pent-up sense of humiliation and injustice that had accumulated during the day built itself into a smoldering rage against this man.

When he reached Pike's farm, Dirk halted the oxen, picked the onion out of the cart and strode to the house. After all, it was Pike's onion, thought Dirk, and he would deliver it to Pike as it had been delivered to him. Pike's wife came to the door, a timid wizened creature with a dirty mobcap.

"Jedediah's sick. He can't see nobody," she said.

But Dirk brushed past her and strode to the lean-to that served as the Pikes' bedroom. On the bed a long narrow cocoon of blanket was topped by Pike's grizzled hair tapering to a queue. A groan issued from the depth of the feather tick.

Dirk held out the onion. "Here's what's left of your load of stuff," he announced, "and that'll be your share of the Riverbrink harvest."

Pike's head emerged from the covers. "Why, Dirk," he cried in a whining tone, "what are you talking about? Whatever 'tis, don't bother me today. I'm a dreadful sick man." And he burrowed under the blanket once more.

"You come out of that bed or I'll drag you out!" shouted Dirk, his voice thick with anger. "Stand up like a man and admit to what you've done and take the beating you deserve."

Out popped Pike's head again, his eyes dilated with fear. "Don't beat me, Dirk! I tell you I don't know what you're talking about. You wouldn't beat a sick, defenseless man, would you?"

The whining voice went on, but Dirk had stopped listening. What satisfaction would there be in pelting a craven, unresisting piece of flesh? Dirk's mind revolted at the thought. Opening his hand, he let the onion fall to the floor and strode away.

In the cottage, Christina was stooped above the hearth, swinging over the flames a crane that carried an iron kettle. At the sound of Dirk's step, she turned, her face aglow with joy.

"Oh, Dirk, Dirk, I feared you were never coming back!"

She ran across the floor with rapid steps and flung herself against him, clinging to his sleeves, to his collar, laughing hysterically and finally weeping in labored sobs.

Peter embraced Dirk's leg and regarded his sister for a moment with puzzled eyes. Then, flinging his head back, he gave Dirk an ecstatic smile.

"Guess what's for dinner," he cried. "Guess what, Dirk. Onion soup! That's what!"

☆ 7 ☆

APPLE BUTTER WAS IN THE MAKING AT RIVERBRINK. ALL morning Dirk and Christina had pared apples. Now the great iron kettle hung over the fire, bubbling with a fragrant mixture of apples and cider. Christina stirred it with slow, deep strokes, her face pink from the heat. Dirk went to the barn with a wooden bowl full of peelings and pitched them into the hog trough.

As he watched the two porkers jostle each other, he fell to wondering what would become of them if he should go to Stonehaven. Perhaps he could best serve Mr. Stone's interests by becoming a rebel and staying here to run the farm. But this would involve a divided allegiance that would be impossible for him to maintain. Here he was again at the same old sticking-point in his thoughts. It was two days now since the interview with Colonel Van Cortlandt and Dirk was as far as ever from a decision.

He knocked the bowl out against the side of the pen and returned to the cottage. Sam was there, talking excitedly, breathlessly, to Christina. As Dirk entered, he turned.

"The fleet's coming, the British fleet!" he panted. "Be in sight any minute. You've got to get out of here."

Dirk only stared.

Sam seized his arm. "Come on! Look lively!" He turned back to Christina. "Get your cloak. Where's Peter?"

The little boy came running at the sound of his name.

"You must take Peter and go, Christina," Dirk decided. "I'll stay with the stock."

"Bring the critters along," said Sam. "That's what I aim to do. Drive them ahead of you."

"I'll stay," said Dirk.

Sam stared at him. "You turning Tory?" he demanded coldly.

"No, I am not," Dirk retorted. "I'm just doing what I set out to do — taking care of Riverbrink. If I should run off now, the British might never come, but thieves and raiders would."

"S'pose the British do come. What you going to do then? Join up?"

"No. I'll just tell them this is the property of a loyal subject, so they won't harm it."

"And then what'll you do?"

"Why then I guess I'll stay right on."

Slowly and reluctantly Sam shook his head. "All along I've said you'd wake up. But I guess I was wrong."

Christina had been gathering up things to take. But now she came to Dirk's side.

"If you're staying here, I'll stay too," she announced.

"You're forgetting Peter," said Dirk sternly. "Now take him and get you gone. Sam is in a hurry."

Sam groaned. "Yes, come on, Tina," he urged. "Maybe after we're gone this big bull-headed mule will come to his senses and overtake us. Look, Dirk, we're going to my Uncle Zebulon's farm. You know where that is?"

"Yes, it's out Crompond way."

"Good. You follow us there. Come on, Tina, Peter."

But the little boy did not want to leave his brother. He clung to Dirk's leg, whimpering. Sam managed to lure him away with the promise that he could ride a pet donkey of the Higgins family called Sophronia. So Sam and Christina departed propelling Peter between them. Each of the two turned to give Dirk a silent signal of farewell, but Peter faced eagerly forward, his high voice chattering of Sophronia until the three figures disappeared.

Dirk turned back into the house to be confronted at once with an odor of burning apples. He sprang to the hearth and caught at the crane to pull the kettle away from the fire, but leaped back with a burned finger.

"Dunderhead!" he muttered at himself.

He seized the poker and swung the kettle around, then stood shaking the injured finger. Such a stupid thing to do! What had Sam called him? A big bull-headed mule. Such a creature would surely be witless and ornery. Dirk could see that he must seem that way to Sam. Was it sheer mulishness, then, that made him stay when everyone else was fleeing? Perhaps. And yet, right or wrong, it was the thing he had to do.

Dirk ran across the fields about half a mile to the western end of the Point. Here the ground fell away in a bluff to a wide belt of shoreline circling the point on three sides. He looked southward. The river lay placid. Not a craft was in sight upon it, not even the ferry. He walked back. Sam was just too excitable, he decided. He almost wished he had not let him carry Christina off so hastily.

Meanwhile, something must be done with the burned apple butter. Dirk spooned up a bit and tasted it. To his surprise the burned flavor had not gone through the entire kettleful. Perhaps if he poured off the unburned part into another kettle and cooked it down some more, it would be fit to eat. He went at the task vigorously, glad of some occupation. When, at length, the apple butter stood cooling in three small crocks, he scoured the two kettles, mended the fire and swept the hearth.

Now he made another trip to see if any ships were in sight. He found three men sitting on a fence that overlooked the river to the south. Their horses were tethered nearby and their weapons proclaimed them to be either soldiers or militiamen. Two turned as he approached. The third continued to gaze through a pair of field glasses.

"Ho there, Big Un," said the older of the two, whose face was pitted from smallpox. "What you doing here?"

"Why, I live here," replied Dirk.

"You'd better be getting out. It's dangerous here," warned the younger one, a boy not over fourteen.

"Yes, better join your militia unit," the older man added.

The third man lowered his field glasses and stared at Dirk. "Maybe he's on the welcoming committee," he suggested and resumed his watch.

"I don't belong to the militia," said Dirk, "but I don't aim to join up with the British either, if that's what you mean."

"What are you here for, then?" asked the pock-marked man sharply.

"I'm guarding that manor house back there at least until the British come."

The pock-marked man regarded Dirk keenly for a moment. Then he said, "Big Un, I believe you. That face of yours would all fall apart if you tried to lie with it. Here's my hand and my name is Shanks, Sergeant Ephraim Shanks."

Dirk proffered his hand and met with a quick, hard grip. He was rather appalled at this ability of his to arouse an instant belief in his word.

A sudden grunt from the man with the field glasses electrified them all. The boy sprang off the fence.

"Are they comin'? Shall I go, Sergeant? Shall I go now?" he shouted.

"Hold on," Shanks roared. "Crawford, what do you see?"

"It's their fleet, all right. Scores of craft — warships, brigs, sloops, everything."

Peering down the river, Dirk could see an indistinguishable mass in the distance. Gradually individual shapes began to emerge — the British fleet! A shudder of excitement seized him. They advanced slowly, almost imperceptibly, but inexorably.

As soon as he could estimate the size of the fleet, Shanks allowed the boy to start for headquarters. With a whoop, he leaped on his horse and pounded across the fields out of sight. The three men who were left abandoned their exposed position on the fence. Crawford elected to climb into a tall maple tree about halfway down the bank toward the river.

"You're goin' to be within shootin' distance of the shore there," warned Shanks.

"They won't see me," said Crawford.

"We-ell, go ahead, then. But put them there spyglasses away. If a beam of sunlight should ketch them, they'd see you for certain."

Without a reply, Crawford made his way down the hill and hoisted himself into the tree. Dirk and Shanks sprawled on their stomachs at the top of the bank under cover of a bush.

As the ships approached the narrow channel where the ferry crossed, the faster ones pushed ahead. All was precision and order, each craft in its place in formation, perfectly controlled. It was a beautiful and frightening sight.

Then a longboat laden with red-coated troops put off from one of the warships and approached the shore. As he watched the rhythmic flash of the oars, the close-packed boat bristling with men and guns, Dirk suffered an instant of panic.

He raised himself from the ground, but Shanks pushed him back.

"Wait," he said, and then in a loud voice, "Crawford, git down out of there. They're a-landin'."

There was no reply from the tree.

"Maybe he didn't hear you," Dirk suggested.

"He heard well enough. He's got to take a last squint through them dummed glasses."

The longboat pulled up to the shore and the men waded to land. There were now a dozen or more boats in the water all converging toward the same place.

Suddenly the bang of a gun made Dirk grip the turf under his hands. Before he could locate its source, there were two more reports. A cloud of smoke floated in the air down at the shore. Then a tree limb cracked sharply — and another. Out of the tree where Crawford had been perched, there fell a heavy bundle of clothes. It made one shallow bounce and was still. At Dirk's side, Shanks erupted a muttered stream of profanity. Dirk twisted the tufts of grass between his fingers, struggling against nausea.

"We better get out of here," said Shanks.

He wriggled backward away from the edge of the bank and Dirk followed. By the time they reached the horses, they were out of sight from the river and could stand erect. Shanks began to unhitch his horse.

"I got to go to headquarters and report this landing," he explained. "You'd better take Crawford's horse and come along."

Dirk stared at Shanks in a daze. He was thoroughly frightened and wanted nothing so much as to run away, yet a strong compulsion held him; he must stay at Riverbrink. He tried to explain this to Shanks but succeeded only in stammering and gesturing toward Riverbrink.

"Oh, you've got your own horse? Well, I'll go on."

Shanks mounted hastily and rode away, leading Crawford's horse by the bridle.

The hoofbeats had not died upon the air before Dirk emerged from his daze enough to regret that he had not gone along with Shanks. A perfect opportunity to escape this oncoming horde and he had let it pass! He took a few steps toward home with a vague idea of driving out some of the stock and starting down the road with them. But he soon turned back; it was too late for that now. He stood for a moment irresolute, then, drawn by a fascination of fear, crept to the edge of the bank and, throwing himself down on the brink again, gazed at the troops along the shore.

Many more had come and still others were pressing in by the boatload. They covered the entire area along the shore line. Some wore the red of British regulars and others green. Dirk tried to count them but gave it up. There were hundreds. He was greatly relieved to note that they seemed to be making camp rather than preparing to advance inland. Arms were stacked, fires built. Even a few tents were erected on the shore.

The fleet, too, was reefing sail and dropping anchor. Men scrambled on the yards as orders were "sung out." A few small craft and rowboats continued to move about from ship to ship and to shore. Toward sunset all was made snug. The fleet rode at anchor. Up and down the river as far as Dirk could see there stretched a forest of masts and spars. It was hard to believe that only a few hours before the river had been empty.

Dirk had momentarily forgotten his own situation in looking at this activity. He was recalled to it by the sound of chopping in a thicket below him. Some British soldier, no doubt, was getting firewood. But would they not soon be sending a party in this direction to look for snipers? Or would not more Continental scouts arrive here to see what the British were doing? In either case, Dirk might find himself in trouble. He wriggled back from the edge of the bank and returned to the manor house. Fleets might come and go, he reflected, but farm chores must always be done. He had put aside the thought of flight.

It was dark by the time he had finished milking and feeding the stock. He locked the stables and went to his cottage where he bolted himself in for the night. Without making a light or a fire, he hunted out some food — cold mush and milk, bread and cheese — then threw himself upon the bed. He slept fitfully.

The next morning he ventured across the point to find the situation seemingly unchanged. Two American scouts were posted at a spot farther inland than the bluff where Dirk had been the day before, as British pickets were occupying the ground directly above the camp. He joined them. They could see little because a heavy fog obscured the far shore and part of the river. The British were still encamped on the eastern bank.

When, at last, the fog lifted, they could see boats carrying troops to the western shore, but how long this had been going on and how many men had been landed there the American scouts had no way of knowing. The sight of buildings burning on the west bank, however, seemed to indicate that the troops landed there had been a mere raiding party and not their main force.

So, as the scouts explained to Dirk, it was assumed that the main force of the enemy was encamped on the east shore and would soon march northward to attack Peekskill. There was nothing for the Americans to do but wait until they started. They waited all day. The enemy seemed continually to be on the point of marching. They arranged their packs, strapped and restrapped them, were drawn up in marching formation and then commanded to fall out. But they never moved from their encampment.

At midafternoon there was a sound of cannonading to the northward. Some time after it had begun, a horseman galloped up to the two American scouts and told them they were ordered to abandon their observation post and rejoin the main body of the army in Peekskill.

"There's a battle on at the two forts across the river," he explained. "We're to be ready to pull back if we lose it."

"But isn't anybody going to watch these enemy troops?" asked one of the scouts.

"Nah, these troops aren't important. Their main body has already attacked us. Landed on the west side of the river and came up and attacked our forts in the rear."

"In the fog!" exclaimed one of the scouts. "They must have landed on the west bank in the fog this morning."

"Well, come on! Look lively!" cried the messenger.

The two scouts mounted and they all rode off with no more than an absent-minded gesture of farewell to Dirk.

"What now?" he wondered. Would the British troops surge up from the shore and swarm over Riverbrink? Though he had become somewhat accustomed to this threat, the new developments intensified it and brought a fresh rush of fear upon him. He took a cautious look over the fence, but the troops seemed as before.

An interminable time passed while the cannon continued to pound. He could accomplish nothing. At length the cannonading ceased. In front of the great house looking north he could hear the sporadic crackle of musketry. Then a shift of the wind took it away. He went to the barn to do the chores. When he returned, the sky to the north was a lurid, shifting red. What was on fire — the British ships, the American forts, or Peekskill? Dirk watched until late in the night when, at length, the red faded to black. Then he locked himself into his cottage to sleep restlessly again until a rainy morning dawned.

That day, in a steady drizzle, the British troops departed. All the long routine of ferrying took place once again in reverse. But this time Dirk watched it with delight, lying in the chill October rain, letting the water course down his back in runnels. In the late afternoon the storm abated and a south breeze sprang up. With a great shouting of commands, the ships hove anchor and sailed up the river.

Dirk noted with dismay the direction they were taking. North! This meant they had won the battle the day before and were advancing into the Highlands. Peekskill must have fallen and the two forts on the river, also. He tried to tell himself that it did not matter which army was in control; they were both alike. Nevertheless, it was most unpleasant to think that he was alone in a deserted country, that his neighbors had fled and that the Continental forces — the scouts with whom he had watched, Colonel Van Cortlandt — were all far away. However, Riverbrink was unharmed and that was his main concern. He slept heavily that night in the knowledge that the manor was safe, at least for a while.

Toward noon of the next day, Dirk was going to the cottage for something to eat when Sam whirled up the lane on horseback. He leaped down, seized Dirk in a wild bearhug and then began pummeling him in the chest.

"So they didn't carry you off, you old stick-in-the-mud!" he exclaimed.

"Why, of course not," Dirk replied, rather startled at Sam's unusual effusiveness. "How are Christina and Peter and all your folks?"

"They're well. Sent word for you to come back with me."

"Oh, no. It's safe here now. The British have gone."

"They've gone true enough — up the river. Our entire army is in retreat. This whole country will be invaded and occupied by the enemy."

Dirk grinned. "I've heard that before. I'll chance it."

"It's no chance, Dirk. It's sure. Come on back. Christina sent me to get you."

"Now, Sam, let's not go through all this again. I'm staying." And Dirk started for the cottage.

Sam followed. "I thought you'd say that. Well, I'll stay with you, then."

Dirk turned joyously and clapped Sam on the shoulder. "Do you mean it? I'd like that fine. But wait. You mustn't take such a risk just to keep me company."

"Oh, I'm not doing it for you," rejoined Sam blandly. "It's for Christina. I told her you wouldn't come but I'd stay and bring her back word whether they shoot or hang you."

Dirk laughed. "Aren't you afraid of being shot or hanged yourself?"

"Oh, no. Never fear I'll fall into their hands."

"Well, there's no need to worry about that just now. Are you hungry? Let's get some dinner." Dirk drew Sam along toward the cottage. "Meantime tell me all about everybody — Christina, Peter, yes and yourself, too. How have you fared, boy?"

Sam began saying that they had reached his uncle's place safely, that his father had arrived there from the battle early that morning.

Dirk watched Sam talk and suddenly, in his joy at seeing that homely but animated face, became aware for the first time just how lonely he had been. He flung an arm across the thin shoulders and they entered the cottage together.

☆ 8 ☆

DIRK AND SAM AGREED THAT THE BRITISH WOULD PROBABLY not invade that area for several days. The King's forces were never noted for their speed in following up a victory and here surely there was no need for haste. The countryside had been evacuated and they could move in at their leisure. But the boys failed to reckon with the British need for foodstuffs and the Tories' eagerness to invade the conquered territory. Thus they were unprepared when the royal forces arrived the very next morning.

Sam had gone across lots to his own house to look for a horse that he had turned into a remote pasture before their flight, thinking him too lame and decrepit to make the journey. So when Dirk heard the sound of slow hoofbeats in the lane, he thought Sam had brought his horse back. Bursting out of the cottage door, he almost collided with two men in green uniforms. Behind them in the lane sat an officer on horseback. The British forces had arrived.

In his astonishment, Dirk instinctively drew back.

"Well?" said the officer on a rising note. He looked Dirk up and down with cool appraisal.

"Are you — is this the, uh, British army?" stammered Dirk.

"Not *British*. We are American loyalists."

"Oh, all the better! I've been waiting here for you."

"To enlist with us, you mean?"

"Not exactly that." Dirk paused for breath. Things were not going as he had planned. "You see, this manor — River-brink, it is called — belongs to Mr. Roderick Stone who is loyal to the King."

"Yes, yes, we know all that." The officer slapped his boot impatiently with his riding crop. "And why were you wait-ing here if not to join up?"

"Why, to tell you about Mr. Stone and then to stay on and take care of the farm."

The officer smiled sardonically. "You needn't worry about that any more," he said. "We'll take care of the farm. We'll butcher the stock or ship them alive. His Majesty's troops must be fed."

"You can't mean that, sir. Mr. Stone is a loyal subject. You propose to treat him like a rebel."

"If he is genuinely loyal, he will be glad to have his prop-erty used in the King's service." The officer slapped his boot again. "And now I have no more time to bandy words with a farm boy. Will you enlist in our regiment?"

Dirk's chin came up. "No," he replied. "I'll stay here and try to protect Mr. Stone's property from his own party."

The officer's lips tightened. "Bring him along, men," he

ordered, and then to Dirk, "I gave you a chance to come of your own will. Now you're our prisoner."

The two soldiers seized Dirk's arms and began propelling him down the lane. The officer rode behind. Dirk knew now with a sudden throat-twisting intensity just how Dr. Huggerford had felt. The humiliation of being hauled along like a criminal!

Worst of all was the possibility that Sam would be captured — Sam who had deliberately risked this fate to try to save his stubborn friend. When they reached the King's Ferry Road, Dirk looked fearfully eastward, half expecting to see Sam being conducted toward them under guard. But there was only a green-coated squad marching in the opposite direction.

The officer now halted the men. "Harkins, take the prisoner to the ship," he said. "Melrose, come with me."

Abruptly, the two groups separated and Dirk was escorted to the riverbank. A ship was anchored in midstream and rowboats were plying between the ships and the shore. Harkins prodded his prisoner into a boat that was about to put off. It was manned by six sailors in navy blue.

"Wot's the cargo, matey?" one wanted to know.

"This?" inquired Harkins. "Just a witless ox that doesn't want to join the loyalist troops."

"A-ow! And can you fancy that now!" exclaimed another sailor in a falsetto voice. "Ye should never have arsked him did he want to join. Just sign him on. That's our way in the navy."

"The very thing, sailor!" exclaimed Harkins. "We'll put this lubber in the navy."

"Why not? We ain't perticular," remarked the tar, whereat the others hooted with laughter.

Dirk tried to keep his face from showing the horror that he felt at this suggestion. He knew these men were only baiting him but he had heard tales of how men were taken by force off the streets and impressed into the British navy. It might happen to him.

They climbed a rope ladder to the deck of the ship.

Here Harkins saluted a green-clad officer and said, "Lieutenant Nash sent this prisoner, sir."

The officer gave Dirk a casual glance and indicated a hatch cover nearby. Harkins lifted the cover off.

"Jump in," he ordered.

And without allowing Dirk time to comply, he gave him a push. Dirk landed with a grunt on a coil of rope in the hold. An instant later the hatch cover was replaced, leaving him in darkness. At once the foul stench of bilge water assailed his nostrils. He rolled to his back and lay half dazed by the rapid sequence of events that had brought him to these straits. Footsteps sounded continuously on the deck overhead and at long intervals there came the musical note of a bell.

Dirk knew he should be planning an escape, but there seemed no possible means. Suppose he should contrive to get out of the hold and even off the ship. What then? The river swarmed with boats. He could not get away. It was hopeless. Hours passed until he lost all account of time and thought it must surely be night.

Then suddenly the hatch was lifted, letting a flood of daylight down upon him. To his astonishment the sun was still high.

"Ho, you down there!" said Harkins' voice. "Can you milk a cow?"

"I'd be a poor excuse for a farmer if I couldn't," said Dirk.

"Come on out, then. You're needed."

Harkins and a sailor hauled him forth. He blinked in the light and breathed great gulps of the sweet air. A glance at the shadows told him it was about four in the afternoon.

Again he was tumbled into a boat and taken back to the east bank of the river. This shore now swarmed with a blatting, bawling, milling mass of livestock that had been collected from the adjacent countryside. Most of the sheep and cattle were sorry-looking specimens that had been left behind by the fleeing farmers, but a few herds were in good condition. Dirk figured that these belonged to Tory families who had remained to throw themselves on the mercy of the invaders. Apparently they had received the same treatment accorded to Riverbrink.

Lieutenant Nash, Dirk's original captor, was awaiting him. "Ah, here you are, farmer!" he exclaimed. "Get busy and milk these cows."

Dirk resented the way Nash said "farmer." In his mouth it was a term of contempt. He stood with set jaw, glowering, and made no move to obey.

"I can't milk without a stool and some buckets," he said.

"Very well. Harkins, go up to the Riverbrink stable and get what he needs."

While he waited, Dirk stood gazing at the activity along the river front. Not far away a party of officers was getting out of a rowboat. One man caught Dirk's eye. There was something familiar in that graceful, arrogant bearing. Then he knew; it was Gerit Van Wyck.

"Oh, sir," he cried to Nash. "There's a man who knows me, who can vouch for me — Mr. Van Wyck."

"Indeed? We'll see about that." And strolling toward Van Wyck, Nash remarked, "Lieutenant, here's someone who claims a previous acquaintance with you."

Van Wyck stared an instant with no recognition on his finely sculptured face. Then he exclaimed, "Ah, yes, the farm boy! You want something of me?"

"Only that you should vouch for my loyalty to Mr. Stone. I am accused of being a rebel."

"Indeed? Well, as for your loyalty to Mr. Stone, I cannot see that it has any bearing on the case. And as for your political opinions, I think they are quite rightly under suspicion. Yes, Nash, the last time I saw this presumptuous lout he was greatly excited over some doctrines propagated by the rebels to the effect that all men are equal. Isn't that right, farmer?"

Van Wyck also said "farmer" as though it was a disgrace to be one. Dirk tensed every muscle to restrain his anger.

"Yes, that's right," he admitted with a deceptive quietness.

"See, Nash? He'll claim, no doubt, that he has had a change of heart since then but don't believe him."

"What do you say to this, farmer?" Nash demanded.

Dirk felt the blood throb in his neck. "I am proud to be a farmer," he said in a voice thick with anger.

"Hear! Hear!" exclaimed Van Wyck. "He condemns himself out of his own mouth. See that insolent expression! He fancies himself right now as our equal. He's a rank stinking rebel."

Dirk flung up his head in defiance. He was swept with a fierce exultation. Though a prisoner, he felt a glorious sense of freedom, for he was suddenly at peace with himself.

"Do you admit you are a rebel?" Nash demanded.

"Yes," Dirk declared, flinging the answer out like a challenge.

"Then why didn't you say so in the first place?" roared Nash.

"I didn't know it," Dirk replied.

"Well, I'm damned," said Nash with quiet fervor.

Van Wyck burst into hard, mocking laughter. "It takes me to bring out their true colors," he remarked, and, still laughing, strode away.

At this moment Harkins returned with the equipment for milking. Dirk thought about refusing to do this task, but all his farmer's instincts impelled him toward it. These cows needed milking. To neglect them would be needless cruelty. Besides, he was in no haste to return to the stinking hold of the ship. He slung his stool under the nearest cow and began milking.

Harkins was detailed to keep guard over him and, having been warned by Nash that his prisoner was an avowed enemy, he kept close watch. Dirk now realized that he had been foolish to declare himself so openly and thus reduce his chances of escape. But he could not be truly sorry he had done so. He felt much better for it, had more respect for himself.

The cattle were restless and hard to manage. Though the slaughter of the other stock was taking place out of sight around the curve of the point, still they could hear the frenzied bawling and smell the fresh blood. This made them exceedingly nervous and, with the feeling of an unfamiliar hand upon them, besides, many refused to give down their milk.

Dirk struggled along as the afternoon waned. When he had finished with the last herd, he realized that the Riverbrink cattle were nowhere among them.

"They're up in the stable," Harkins volunteered. "Guess captain thought he'd leave them there till time to ship them."

"I'll milk them up there, then," Dirk decided.

"Oh, no, you won't," declared Harkins. "I'm tired of being escort to a milkmaid. Besides, we don't need any more milk."

Dirk was also weary. For an instant he wondered why he

should be concerned over taking care of this enemy property. But the long habit of responsibility for Riverbrink's welfare could not be so readily shaken off.

"I'm tired, too," he remarked, trying a different approach, "but the Riverbrink herd is very valuable. The lieutenant will be angry if we neglect them."

"Well, be quick about it, then," ordered Harkins. "It's past my mess hour."

Dirk had had no food since morning and the savory odor of beef frying over the campfires was tantalizing. One of Harkins' comrades gave him a slab of steak on a long fork. The sight of it dripping succulent juices brought the saliva gushing into Dirk's mouth.

At Riverbrink, Dirk found the great house had been opened. Smoke rose from every chimney. Officers lounged on the porch and orderlies were busy in the kitchen quarters. There was considerable activity also in the horse stables. But in the cow stable all was silence and semi-darkness.

"What a stink!" exclaimed Harkins. "Make it quick, rebel. I can't stand this foul smell for long."

"A cow stable smells good," said Dirk resentfully.

While he milked, the soldier paced restlessly about the stable, constantly urging him to hurry.

At length he said, "See here, rebel, I'm going to stand outside the door where I can get some fresh air for a moment, but let me hear the milk falling steadily into that pail. Not a false move, mind you, or I shall come in and shoot you."

Dirk's back was toward the stable door. He heard the

soldier cross the floor. He continued to milk steadily, but his eye flashed about the stable, looking for a possible weapon. This might be his best chance to escape. Let Harkins once turn his back and Dirk would have his opportunity.

Suddenly he was aware of a small scuffling noise toward the back of the stable. Without moving his head, he swept his eyes about the whole range of their vision. Some chaff was sifting down from the square aperture in the ceiling that led to the hayloft. It gleamed briefly in the horizontal shaft of light from the doorway. Then appeared a pair of clumsy leather shoes dangling at the ends of skinny legs. Dirk caught his breath and missed a beat in the rhythm of his milking, for the figure swinging there full length now before his startled gaze was that of Sam Higgins.

Dirk's lips made the words, "Back, Sam! Go back!"

But he did not utter them. He could only pray mutely that this dangling target was not visible from the door, or, if it was, that Harkins was not looking. Sam swung a moment by his hands, caught sight of Dirk and gave him a bold wink. Then he dropped to the stable floor. Though there was some hay to break the impact, a loud thump resulted. Sam sprang up at once and dodged between two cows.

"What was that?" roared Harkins, charging in with his musket at the ready. He peered about intently, but it was evident he could see very little after the brighter light outdoors.

Dirk rose and looked in the opposite direction from the one where Sam was hiding. "It was a thump," he said helpfully. "It might have come from over there."

"Go over and see what it is," Harkins ordered. "And no nonsense. I have my gun on you."

Dirk walked down the center of the stable with Harkins following closely behind him. They passed the place where Sam was concealed. An instant later there was the sound of a dull impact and a grunt. Dirk was jostled forward. He turned to see Harkins lying on the floor and Sam standing over him with a wooden manure shovel in his hands. For a moment the two boys could only gaze down in stupefaction at their victim.

Sam was the first to break out of the spell. "Let's get away from here!" he panted. "Let's take his gun and run for it."

But Dirk held him back. "Not so fast!" he urged. "He isn't dead, just stunned. We'd do better to bind and gag him so he won't make any trouble when he comes to. Then we can stay right here till it's dark enough to get away safely."

So they trussed the soldier up with articles of his own clothing. Scarcely had they finished when he began to regain consciousness. He rolled his eyes angrily and twisted against his bonds.

"Guess they'll hold," muttered Dirk. "Sorry you don't like the smell here, soldier, but it's a sight better than the hold of your ship."

The two boys now began to fill themselves with milk, taking turns drinking it from a wooden grain measure. They moved to the opposite end of the stable from Harkins and conversed in whispers.

"We'd better plan out where we're going," said Dirk.

"Where!" Sam lowered the grain measure and stared, his upper lip moustached with milk. "Why, we're going back to our folks, aren't we? What else would we do?"

Dirk was thoughtful. "I hate to leave these cattle. They aren't going to take any proper care of them. I can see that."

"Well, but, land o' goodness, we can't take them with us. We'll be lucky if we can get away ourselves."

"Let's stay nearby for a while, Sam. It won't be very risky. They won't bother themselves to look for me. Maybe I'll think up what to do about the cattle."

Sam hesitated, then said, "Well, I'll tell you a place we could hide. I figured to spend tonight there if I didn't find you — in the tree house."

"Just the place!" Dirk exulted. "We can reach it easily from here."

It was fortunate for their purposes that the stable faced away from the great house. They could slip out and follow the cow lane down to the night pasture with little danger of being seen. They walked rapidly, Sam carrying the soldier's gun, and arrived safely at their hiding place.

The tree house was nothing more than a rough platform that the boys had built a number of years before in a pine tree on the southeast side of the manor. About ten feet from the ground, it was entirely concealed by low-hanging branches. Here the boys had often played in their childhood, sometimes that they were Indians about to attack the manor house, sometimes that they were pioneers defending their wilderness cabins. Now they swung themselves up into its dark shelter with a far keener sense of escape than they had ever achieved in play. But at once they encountered difficulties.

"This place never seemed so small when we used to play here," grunted Dirk, trying to dispose his legs comfortably. "The tree must have grown in on it."

"Could be you've grown *out*," chuckled Sam. "I feel some cramped myself."

After much shifting about, they finally disposed themselves in fairly comfortable postures, Dirk with his legs looped over a convenient limb. For long they lay breathing the pine fragrance and savoring their freedom.

"How'd you come to be in the barn?" demanded Dirk at length. "Hadn't you got home when the redcoats came?"

"Yes, I was just bringing my old horse from the pasture. I dropped behind a stone wall and watched them pass the house. Then I started across lots for Riverbrink."

"Why didn't you hit out for your uncle's place, Sam? You could have got away easy."

"And what would I have told Christina when she asked what happened to you? No, it wasn't that I cared a rap about your skin, Dirk. I just didn't dare face her and say I had deserted you."

Dirk pounded his friend affectionately. "You lying old rascal!" he chuckled. "Did you see them leading me off?"

"No, I was too late. I hid up in the haymow all day and

131

watched the grounds out of that little window in the peak of the roof. When I saw you coming back, I worked my way down to the stable."

Again they lay in a companionable silence.

"About those cows," Dirk began, "why couldn't we drive them off, say, around to that swamp pasture tonight? The enemy'd never find them there. Then tomorrow night we could start driving them to your uncle's."

Sam roused up abruptly. "You don't get me back to that stable tonight," he declared. "We were lucky to escape as easy as we did."

"Well, maybe we should wait till tomorrow night to get them, when things have quieted down," Dirk conceded.

Both were sitting upright now in the darkness.

"Anyhow," Sam added sharply, "just this morning you were claiming the redcoats were really entitled to those cattle."

"They're Mr. Stone's," said Dirk. "He'll never see them if they get hold of them."

"Do you mean by this that you're a patriot, Dirk, or just that you're not a Tory?"

For a moment Dirk did not answer. Then he said, "We've got to fight them. I see that now. We've got to fight them and beat them. They don't understand about us."

"So then, Dirk, you *are* one of us!" Sam grasped his arm. "You have finally waked up, thank heaven. What made you change your mind — their arresting you?"

"No."

"Well, what did they do that made you come to your senses?" And Sam shook his arm impatiently.

Dirk was silent a moment. Then he said, "They called me a farmer."

"Well, you are one, aren't you?"

"Yes, of course. It was the way they said it, as if they were better than I was on that account."

After a moment, Sam remarked, "You're a queer sort, Dirk. When you had all manner of *good* reasons to join us, you couldn't make up your mind. Now they call you a farmer, which you are, and that — *that* decides you."

"It must sound foolish to you," Dirk admitted. "I guess I just can't make you understand my reason. But, Sam, I can only say to me it is a great reason — truly the greatest."

☆ 9 ☆

DIRK OPENED HIS EYES AND LOOKED AT A CURTAIN OF green needles. He stirred sleepily to find that every muscle was stiff. His movement aroused Sam and both groaning boys hauled themselves to a sitting posture.

"We ought to have spent the night on the ground," remarked Dirk. "By the time we've stayed here all day, we'll be so stiff we won't be able to move."

"It's a perfect place to hide, though," said Sam. "We're on a little hill. Can see the manor house and yet not be seen."

Dirk agreed and they both peered out through the screen of branches. Even so early there were signs of activity. A horseman cantered up the driveway and smoke rolled from the chimneys. The boys grinned at each other, enjoying their sense of security.

"Now if I only had a nice rasher of bacon — " Sam began, but Dirk protested that this suggestion was torture.

From the ground directly below them came a sound of panting. Dirk peered over the edge of the platform into the uplifted muzzle of a shepherd dog.

"It's your dog, Sam," he announced with quiet despair.

134

"Not Pluck!" Sam gazed downward in horror, and the dog, tail thrashing, gave a delighted woof of greeting. "He's followed me from Uncle Zeb's. What'll we do with him, Dirk? We can't bring him up here."

"Well, we certainly can't leave him down there," said Dirk.

"What in the world shall we do?" Sam pondered while the dog circled beneath him, looking up with mouth open and long tongue flapping. "I'll have to shoot him, that's all." He reached for the gun lying across an adjacent limb, his face puckered with emotion, then drew back his arm. "Oh, Dirk, I can't."

"Bring him up here, Sam. The two of us can keep him in hand."

Sam brightened. "We can try it," he agreed.

After a look all around, he scrambled down from the tree and hoisted the dog to where Dirk could get a grasp on him. It was a hard tussle and all three were panting heavily when they finally achieved the platform. If this had seemed small for the two boys only, now, with a large and struggling dog between them, they were both in constant danger of being crowded over the edge. They finally arrived at an endurable arrangement with the dog on the higher side of the platform, from which he did not dare to jump, and the two boys ranged along the lower side where they could restrain him. Gradually, Pluck became resigned to his captivity and they all settled down for a long day.

Shortly afterward, a troop of green-coated horsemen cantered down the driveway and at the same time another detail of troops appeared on foot. At the edge of the manor house grounds, the infantrymen fanned out and proceeded across the fields, their bayonets fixed. They followed stone walls, poked into fence corners and generally made a search of all possible hiding places — except treetops.

"They're looking for you, Dirk!" exclaimed Sam. "And those mounted men will search the highways."

"I didn't know they needed me so bad," said Dirk with his slow grin. "Probably can't get anybody else to milk their cows."

But though he joked, it was a frightening sight and the boys drew closer together on their perch.

"If this fool dog doesn't betray us, we'll probably be safe," Sam remarked.

One by one the foot soldiers disappeared from the boys' range of vision. A couple of hours later they began straggling back. The boys kept count until all had returned but one. This trooper finally appeared cutting across the very field where their pine tree was located. His course indicated that he would pass directly under it. Dirk reached down the gun and kept him covered while Sam held Pluck's muzzle. The green cocked hat passed beneath them. Its owner walked on, scaled a stone wall and was gone. The two boys collapsed with relief. Like a flash, Pluck scrambled past them. Eluding Sam's frantic clutch, he ran along a drooping branch and sprang to the ground.

Sam began to mutter angrily, but Dirk said with a laugh,

"I'm glad he's gone. Now we'll have a little more room."

"But if he stays around down below us looking up —"

"He won't. He didn't like the way we treated him."

Nor did he stay or return the rest of the day.

As soon as darkness set in, the boys climbed down out of the tree. It was a sheer pleasure to get their feet on the ground once more and walk about freely. Dirk now set in motion his plan to recover the Riverbrink cattle. Since Sam did not fully approve the idea, Dirk was determined he should bear as little of the risk as possible. The arrangement was that Dirk should go to the stable and first bring out the grain, then the cows. He was to lead one at a time down the lane and across a meadow to a break in the stone wall near the river on the eastern side of the manor. Here Sam would meet him and conduct the cow to the swamp pasture while Dirk returned to the stable for another. Thus Sam's route would be rougher but Dirk's more hazardous.

In the late evening, Dirk made his way to the cow stable and crouched in the shadows outside waiting to see if a sentry would pass. There was no moon but bright starlight. At length a dark figure came thumping down around the corner of the barn, crossed the lane, and continued out of sight around the horse stable. The creak of a leather gun sling identified him as a sentry.

Dirk entered the cow stable. The door was not locked, but it squeaked sharply. He paused motionless inside. There was no sound but the stirring of the cattle, all of which he found to be still there. He groped his way to a room at the back of the stable where grain was stored, hauled forth a sack and carried it to the end of the cow lane where Sam waited to take it another hitch. There was sufficient time for two trips between passings of the sentry. The whole process was accomplished without incident.

Getting the cattle out was more difficult. As Dirk led each cow down the lane, their passage caused considerable clatter and sometimes she would try to turn back to the stable. However, he successfully escorted a dozen to the point where Sam took charge. Then the lightening horizon warned him that there would be time for only a few more trips. He became reckless. Whereas each time before he had waited in the stable until the sentry passed, even though it might mean the loss of a quarter hour, this time he took a chance and started out with two cows.

When he was halfway down the lane, there came the harsh challenge, "Halt! Who goes there?"

Dirk tried to stop, but one cow edged around sidewise while the other jerked back on her halter.

"Answer or I'll fire," warned the sentry.

Dirk could hear the gun being cocked. He crouched between the two cows. There was a sharp blast and one of the cows staggered against Dirk, almost knocking him down. Then with loud agonized bellows, she bolted away and galloped down the lane. Under cover of the racket, Dirk scurried over the stone wall and crouched behind it. In an instant two men ran up, apparently from the horse stable and demanded what all the noise was about.

"I guess I've shot a cow," the sentry admitted.

One of the men guffawed. "She didn't advance and give the countersign, I suppose."

The other exclaimed, "Well, clumsy, go shoot her again. Put her out of her agony."

The bellows of the wounded animal could still be heard nearby. The sentry clumped down the lane after her.

"Where did she come from?" asked one of the remaining men of the other.

"Why, the cow stable's right here. Some careless fool left the door ajar."

The hinges creaked. Then voices came from inside.

"Are any others gone?"

"Yes, here are several vacant stalls, a dozen or more."

"Well, there can't be as many as that astray. They would be all about the place. They must have been driven down to the shore."

"Then it's no further concern of ours. Let's get back to our game."

The stable door squeaked shut, its wooden bolt slid home. The voices receded in the direction of the horse stable. A gun crashed, putting an abrupt end to the bellowing of the cow. A moment later, the sentry clumped past and resumed his beat.

Dirk stood erect. All about him the night was still once more. He scrambled over the wall and hurried down the lane. In the middle of the meadow he met Sam plunging over the ground with Pluck at his heels.

"Those two shots!" Sam gasped. "I thought they had you for sure. I was way back in the swamp meadow."

Dirk explained what had happened. "And now let's get that grain to a safer place before daylight," he added.

They carried the sacks to a secluded fence corner and covered them with brush. Then they started for their hidden pasture. This took them back over the route that Sam had now traversed so many times — through the meadows, across a shallow inlet of the river, and finally through a field overgrown with brush that bordered on the pasture they had selected. In this swampy area there was still some green grass and some of the cows were grazing, for dawn had come.

The boys took turns milking and keeping watch over the fence toward Riverbrink. They drank their fill of milk and then sought out a secluded fence corner near the river where they alternated sleeping and standing guard all day. At nightfall, Sam was ready to start driving the herd toward his uncle's farm, but Dirk had another proposal.

"I've been thinking, Sam," he said. "Why not keep the cows right here? They'd be safer than they would be on the road. Those soldiers won't be looking for them. They'll think they've been taken down to the shore with the others — just as those men did that I heard talking last night. Besides, driving them all that way would be bad for them, the milk and meat both."

"Oh, you and your tarnation cows!" Sam exploded. "I don't care what would be best for them. I want to go back and see my family and — and Tina."

"Why don't you go, then, and I'll stay," Dirk suggested. "If I get lonesome or decide the enemy's going to stay all winter, I'll come along later."

It was finally settled this way although Sam was reluctant to leave his friend in such a dangerous post. Dirk insisted, however, that even though the enemy might find the cattle, they would not catch him again. So at length Sam went off with Pluck at his heels and Dirk was left with his flock.

He soon established a routine. He milked before daylight and after nightfall. The rest of the time he kept away from the cattle. Much of his time was spent at the edge of the river on a tiny inlet where a thicket screened him from sight. Here he fished and sometimes slept. Besides fish he had rabbit to eat, which he caught with a snare.

At night he sometimes prowled around Riverbrink. Once he went to the Higgins barn and hunted out a couple of blankets to keep him warm sleeping in the crisp October weather. A number of nights were spent contriving a thatched shelter for the stack of grain bags. So a week passed.

Meanwhile the weather became increasingly cold and the enemy showed no signs of leaving. Dirk was chilly and lonesome. He decided to drive the cattle to Sam's uncle's farm. At the very point of departure, he jumped from a stone wall and wrenched his ankle severely. It swelled up and caused him intense pain. He bound it with a strip of blanket. There was no more question of walking the eight miles or so to Crompond. He could scarcely hobble around to do the milking.

And now, for the first time, he began to fear capture. Before his injury he had been confident that he could keep out of the enemy's hands, but now he felt helpless. For long hours he sat in his thicket shelter prepared, if discovered, to jump into the river and swim for safety. So passed another week and more.

One morning he awoke with a cold rain beating on his face. His blankets were soaked. The cows huddled under the trees too miserable to eat. That decided him. He would start with the cattle for Crompond that night. His ankle was on the mend and he had fashioned a crutch from a tree branch. Along in the afternoon the rain ceased and a biting wind came up. He took shelter in the angle of a stone wall.

Suddenly, he became aware of hallooing in the distance. As it came nearer, he could distinguish his own name in Sam's voice. Was Sam trying to shout a warning, he wondered. Should he hide? While he stood irresolute, Pluck broke through the bushes to the south and after him came Sam. At sight of Dirk, Sam tossed his cap in the air and uttered a shout of delight.

"Dirk, you old pirate, I thought they had got you again for sure," he cried.

"They'll have us both if you don't stop bellowing," said Dirk. "Have you lost your mind, shouting like that?"

Sam gazed at Dirk with a puzzled expression. "Don't you know?" he asked. "They've gone."

"Who's gone? The enemy?"

"Two days ago, bag and baggage. Didn't you see them?"

"No, I haven't been over there lately. Twisted my ankle. What made them go?"

"Seems there was a battle somewhere up the river — Saratogy or some such place. We whupt them and chased them clear back down the river. There's Continental troops back in Peekskill right now."

"Well!" exclaimed Dirk inadequately. "Well! Let's go home. Give me some help, will you? This old ankle!"

They started back for Riverbrink, Dirk with a hand on Sam's shoulder.

"It's good you kept your cows here," Sam remarked. "The enemy got ours."

"No! Way out there?"

"Yes. Four Tory soldiers came one day. I was away on my horse at the time so they didn't get him. Pa was there. He herded all the women into the house and stood guard over them with a musket but the men never went near the house. Took all the stock they could drive away. All we've got left is an ox they didn't want and some sheep and three heifers that had wandered back in the hills. Got my uncle's critters, too."

Just as they reached the cottage, Dirk asked, "How did you leave Christina and Peter?"

"I didn't!" cried Sam and flung open the door.

It was a merry reunion. Peter squealed with ear-piercing elation. Dirk tossed him to his shoulder and hugged Christina while Sam looked on with a grin.

When the frenzied greetings had subsided, they began

143

to note the condition of the cottage. All of the furniture had been left. Some of it showed the marks of rough usage — the rakes of spurs and knife gouges. But it was still serviceable. Only the foodstuffs were taken, of which there had been no great supply — salt, spices, smoked meat hanging in the rafters.

At the great house many small articles of value were gone and even some of the lighter pieces of furniture. A few hangings and pictures had been taken. The wine cellar was empty and all the foodstuffs in the house had been carried away. The only food left at Riverbrink was in a vegetable cellar dug into the slope of a bank on the east side of the grounds. Situated at some distance from the house and barns, this had been overlooked. As it was stocked with potatoes, carrots, beets, and turnips, it might well stand between the Hollenbecks and starvation during the next winter.

The ranks of the livestock were heavily depleted. Horses, sheep, and hogs were gone, and the cows that Dirk had had to leave. A pair of oxen was left. The flock of chickens had been taken, but in his inspection of the grounds, Dirk spied a few running wild which had apparently escaped their captors. With luck he could find where they were roosting and, in a couple of nights, would have the beginnings of a new flock.

Altogether, Dirk and Christina figured, as they sat in the cottage over a late meal of milk and baked potato and stewed rabbit, they had come through the invasion not too badly. They were all three together once more, safe and well, with a roof over their heads and enough food for the winter.

Suddenly Peter roused up in bed and began to call for Dirk, who promptly picked him up, slung him over his shoulder and resumed his place. Peter took a firm grip on Dirk's ear, then, with a long, shivering sigh, went back to sleep.

"Poor little fellow!" said Christina. "You can't believe how he's missed you, Dirk. I do hope you need never be separated from us again."

"I expect I will, though," said Dirk reluctantly, "and quite soon, too. I must go down to Stonehaven and tell Mr. Stone I've joined the American side."

"Now, Dirk, what good can that do? You'll only make him angry."

"Probably. But I told Miss Ellen I would and I must keep my word."

☆ 10 ☆

It was not until the following January that Dirk finally set forth on his journey to Stonehaven. The day was intensely cold, dark and threatening. Dirk was wearing the rusty greatcoat and blue knitted cap that he had worn on the same journey more than a year before. He was mounted on a chestnut horse called Highboy that belonged to Sam.

At the Higgins farm the horse wanted to turn in, but Dirk hauled him back onto his course. He had no desire to see Sam this morning, for Sam did not approve of this trip. He thought it dangerous and futile. But when Dirk had insisted and had planned to walk, Sam had lent him the horse. He had also offered to do the chores at Riverbrink for the two or three days Dirk would be gone. This would not be necessary since Christina could milk. Still, it was a comfort to know the Higgins family was near if she should need them.

Many things had delayed his starting. First, he must get the Riverbrink farm in running order again. Then it soon developed that the entire countryside had been seriously disorganized by the invasion. Many families returned to find their homes burned. Even those whose buildings had been spared were, in many cases, almost destitute of food and fodder. Dirk found himself serving on a committee to provide for these people by collecting foodstuffs from the more fortunate. This meant, of course, that the Riverbrink supplies and even its stock must be shared.

It was, therefore, as a well-established and active patriot that Dirk set out at length upon this journey into the Neutral Ground. It had been much to accomplish in two months. But during that time, also, winter had set in. A foot of crusty snow lay on the ground and more began to fall shortly after he left Peekskill. It fell in a quiet, direct, businesslike manner. In no time the horse's footsteps were muffled into silence and the only sound was the creaking leather of the saddle. The snow made a moving veil across Dirk's vision; fence rails and nearby buildings were blurred, the farther landscape entirely blotted out. He knew that he ought to turn back at once, but stubbornly he set his mind against it. The events of the last two months had seemed a deliberate conspiracy to keep him from Miss Ellen and now that he had actually achieved a start, a little matter of snow was not going to deter him.

He did not deny to himself that the chief object of this journey was to see Miss Ellen — just that, only to see her. Perhaps they might not exchange a word but he would know that she was safe and well. It had occurred to him in anticipating this trip that he might not get to see her at all. He must go first to the tenant house, of course. That was where he would be lodged. Then Matthew East would arrange for him to talk with Mr. Stone at the great house. And somehow, either before or during or after the interview, he must see Miss Ellen. He would not start for home until he had.

A wind sprang up out of the north and beat down in short, vicious gusts. Each attack enveloped horse and rider in a whirl of snow so that Dirk could not see beyond the horse's head. Sometimes Highboy would stop and wait for the onslaught to pass; sometimes he forged on, only to plunge into a ditch at the roadside. Dirk then seriously contemplated turning back, but this shift in direction would bring the wind straight in their faces and he knew the horse could then make no headway at all. So he continued.

On Pine's Bridge he met a rider, the last he was to see that day. The man was muffled to the eyes. He and his mount were plastered over completely with snow. They maneuvered their horses past each other on the narrow planking and Dirk was alone again in a wilderness of snow. As the day wore on, the storm intensified. It attacked now from every quarter and sometimes seemingly from all quarters at once, whirling down upon him with an eerie whistle and sucking the very breath out of his nostrils. At such times Highboy would whirl about, trying vainly to get the storm at his back, so that when the tempest subsided Dirk would have to dismount and locate the horse's tracks (already nearly obliterated) to avoid doubling back upon them.

His one thought now was to find refuge. He came upon a house near enough the road so that its dark bulk was visible through the storm, but there was no track to it between the gateposts. That meant that it was unoccupied. Dirk sat a moment debating whether to go in but decided against it. This blizzard might take a week to blow itself out and a man could perish waiting so long in an empty house. He would keep on until dark.

All the time the snow had been piling up rapidly and now Highboy had trouble wallowing through it. His pace, never more than a walk, became slower and slower. Finally he stopped. When Dirk slapped him on the flank, he took a few steps, then halted again and would not budge. There was nothing to do but dismount and lead him.

So another phase of the journey set in. Dirk soon found that the greatcoat impeded him too much. He took it off and slung it across the saddle. Then there were miles of plunging and staggering through the snow with the bridle looped around his arm. Often the drifts came as high as his hips. He swung his arms ahead, scooping the snow aside. Soaked to the skin all over, he was scarcely conscious of the cold, so violent were his exertions.

When his strength had begun to fail and the light was waning, he came upon a small house. Occupied or not, this must be his refuge for the night. He dragged himself to the door and pounded loudly.

"Go away!" called a masculine voice from inside. "Go away or I'll shoot you."

"Great heavens, man!" cried Dirk. "Would you turn a human creature away in this storm? Let me in or I'll die."

The top half of the door swung open and a musket barrel was thrust out. Behind it appeared the grisly, unshaven face of a man.

"Go away, I say," he repeated. "I care nothing whether you live or die, just so you're not in here eating my food."

For a moment Dirk stood so taken aback that he could not think. "Well, then," he said at length, "would it be too much for you to tell me where Stonehaven is from here?"

The man's face expressed instant relief. "Not far!" he exclaimed. "Not far. Continue down this road to the four corners. Turn right and you're there." With that he hauled in the gun and shut the door.

Back on the highway, Dirk reflected in horror upon what he had just seen. This was indeed life ruled by stark fear and hunger when a man would refuse another shelter from a blizzard because of the few bites he might eat. What sort of country was this Neutral Ground? No place for a woman surely.

Dirk's progress now became a race with nightfall. If he did not reach the crossroads before dark, he would pass right through without seeing it and be hopelessly lost on beyond. In fact, it was a grave question whether he would recognize the intersection even by daylight, so limited was his range of vision in the welter of snow and wind. The storm rose to new heights of fury, and darkness advanced inexorably. At length he stopped, breathing in great gasps, and looked again to either side for some sign of a road or a wall bordering a road, but there was only the eternally falling veil of snow.

He must have passed the crossroads. Should he go back and look more closely or should he go forward until he fell in his tracks and the horse trod upon him?

He took a last despairing look ahead, and there, looming up, was a figure like a tall man with arms outstretched. He staggered forward and clutched at it. His hands encountered the wooden arms of a signpost. He was indeed at the very center of the crossroads. With a hoarse shout, he plunged into the right-hand lane. A few moments later, the last rays of daylight showed him the gambrel roof of Stonehaven.

In response to his knock at the great house, a yellow glow appeared in the fanlight over the door and a feminine voice asked who was there. As soon as he shouted his name, the bolts were drawn and the door swung open. He had a momentary glimpse of Miss Ellen holding a candle and looking up at him with surprise and pleasure on her face. In that instant he was fully rewarded for all of the day's hardships. Then the storm swept into the room, snuffing out the candle and whirling snow to the opposite wall.

"Close the door, Dirk," said Miss Ellen. "I'll get another light."

He looped the bridle over the inside door latch and brought the door to upon it.

"I've got a horse out here, Miss Ellen," he said when she came back. "What shall I do with him?"

"Why, take him to the stable, of course."

"Yes, but, ma'am, I'm afraid I couldn't find it tonight. Perhaps if Mr. East is about, we can manage together."

"He's not here." Miss Ellen paused in thought. "There's a shed at the back of this house running from the kitchen out to the well house. It's enclosed in winter. You could lead your horse around there and leave him for the night."

"Yes, ma'am."

Dirk opened the door. As if lying in wait, the storm swooped in again. Out went the candle. He felt Miss Ellen beside him pushing the door shut.

"You must not step a foot out into that tonight," she declared. "There's nothing for it but to lead the horse through the house. Wait until I get a track cleared."

A moment later Dirk was escorting Highboy with a noisy clumping of hoofs upon the wooden floor through the hallway and into the living room. Here the hard-packed snow upon his hoofs made the horse slip. His leg crashed against a small stand which went down in splinters. The wider spaces of the kitchen were negotiated in safety, however. In the shed Dirk removed the saddle; then he returned to the kitchen. Miss Ellen was sweeping up the heaps of snow that had fallen during their passage.

Suddenly a high-pitched ranting voice came down the back stairs. Dirk scarcely recognized it as a weakened and querulous version of Mr. Stone's. "Ellen! Ellen! What in heaven's name is going on? It sounds exactly as if a horse was walking around down there."

Dirk and Miss Ellen looked at each other rather guiltily. Then she began to laugh and Dirk grinned in response.

"That's just what it was, Father, a horse," she called up, "but we have him outside now."

"Is the boy here, Ellen?"

"No, it's Dirk Hollenbeck from Riverbrink."

"Oh, very well. Have him go directly to the barn and do the chores."

The shuffle of slippered feet diminished in the upstairs hall.

"He doesn't realize what the weather is," Miss Ellen explained in a low tone, "and there's no need to upset him by telling him tonight."

"Is he sick, ma'am?"

"Yes, it's his stomach again. He's been ailing all winter."

"Then you have to care for him and your grandmother, too?"

"Oh, no. Grandmother passed away nearly a year ago. There are only the three of us here now — Father and Mr. East and I."

"But I thought you said Mr. East was away."

"Yes, for a few days only, I hope. You see, his wife went to New York to live last spring. And this morning he received word that she was ill. So he started out at once to go down to her, intending to arrange on the way for a man from White Plains to come here and do the chores in his absence. When you knocked just now, I thought of course it was the man. I was pleased to find it was you." And Miss Ellen smiled warmly.

Dirk did not respond, however. He was too shocked by what he was hearing. "But who does the work here, cooks the meals and all?" he asked.

"I do," she replied, still smiling. "But what am I thinking of to let you stand in those dripping clothes? This is Mr. East's room here off the kitchen. Put on some clothes of his and bring yours out to dry."

Dirk found in a chest a brown homespun shirt, leather breeches and woolen stockings, which he put on. The shoes were too small but he didn't need them indoors. The warm dry clothes were immensely comforting, though they relaxed his muscles and so made him more aware of his exhaustion. He was trembling all over and his knees felt rubbery.

Back in the kitchen, he found Miss Ellen preparing supper. The delicious odor of frying ham filled the room.

"I'd better look after my horse," he said. "Have you a stiff brush I could use?"

Miss Ellen produced a hearth brush, which Dirk cut down to stiffen the bristles. Then he went out to the shed and set to work on Highboy's coat. It was a hopeless task. Ice had frozen into the hair. At length Miss Ellen came out to see how he was progressing.

"You'll have to melt it loose," she decided. "Bring the horse into the kitchen."

So back they trooped with Highboy clumping across the brick floor to stand in front of the hearth. Dirk put on Highboy the feed bag he had brought along for a noon meal. While the horse munched the grain, he brushed and picked the coat. When he had finished, Miss Ellen got an old blanket to strap over Highboy's back and he led the horse back to the shed.

By the time he had washed up, the meal was on the table, which was set with china and silver. A glass of wine stood at each place.

"Sit down, Dirk," said Miss Ellen.

But he protested, "It's not fitting that you should serve me nor that I should sit at table with you."

"Now, Dirk, let's be sensible," said Miss Ellen. "In our present circumstance it would be foolish to stand on ceremony. You have come through twenty miles of blizzard in my father's service. The least I can do is offer you a place at my table. I am very glad indeed to have you here this night."

So Dirk sat down and applied himself heartily to the meal. As he sipped the wine and ate the solid, warming food, he became filled with a delightful sense of comfort and well-being. It was a pleasant room, this kitchen, with its great oak rafters, broad fireplace, and red brick floor. Outside the storm howled and whistled, occasionally sending a puff of smoke down the chimney into the room. It only served to emphasize the warmth and peace within. Dirk's wet clothes hanging beside the fire added to the impression of domestic intimacy.

He looked across at Miss Ellen, letting his eyes dwell upon her dark, lowered lashes, the curve of her cheek, her mouth. Why, he thought to himself, it was as though they were a married couple sitting at supper beside their own hearth. At that instant Miss Ellen looked up and he felt himself blushing. Suppose she should guess what he had been thinking!

To cover his confusion, he inquired about Mr. Stone, whether he was well enough to get downstairs.

"Yes, he can come when he likes, but he is weak; it tires him to get back. So I take his meals up to him. Often I eat upstairs with him, but at night he has only milk. I gave him the last in the house an hour ago."

"I'll get to the barn in the morning," Dirk promised. "He'll have some more tomorrow."

"Oh, Dirk, if you hadn't come!" exclaimed Miss Ellen. "Isn't it odd? The weather always conspires to keep you from Stonehaven."

"But I come anyhow," said Dirk with a grin.

"What brought you this time?"

Dirk found himself reluctant to explain. "You see, ma'am, you told me you thought I had a right to change my politics but that I ought to come and tell your father if I did. Well — "

"Dirk, you've joined the rebels!"

"That's about the size of it, Miss Ellen."

"Oh, Dirk!"

"I'm sorry, ma'am, sorry to set myself against you and Mr. Stone, but it is something I have to do."

"I'm afraid Father will take this hard." Miss Ellen looked worried. "Things upset him so much now."

156

She arose and began clearing the table. Dirk thought of offering to help her but was afraid of breaking some dishes. He had suddenly become very drowsy. Getting up shakily, he scrubbed the icy slush from the floor where he had been grooming Highboy and banked the hearth fire for the night. By the time he was through, Miss Ellen had finished washing the dishes. She took a candle from the mantel shelf, lighted it from the one on the table, and, bidding Dirk goodnight, went upstairs.

Stumbling with weariness, Dirk brought his saddlebags into the kitchen to get out his night things. The first article he found in them was a snow-encrusted napkin wrapped around two hard biscuits and a pat of cheese — the lunch that Christina had packed for him early that morning. Dirk could never see food without the impulse to eat it. He sat down on the settle before the fire with a biscuit in one hand, the cheese in the other, and took bites from them in alternation.

Suddenly sleep pounced upon him. He slid sidewise, his legs sprawling across the long bench. The biscuit rolled in one direction, the cheese in another. In that instant he was sound asleep.

11

"DIRK! DIRK!"

A hand shook his shoulder. A candle flame plagued his eyes. He tried to rouse up quickly but was all entangled with the settle, having slid one arm between the spindles at the back and his feet through the armrest at the end. Miss Ellen stood laughing at his efforts to extricate himself.

"Didn't you go to bed?" she asked.

"Must be I didn't," he remarked, as surprised as she. "Is it time to get up? Pretty dark yet."

"It's eight o'clock and daylight upstairs. The reason it's dark down here is that we're snowed in."

"No! It can't be to the tops of the windows!"

Dirk strode to the kitchen door and pulled it open. He found himself confronting a solid wall of snow from threshold to lintel. Miss Ellen gave a little gasp of horror. He closed the door quickly.

"Must be drifted against this side of the house," he muttered and hurried to the front hall.

From this door the view was somewhat more reassuring. It had stopped storming. The snow at the threshold was only

two feet deep but then it swept up in the immediate fore-
ground to a drift eight feet or more at its highest point. Along
this nearby horizon Dirk could see the wind playing cease-
lessly, moving the snow in whirling patterns like sand.

Miss Ellen appeared at his side.

"See, ma'am, it's as I thought," he said cheerfully. "Those
were just drifts at the back of the house. Why, I'll wager it's
not more than three feet on a level."

"Three feet! But Dirk, you can never get to the barn
through all that."

"Just watch me," he promised recklessly.

After a breakfast of hot mush, coffee, and thickly buttered
toast, he set forth with a shovel from the front door. This
was, of course, at the end of the house farthest from the
barn, so he first worked his way around the house and then
struck off toward a row of trees that bordered the road to the
barn.

His progress was slow. He circled around the highest
drifts, wading where possible, shoveling where necessary. By
a direct route the distance to the barn was about a quarter
of a mile but he was making a mile or more of it, he figured.
Sometimes, when an especially vicious wind swept down, he
could only stand humped over, his nose in his muffler, until
it passed over.

His worst handicap was his lack of knowledge of the ter-
rain. He would sometimes choose a route where the snow
seemed shallow only to discover that the ground beneath
fell sharply away, plunging him deep in a drift. Once, when

this happened, he found himself suddenly in snow to his armpits. The shovel had slipped from his grasp and skittered two yards away across the top of the drift. For a few moments he floundered wildly, driving his legs deeper with every movement. Then he checked himself, took stock of the situation. He found he had been working farther into the drift while reaching for the shovel. He now flung his body toward the shallower side, drew one leg up, whereupon the other sank deeper. Again he threw himself sidewise. He was now almost horizontal on the snow but had worked out of the deeper part of the drift. He wormed his way along as though swimming, until finally he reached shallower snow.

Panting heavily, he stood and looked at all the marks of his floundering. A man could perish in such a situation, sink out of sight forever. He must go more cautiously. He skirted the drift and reached the shovel from the opposite side.

Soon afterward he came out upon a rise of ground from which, between gusts of wind, he could see over the countryside. It was a wide expanse of snow dotted with a few trees. The snow lay in dunes like sand on the desert and, like sand also, it was constantly blowing and shifting. The barn and all its outbuildings lay ahead.

Once there, his unfamiliarity with the place delayed him. It was dark in the stables, and he could find no lantern or flint to strike a light, so he had to go prowling about in search of the things he needed. He was shocked by the small amount of stock. There were only three cows, all bawling pitifully, a pig, a few chickens, and no horses. But at least, he thought, the small number had its advantage just now. He needed less time to do the chores.

On the return trip he was faced with the problem of getting some milk back to the house for Mr. Stone. Twice he started out with a bucket half full and twice he lost his balance, dumping it into the snow. On the second trip back to the barn Dirk pondered his problem. As he passed the place where he had spilled the first batch, he noticed that it had begun to freeze. The sight gave him an idea. Frozen milk could be carried easily. He set the remaining supply outside the barn door in a covered pail. This would be frozen by the time he returned in the afternoon and now he would carry back some grain for Highboy instead.

It was noon when Dirk arrived at the front door again. He felt as if he had been gone on a long journey. He ran through the house looking for Miss Ellen but when he came upon her in the kitchen bending over the fire, he halted abruptly, embarrassed at his eagerness. In the name of common sense, what had he expected, that she would fall upon his neck with joy because her farm hand had returned safely from the stable? She was disappointed that he had not brought any milk but accepted his explanation readily and even expressed admiration at his ingenious solution to the problem.

"I'll give Father some mush this noon instead," she declared. "Oh, Dirk, he wants to see you. Will you go up now while I'm preparing his dinner?"

Dirk hung his snowy wraps near the fire. He faced the

161

coming scene with misgivings. But after all, this was the purpose for which he had made the journey. He brushed a hand back over his hair and mounted the stairs.

Mr. Stone was in a large front bedroom. He lay back in a wing chair, his feet on a hassock. A bright brocaded dressing gown emphasized the ghastly pallor of his face. Without a wig, his wispy reddish hair was inadequate covering for a parchment-white skull. His eyes were sunk under stiff brows. Deep lines from both nostrils to the corners of his mouth expressed a world of irritation, pain, disillusion. Dirk stood before this broken man shocked beyond words.

"Well, Hollenbeck, what brings you here?" Mr. Stone rolled his eyes up at Dirk without raising his head. "What's gone wrong at Riverbrink? You need money, I suppose. Well, let me tell you right now if it's money — "

"No, sir. It isn't money. Nothing like that. Sir, I — I came down to tell you I've had a change of politics. I've joined the American side."

"So that's it! Well, I am astonished. And I suppose the 'Americans' have rewarded you for joining them by giving you my confiscated estate."

"No, sir. That's something I want to explain to you. I am running the farm now but at the end of this war, if my side wins, I'll see that you get it back or are paid for it."

Mr. Stone raised his head and gave Dirk a look of cold hostility. "Of all the impudence!" he cried. "With what, pray, would you pay me for my manor? Perhaps you would sell off my stock and send me part of the money."

162

Dirk had not thought just how he would pay for the property. Of course it would have to be with something that the farm had produced; there were no other resources. And that, apparently, would not be honest. He moistened his lips, uncertain what to say.

But Mr. Stone was not waiting for a reply. "Ah, such ingratitude!" he cried. "Was it for this that I supported you and your whole family for years when you were not earning me a farthing?"

"Oh, sir, please don't say that! I am indeed grateful." Dirk took a step forward and extended his arms in helpless appeal, then let them fall at his sides.

"Father, of all things don't accuse Dirk of ingratitude. *We* are the ones who are indebted to *him*." Miss Ellen swept in with a tray carrying her father's dinner.

"So now you turn upon me too, my own daughter! Well, I'm still master in my own house, and as such, I command you, you young upstart, to leave." Mr. Stone leaned forward in his chair and shook a threatening fist at Dirk. "Get out! Get out this instant!"

"Now, Father, Dirk couldn't leave even if he wanted to. We're snowed in." Miss Ellen moved forward and set the tray down upon Mr. Stone's knees. She spoke soothingly as one would to a child. "Besides we don't want him to go. We couldn't get along without him. Why, he's been to the barn this morning and taken care of the stock. Without him you couldn't have any more milk."

Her last words seemed to make some impression on him.

He leaned slowly back and his eyes fell upon the bowl of mush in his lap. Then he was upright again.

"Where is the milk?" he demanded.

"You'll have it tonight, Father. Dirk couldn't — "

Mr. Stone was not listening. "Get out! Get out both of you," he screamed. "And take this slop along." He thrust the tray at Miss Ellen. Again he shook his fist at Dirk. "As for you, you ungrateful whelp, leave these premises at once. If I ever lay eyes on you again, I'll run you through with my sword."

Miss Ellen walked out of the room, her cheeks a deep red, the tray in her hand. Dirk followed her. As they went down the stairs, he could hear Mr. Stone muttering in a voice that trembled with self-pity.

"I've lived too long. I've fallen upon evil days. My servants have all deserted me. Even my own daughter takes their part."

In the kitchen Miss Ellen set down the tray and turned to Dirk. "You mustn't mind what my father said," she whispered. "He isn't himself. He's very ill and all that has happened has warped his mind." Her voice trembled and tears welled in her eyes.

"Oh, ma'am, I understand."

Dirk's heart contracted with pity for Miss Ellen. She had so many troubles, and here he was adding to them. His presence was making her father unmanageable.

"Look, Miss Ellen, why couldn't I stay down at the stables?" he suggested. "I could bring up milk for your father

164

once each day. Then you could truthfully tell him I wasn't in the house any more."

"No, you'll not sleep in the stable like a tramp," Miss Ellen declared with vehemence, "unless, of course, there is real danger that Father might harm you."

"Ma'am, a child could defend himself against Mr. Stone the way he is now."

"But at night, Dirk, when you're asleep, he might — " Her voice broke. "Oh, it's horrible to think such things about one's own father."

"Ma'am, I don't think your father would do anything violent even if he had the strength. You know, he always did rather like to make a fuss and frighten people."

"Oh, Dirk, you're so calm and sane." Miss Ellen's hand rested fleetingly on his sleeve. "Sometimes when I've been with Father day in and day out, I begin to wonder what is the sensible way to think. You counterbalance him wonderfully."

She looked up at Dirk and smiled. He found the effect dazzling at close range. His heart turned over slowly, sensuously, like a kitten being stroked.

Then, abruptly, she was away across the room, calling back over her shoulder, "Let's have dinner. Oh, it's so dark in here! Light another candle, will you, Dirk? It's quite exciting being snowed in like this, isn't it? And cozy — but frightening, too."

As she talked, Miss Ellen whirled about the kitchen preparing their meal. Watching her, Dirk's eyes darkened, for he recognized this as a gallant effort to rise above her troubles.

His own mood was serious as he lit the extra candle for her and went out to feed his horse.

Before they sat down to dinner, Miss Ellen ran upstairs with her father's bowl of mush, which she had kept warm on a trivet at the edge of the fire. When she came back, her gaiety was subdued. Dirk asked how her father was.

"He's still angry and in great pain," she replied. "He'll feel better, though, as soon as he eats. It's always that way."

Dirk drew out Miss Ellen's chair as he had seen her father do and they seated themselves.

"Tell me about Riverbrink," said Miss Ellen as they began to eat. "I want to know all that has happened there."

"Well, ma'am, we were invaded."

"Not at Riverbrink! Do tell me about it."

So Dirk told the story of those grueling days, and after the first self-conscious hesitancy he told it well. Miss Ellen listened, exclaimed, commented.

When he had finished, she said, "Dirk, those cows are yours. I'm not sure but that the whole farm is at least as much yours as ours. But the cows you saved at great risk and you're entitled to keep them."

As Dirk began to protest, she broke in with a question. "Was that what made you join the rebels, the way the British army treated our property?"

"No, ma'am. I've seen bad actions on both sides when it comes to property. It was more the way they treated me, as if all I was good for was to milk cows. Well, maybe it is, but a man likes to think he's worth more than that. A man likes to think he can own his own farm or become a — well, say a lawyer, or even be governor of his province — I mean *state* — if he's capable of it. That's what we Americans think. The British think if a man starts out as a servant, he can never be anything better, or want to be."

Dirk paused, a little abashed at having delivered such a speech, yet meaning every word of it deeply.

"Then you do truly think that document was right, that all men are equal?" she asked. "You think that you are the equal of my father?"

"Miss Ellen, you know I wouldn't set myself up to be the equal of an educated gentleman like Mr. Stone. The declaration doesn't say all men *are* equal. It says all men are *created* equal. I take that to mean that I wasn't born to be Mr. Stone's servant nor was he born to be my master. We were born equal. We Americans, if we can get free of England, mean to form a nation where any man, no matter how low he was born, can get to be anything he is capable of. See what I mean?"

"Yes, I see." There was a touch of condescension in Miss Ellen's smile. "I suppose it's natural enough for the people in the — uh — servant class to want to reverse the social scale and get into power themselves. But it wouldn't work. If your faction should succeed with this revolution, which I trust you won't, you'd soon be in a state of anarchy. You'd be begging for the ruling class to take control again."

"But, ma'am, we're already ruling ourselves. We set up a state government last summer. And as for what you call the ruling class, we've got the best of them in office right now alongside of men as humbly born as I. Colonel Van Cortlandt, for instance, is our lieutenant governor."

"Colonel Van Cortlandt is a traitor to his class, my father says." Miss Ellen's condescending smile had disappeared. "And you don't think for a moment, do you, that *he* truly believes in this nonsense of equality?"

Dirk grinned. "He was the person who persuaded me of its truth."

"You! Colonel Van Cortlandt talked to you?" Miss Ellen's incredulous tone was not flattering.

"Is that so surprising, ma'am?" asked Dirk, letting some of his hurt into his voice.

"Well, I suppose he must pretend to believe in this equality," she said, "so that he can persuade the lower classes to take arms against their king!"

Dirk rose abruptly. "Ma'am, Colonel Van Cortlandt is the finest man I know," he said in a vibrant tone. "He wouldn't pretend about anything. And now, ma'am, I think I'll go back to the stables."

Picking up his wraps, he walked out of the room. In the front hall he put them on and went out.

So Miss Ellen was surprised that a gentleman would talk to him, was she? And she didn't think that the colonel truly believed in equality. And — this hit him the hardest — she considered Dirk one of "the servant class."

He plunged blindly into a drift and nearly foundered. The snow whipped against his face stinging him back to a sense of reality. He worked out of the drift, then started ahead more steadily.

After all, what was he so upset about all of a sudden? Nothing was any different from what it had been all along. Miss Ellen had never pretended that she considered him anything more than a servant. She waited upon him and let him sit with her at table because it was the sensible and convenient thing to do in the circumstances. It was good that this discussion had come up. Now, perhaps, he would remember his place.

His heart was bruised, however. He slogged along through the snow with none of the zest and high spirits he had felt that morning. And at the barn he attacked the chores sluggishly, feeling no eagerness to finish and return. Several times he found himself sitting idly on the milking stool, brooding, while scraps of their conversation floated through his mind. So it was not surprising that when he had finished and prepared to start back, darkness was at hand.

The sight of the lengthening shadows brought him at last sharply to his senses. Was there time to reach the house before nightfall or should he remain at the barn? Miss Ellen would worry if he didn't return. In the face of this new problem, her political views became unimportant. With a careful eye, he gauged the degree of daylight and decided to take the risk.

The blowing snow had shifted the pattern of the drifts so that Dirk could not follow his previous course. He must gain the crest of the slope where he could see the house before dark. But as he fought his way along, the night descended rapidly. When he reached what he judged to be the crest, there was only snow swirling in the dusk. He tried to set himself a straight course in the direction where the house should be, but turning out for snowdrifts threw him off from it until he lost his bearings entirely.

He stopped. Panic hovered at the edge of his mind. He fought it off. What now? It would be best to bear to the right. Then if he missed the house, he might come across the stone wall that ran in front of it. One last look around before he started again. What was that to the left? A faint, wavering, almost indistinguishable glow. He started toward it, half afraid it would prove to be some luminous effect of the wind and snow. But it strengthened, became a candle flame in a window. As he approached, he could see candles in every window on that side of the house. Miss Ellen, bless her, was lighting him in. He flung open the front door and set down the milk pail.

She came running along the hall. "Oh, Dirk, I thought surely you were lost."

"Not me, ma'am, not with such good signal lights to guide me."

Together they closed the door on the darkness and snow outside, then turned and faced each other.

"Oh, Dirk, I'm so relieved."

Miss Ellen let her breath out in a long sigh. She was standing near him, looking up with undisguised pleasure. It would have been easy to take her in his arms. Instead, Dirk dragged off his mittens and forced his hands up to untie his muffler.

"It was the candles in the windows that fetched me."

"Oh, we must put them out!" Miss Ellen hurried into the living room and clipped each flame with a snuffer. "Then I'll get some dinner. You must be hungry."

It was an evening Dirk never forgot. His recent brush with danger gave him a delightful sense of release. To be enjoying Ellen Stone's company had lost none of the unbelievable dreamlike quality it had had the night before, only now he was able to enjoy it more fully, not being exhausted physically. Miss Ellen, too, was very gay as they prepared the meal. She laughed at Dirk's clumsy attempts to help her and he joined in with good-natured chuckles.

After dinner they sat long at the table chatting. Miss Ellen inquired about Dirk's family and he told her in detail about Christina's many activities and Peter's droll sayings.

"Father and I have missed seeing your little family," Miss Ellen remarked. "We have often spoken of you all."

"He'll speak of me no longer, I fear," remarked Dirk in a soberer vein.

"He's become so bitter about the war. It frightens me," said Miss Ellen. "If only he would come downstairs and live more normally, I think his health might improve. He just sits up there and broods."

"But last night you said he wasn't strong enough to come down," Dirk protested.

Miss Ellen did not answer for a moment. "That's his excuse and I accept it," she said at length. "But I think the truth is that he can't bear to come down here and see me doing housework. If he stays up there, he can pretend to himself that everything belowstairs is the same as it used to be, that a servant prepares the food and I just carry it up to him."

"I can understand that," said Dirk, remembering how he had at first been taken aback at the sight of Miss Ellen working.

"That is an odd attitude for you to take," remarked Miss Ellen abruptly. "With all your revolutionary talk about people being equal, I would expect you to enjoy seeing me work." Although she smiled and spoke jokingly, Dirk sensed a hostility in her tone. "Why, I am truly surprised that you show me so much respect, that you continue to call me 'miss' and 'ma'am.' There is nothing to hinder your assuming an equal footing. I am in no position to object."

"That is exactly why I would not think of doing so," said Dirk stiffly.

He was astonished and thoroughly angry. Why should she assume he would seize the first opportunity to become familiar with her? She was acting childish, he thought, and deserved nothing so much as a sound spanking. He became aware of a protracted silence.

Suddenly, Miss Ellen sprang to her feet. "What is the matter with me?" she cried in a shaken tone. "Dirk, you didn't deserve that thrust and I apologize. You are conducting yourself much more like a gentleman, I must confess, than I am like a lady."

172

Dirk stepped to Miss Ellen's side, his anger forgotten. "You are tired, I think, and overwrought about your father."

"Ah, yes — Father. I am neglecting him. If the milk is melted, I'll take some up."

She spoke in haste and abstraction as if seeking a pretext to get away. Dirk suspected that she was even more ashamed of her outbreak than she had admitted.

He helped her pour some milk from the pail into a pitcher.

"When you take Mr. Stone the milk, he'll know I haven't left yet," he reminded her.

"I think he knows it already," Miss Ellen said. "You see, he doesn't truly want you to go because he knows we need you. If he doesn't see you — it's like his not seeing me work — he can pretend you're not around and at the same time enjoy the advantages of having you here."

Miss Ellen put the pitcher and glass on a tray along with a lighted candle and went upstairs. In a few moments she was back.

"He wants me to read to him," she announced. "I'll just clear away the supper and then go back."

She bustled around as if, Dirk thought sulkily, she could not get out of his company fast enough. Soon he found himself sitting alone before the fire, gloomily contemplating the toes of his brown woolen stockings. It was unendurable that he must waste this evening sitting here while Ellen Stone remained upstairs reading to her father. Though she might ridicule or insult him, even that was far preferable to this loneliness.

Dirk recalled incredulously the many long years that he had lived near Miss Ellen, content to see her occasionally even at a distance. And he had thought himself in love! It had been little more than a boyish admiration. But now this need of Ellen Stone had become the strongest force in his existence.

Dirk rose and, groping his way across the living room, stood in the cold darkness of the hall until he could hear Miss Ellen's low voice between the measured ticks of the nearby clock. He could not distinguish her words, only a smooth flow of sound. With a sudden decision, he returned to the kitchen, donned his greatcoat and then padded silently up the stairs. Before the door of Mr. Stone's room he dropped to the floor, his ear against the panel. Here her voice was clearly audible. Dirk curled his feet up under him and settled to listen.

At first he paid little heed to the substance of what she read, listening only to the cadences of her voice. But gradually he became aware that she was reading a conversation. She would first give the name of the speaker and then what the speaker said. For a time Dirk floundered helplessly, making little sense of it all.

Then a story began to emerge. There was, it seemed, a masqued ball being given, at which a young man, an enemy of the host, was present, uninvited. He had come to find a young lady with whom he thought himself in love, but while looking for her, he spied another girl, the daughter of the host, and fell in love with her. In a brief and bantering conversation, he kissed her. To Dirk's astonishment, the young lady seemed not to object. A loose-mannered parcel of folks, he decided.

Somewhat later the two lovers were conversing through a window, she upstairs, he in the orchard without. Their conversation seemed to Dirk full of a great deal of flowery nonsense. He could not imagine a man saying such extravagant things even to the girl he loved. But it all sounded pretty in Miss Ellen's low, well-modulated voice.

At length came time for the lovers to separate.

"Good night, good night: parting is such sweet sorrow,
That I shall say good night till it be morrow.

.   .   .   .

Sleep dwell upon thine eyes, peace in thy breast! —
Would I were sleep and peace, so sweet to rest!"

Miss Ellen's voice dropped lower, but still her tones came clear and vibrant, as though she were speaking to Dirk alone. His spine tingled at the unexplainable magic in the words.

Miss Ellen stopped reading and there was silence inside the room. Suddenly with a click of the latch, the door began to move back from Dirk's shoulder. He scrambled to his feet just as Miss Ellen appeared on the threshold. At sight of Dirk's great bulk looming before her, she gave a startled little cry and wavered backward, toppling out of its stick the lighted candle she was carrying. Dirk caught the candle in one hand while with the other at her back he steadied her. An instant they stood in arrested motion. Her head, though flung back, was in deep shadow so that Dirk could not see her expression. With a compulsive movement his arm tightened and he stooped toward her lips.

"Ellen! Ellen! Did you call?"

At the sound of her father's querulous voice, the girl stiffened and thrust herself violently out of Dirk's embrace.

"Yes, Father," she replied breathlessly. "I — I nearly dropped my candle."

"Well, be more careful. This is no time to set the house afire."

The bed curtains swayed as a skinny hand drew them aside. Dirk stepped into the hall out of Mr. Stone's line of vision.

"Yes, Father. I'm sorry I awoke you."

"Tush, I wasn't asleep."

"Goodnight, Father."

Miss Ellen crossed the threshold and drew the door shut behind her. Dirk handed her the candle, which she replaced in the candlestick. They walked down the hall in a strained silence. At the head of the stairs they stopped.

"Dirk, how did you happen to be at the door just now?" asked Miss Ellen in a whisper.

"Why, I was listening to you read," Dirk explained. "I'm sorry I startled you. I had no thought you'd come out so sudden. Thought you'd bid goodnight to Mr. Stone."

"No, I read until he falls asleep each night, then draw his bed curtains and come away."

They fell silent, remembering tonight's sequel to that procedure.

"Well, goodnight," said Miss Ellen abruptly and continued along the hallway toward her room.

Her tone was matter-of-fact, almost brusque, but as he groped his way down the stairs, Dirk recalled how she had said goodnight only a few moments before, the gentle modulations of her voice, the intimate loving tones. He smiled into the darkness as he repeated the words to himself.

"Good night, good night: parting is such sweet sorrow,
That I shall say good night till it be morrow."

12

THE NEXT MORNING MISS ELLEN WAS VERY MUCH THE lady of the manor. Gone was the easy friendliness of the day before. She spoke to Dirk in a kind but dignified manner. It was obvious that she was reminding him of his place so that there might be no repetition of such an incident as had occurred the night before. Dirk felt rebuffed but decided to ignore this change of attitude.

"Where's your woodpile, Miss Ellen?" he asked as they sat down to breakfast. "The box needs filling. I took all that was left to build the fire this morning."

"Dear me, we can't get any more!" exclaimed Miss Ellen. "The woodpile is outside that door that's blocked with snow."

"How far away is it, ma'am?"

"Why, only a few steps, but — "

"I can tunnel out to it, then."

Silence fell.

Suddenly Miss Ellen said, "Gerit Van Wyck enlisted with His Majesty's forces. Did you know?"

The remark struck Dirk with the impact of a physical

blow. For the time he had forgotten Van Wyck. His world had consisted of Miss Ellen and himself with Mr. Stone vaguely in the offing. And now a most unwelcome person had intruded.

"Yes — yes, I know," he stammered.

"If only *he* had been with the King's forces that took Riverbrink," said Miss Ellen, "all that looting would never have occurred."

"But he *was* there. I saw him."

"He was there!" Miss Ellen's astonishment quickly changed to relief. "Why, then we need distress ourselves no longer. He has taken charge of our property and is keeping it safe for us."

Dirk was so taken aback by this startling conclusion that he could only stare at Miss Ellen in astonishment.

"You see," she added. "Gerit and I — well, Gerit has a very special reason for protecting our property."

She flung out this information with a sort of defiance. Then, under Dirk's silent gaze, a hot wave of color suddenly suffused her face. Dirk's appetite left him. He pushed back his chair.

"Is there a shovel handy?" he demanded gruffly. "I'll dig out to the woodpile."

He attacked the digging violently, making the exercise an outlet for his pent-up feelings, but soon he steadied to the work. His method was to cut out chunks of the hard-packed snow, shovel it into wooden buckets, and carry it through the house out at the front door. Miss Ellen helped. Clad in a red cloak and mittens, she carried blocks of snow in her arms. Under her instructions, Dirk swung his tunnel sharply to the right toward where the woodpile stood, as she said, at a right angle to the house wall.

As they worked together, they found themselves slipping into their former companionship. Miss Ellen became once more her friendly self. And Dirk's mood of anger mellowed. After all, he realized, Miss Ellen had simply reminded him of something he had chosen to forget. Well, he would not forget again. He must see that she was not annoyed by any such awkwardness as had arisen the night before.

As though her thoughts had been running in some similar channels, Miss Ellen asked abruptly, "Did you like the play I was reading, Dirk?"

"I liked to hear you read. As to the story, it was well enough."

"Well enough!" Miss Ellen laughed gaily. "That is faint praise indeed for England's greatest dramatist. To what did you object?"

Dirk was shaping off a corner of his tunnel roof. He continued the work as he replied. "Well, ma'am, it seemed to me a pretty trifling affair for so many fine noble words."

"Why, Dirk, that is one of the greatest romances of all time."

Dirk sniffed derisively. "I know nothing of such matters but it seemed to me to be about a young man who didn't know his own mind. He went to a party chasing after one lady and as soon as he saw another, he started chasing her instead."

Ellen laughed. "When you put it that way, it does seem that Romeo was somewhat fickle."

"And the lady too, ma'am, I would call light-minded and flighty. But I am only a rough farmer who doesn't understand such grand works. The people in this story were of a foreign country, judging from their names. Perhaps where they lived such actions were thought well of."

"That may be so," Miss Ellen agreed. "The Latin races are more violent in their emotions. You with your Dutch heritage and I with my English can scarcely expect to understand them."

"Are you forgetting, ma'am, that you, too, are half Dutch?"

Miss Ellen spoke bitterly. "When I think with whom that Dutch blood connects me, I should like to forget."

Dirk plied his shovel silently for a moment. "Well, Miss Ellen," he said at length, "it is no use to discuss Colonel Van Cortlandt again. We would both become angry to no avail. But I must, out of loyalty to him and to you, remind you that your father has set you against your mother's people and — "

"Dirk, you forget yourself!"

He turned to find her eyes blazing angrily into his. "Perhaps, but there is no one else to speak for your mother's people so I must do it. Political differences are all very well, Miss

Ellen, but there need not be this bitter personal hatred that your father has tried to arouse in you toward the Van Cortlandts. I can assure you the colonel feels no such sentiment toward you or your father."

"I am not interested in the colonel's feelings nor — "

"Why, the last time I talked with him, he spoke very highly of you, Miss Ellen."

"Of me! I can't conceive how or why any reference to me could have occurred in your conversation."

"Quite simply. I was speaking of how I felt in your father's debt and on that account that I didn't like to go against him in this war. But I told the colonel you said I had a right to.

"Ma'am, the colonel smiled very happily and said you spoke like a true Van Cortlandt!"

Miss Ellen sniffed. Dirk knew she was searching her mind for a scathing comment but at that instant the shovel rang against the woodpile. The subject was never resumed.

The completion of the tunnel seemed to add the last touch to the snugness of their situation. They now had easy access to a winter's supply of wood; the cellar was adequately stocked with food, the stable with grain. But Dirk's pleasure in it was gone, driven away by Miss Ellen's mention of Gerit Van Wyck.

As soon as he had finished the tunnel and filled the woodbox in the kitchen, he went to the barn. It was an easy journey this morning, for the wind had gone down, leaving the dunes of snow standing in fantastically sculptured rigidity. His route was now familiar and he made his tortuous way across the field, squinting against the blinding glare of sun on snow. A sharp cold had set in. After the chores were finished, he lingered in the stable, reluctant to return to the scene of his tortures yet drawn there, too. Being a man of strong, simple impulses, he found these complicated emotions confusing. He began to wish desperately for a release from this situation. Yet when it came that very night, his disappointment was keen.

At twilight he was returning for the second time from the stable when a mounted man appeared at the gateway, his horse floundering wearily through the snow. Dirk waded forward to meet them, wishing for his gun. It was not until he had reached the man's side that he recognized him as Matthew East.

"Well, Hollenbeck, you here?" cried East. "Thank God! Get me off this beast. I'm stiff as a dried mackerel. Here, take this shovel first."

Dirk helped East into the house and led his horse to the stable.

So now the brief interval of life alone with Ellen Stone was over. It had been so much more than he had ever dreamed of — and so much less than he now needed with his whole being. His mind groped toward the future and recoiled. To go home to Riverbrink without her, not to see her for months, years perhaps — or even a lifetime.

He returned to the house with a heavy spirit. Miss Ellen was preparing supper and East was telling her what had happened since he left Stonehaven. He had scarcely reached the home of his friend in White Plains when the storm halted his journey toward New York. At the same time, of course, neither his friend nor he could return to Stonehaven. Torn between a desire to reach his wife's bedside and a frantic concern over what might be happening at Stonehaven, East had decided that since his wife was probably receiving good care, his first duty lay back at his post where he was no doubt desperately needed. The day after the blizzard he had set out for Stonehaven but soon had been obliged to turn back. On this, the second day, with a stout horse, he had managed to push through by dint of much shoveling and circling through fields to avoid drifts.

"I'm glad to find you here, Hollenbeck," East added after speaking of his journey, "but I could wish I had known you were here and so been spared the trip. I'm sure it shortened my life ten years."

Despite his fatigue, however, East sat in the kitchen for a while in conversation with Dirk after Miss Ellen had gone upstairs.

"This is no place for a woman," Dirk said. "Miss Ellen should go back to Riverbrink with me."

"Mr. Stone would never consent to it," rejoined East.

"Then he should be overruled."

"I can protect her."

"And if something happens to you?"

East ignored the question. "Look here, Hollenbeck," he said. "No place is absolutely safe these days. Why, you were invaded at Riverbrink. Suppose Miss Ellen had been there?"

"I would have looked after her, Mr. East. She'd be much safer up there because I —"

He broke off, aware that East was gazing at him with one shaggy eyebrow cocked.

"So that's the way it is," said East slowly.

Dirk's eyes did not waver. "Yes, that's the way it is with me. I've got to know she's safe."

East considered the matter a moment. "Well, this much I'll promise you, boy," he said at length. "I won't leave her again — for anything. She needs me more than my wife does and I'll stay with her. That I promise you."

"Thank you, sir."

Their hands met in a powerful grip.

☆ 13 ☆

WHEN THE TIME CAME FOR DIRK HOLLENBECK TO RETURN home, Ellen was disturbed to an unaccountable degree. She told herself it was because she and her father had been so dependent upon him during the two days after the storm. Then, too, she half-wanted to go back with him to the comparative safety of Riverbrink. This he had urged strongly. But her father went into a violent rage at the mere suggestion. She must stay at Stonehaven.

On the morning of his departure, Dirk rode Highboy up from the stable and dismounted before the door. Ellen thought to herself that Dirk always looked so clean. It was his fair complexion, she decided, and the shining hair brushed back so smoothly.

"Well, Miss Ellen, I'll bid you good-by," he said.

He was smiling, but his blue eyes were serious. He stood on a step below her, which brought their faces almost on a level.

Impulsively, Ellen extended her hand and Dirk enveloped it in a warm grasp. "Good-by, Dirk. I — we can never thank you enough for — "

"Please, Miss Ellen, I don't want to be thanked."

Their hands slid apart. Ellen wanted to draw back but found herself held by the blue intensity of his gaze. His expression was not the gentle good-natured one to which she was accustomed. It was severe almost to the point of being fierce. So strong was her sense of his domination that she swayed slightly toward him as though he were sweeping her into a violent embrace. But he made no move to touch her. Suddenly, he turned and strode away, replacing the cap on his head. As he swung upon his horse, it moved off. At the gate, he waved an arm in farewell. Then he was gone.

Ellen returned to the hall, somewhat out of breath. She stood a moment struggling with an impulse to run to a front window where she might see Dirk riding past. Though she mastered it and went dutifully upstairs to her father, she found it was not so easy to put the young farmer out of her mind. During the rest of that day and all of the many dull winter days that followed, her thoughts recurred frequently to him.

Especially did she remember that instant in the upper hall when he had caught her from falling and very nearly kissed her. What troubled her was not so much that the thing had occurred but that she had allowed it to. Why, if her father's voice had not recalled her to her senses — well, it was past thinking on. And so saying, she continued to think on it.

Another troublesome memory was that of her having pretended a betrothal with Gerit Van Wyck. She was ashamed of this, ashamed to have been so dishonest with Dirk. But, on second thought, it was no affair of Dirk's what her relations might be with Gerit. Dirk was only a farm boy, her servant. What ailed her anyhow that she had come to spend so much time thinking about him?

The reason, she decided, was that life was so very dull at Stonehaven. Week after week flowed past with no variation except in Roderick Stone's moods or the weather. No one ever came to the house or seldom even passed on the road. Boring as this situation was, however, Ellen and East were glad of it. Snow and cold were a welcome protection to dwellers in the Neutral Ground.

With the coming of spring, marauders were on the prowl once more, bolder than ever. East had a gun continuously at his side, and, when he was out of the house, Ellen kept the doors locked and a pistol handy. East was sure that with these precautions they were safe. He thought the marauders would give way before a householder determined to defend his property.

It was not long before an event occurred that shook this belief. One spring night Ellen was awakened by the distant sound of shouting. It seemed to come from the direction of Mr. Blodgett's house, where the elderly owner lived alone. He was the only one of their neighbors remaining in that vicinity. Ellen ran downstairs to find East already outdoors. Smoke and sparks were billowing up into the night sky.

"That's Blodgett's house! It's on fire!" she shouted at him.

He nodded without taking his eyes from the scene.

"Well, but you should go and help him," she cried.

Still East stood with gun gripped in hand. The red glow illumined his rugged profile.

"I can't go, Miss Ellen. God help me, I can't leave this place. Those devils that set the fire may come here next."

"The fire was set?"

"Certainly, ma'am. Can't you hear 'em yelling? The demons! I couldn't help Blodgett if I went. I'd be one man against Lord knows how many."

For an hour or so they watched the flames and listened to the shouting. Then a clatter of hoofs sounded on the road. The two drew back into the shadows as five horsemen came up outlined against the red sky. To Ellen's horror, they stopped before the gate of Stonehaven.

"Whoa! Hold on!" roared one. "Why don't we touch off this place? 'Twould make an almighty blaze."

"Yes, we'd ought to," another agreed in drunken accents. "Owner's a damn Tory. Fled to New York."

One man was dismounting to open the gate when a third protested. "Don't burn this yet, ye plaguey fools. It's the manor house. There'll be good loot to take out first."

"I vote with Lem," said someone else. "I'm sleepy. Let's get on home. We can come here some other night. Come along, Abe."

The man at the gate remounted and there was a scuffle of hoofs.

"Ah, rats!" grumbled the first speaker as the party rode away. "I never get my way. It would have made a mighty big blaze."

Ellen let out her breath in a long, quivering sigh.

All was silent now in the direction of Old Blodgett's and the fire was dying. East ventured down the road while Ellen waited, shivering in the cold dawn. He returned with a grimly set face.

"It's as I thought. They shot him," he said. "I'll dig a grave tomorrow. Meantime, get you to bed, ma'am. And try to sleep. We're safe for now."

Back in her room, Ellen crept beneath the blankets and lay trembling with a nervous chill. It was broad daylight before she slept, only to be aroused shortly afterward by her father shouting for his breakfast.

When she went to the kitchen, East was nowhere about the house. She could too easily guess where he was and what he was doing. He returned at length leading a horse, his manner surprisingly brisk.

"This horse was down in the lot below Blodgett's barn," he said. "Let me catch him easy. Now we've got two horses so I can take you out of the Neutral Ground to a safe place."

"But you've always said you and Father could protect me here," said Ellen.

"Yes, ma'am, I did in my ignorance, but we'd be no match for a party like that one last night. Poor Old Blodgett taught me a lesson."

"But Father wouldn't permit me to go. Besides, he really needs me, sick as he is."

"He is that, ma'am. He's too sick to judge what's best for you."

"Oh, dear, I don't know what to do," cried Ellen. "Let me think about it."

Grimly, while working, she pondered the question. At first it seemed that the only thing to do was to flee to safety. Her memory of the night before was vivid — of the drunken, lawless men ranging at will, pausing before Stonehaven ready to pillage or burn as the whim might take them.

And it would be pleasant to be home at Riverbrink once more in comparative safety and in the cheerful company of young people. But there would be bitterness with the sweet, for she would no longer be truly the lady of the manor. She would be a refugee who had fled to the rebels for protection, penniless, helpless, dependent upon her former servants. Her pride revolted at the prospect.

And most important of all was her father's situation. Could she leave him lonely and in pain, needing the kind of comforting services that only she could give? It seemed heartless to abandon him for a servant to tend.

At noon she had made her decision. "I'm not going," she told East.

He accepted it quietly. "Well, then, ma'am, let's figure how to make ourselves as safe as possible. I think we'd best move to my cottage. It's under the hill, out of sight from the road. If any raiders should come along, they'd attack the great house first. It would give us time to get ready for them."

"But, East, your cottage is so small."

"We can make it do. Your father can have my bedroom and there's a room finished off in the loft that you can take.

I'll bed down in the main room where I can look after things."

"But Father would never consent to move."

East's strong features set in determined lines. "I think he will, ma'am. I told him about Blodgett this morning. It shook him bad."

"Did you suggest our all leaving?"

"Yes, he won't hear of that — yet."

As East had predicted, Roderick Stone accepted the shift with only minor protests. In a few days they were established in the cottage. Ellen was pleased with the change. Her work was halved by the convenience of her new quarters. Everything was near at hand in the main room where she prepared meals. And to reach her father, she need only step into the adjoining room instead of traveling the length of the house and climbing a flight of stairs.

For Stone, also, the change was beneficial. As he could no longer keep aloof from the realities of his situation, he now accepted them. He spent most of his time in an easy chair before the fire watching Ellen at her work. Sometimes in fair weather he even went out and strolled about the estate.

The return to his own cottage brought East nearer to the barn and stables. This was not, however, as much of an advantage as it would ordinarily have been, for with the warmer weather he had taken the little remaining stock out of the stables and tethered them in a woodlot two fields below the farm buildings. Thus they were hidden from raiders who might then search the barns and stables in vain. East must carry grain twice daily to these hiding places and bring milk back.

They had been in their new quarters a little more than a week when one night Ellen was awakened by East's calling up to her in a guarded tone, "Raiders are breaking into the great house, I think. You'd better dress and come down."

She scrambled into some clothes and as she felt her way down the ladder from the loft, she could hear East urging her father to dress.

"I'll not stir a step from this bed," roared Roderick Stone. "You persuaded me to abandon my manor house to those wretches and now you want me to leave this cottage for them, too. I say let them come. I'm ready for them." And he snapped the hammers of a pair of dueling pistols.

"As you will, sir," said East. "I'll take Miss Ellen to a safer place."

Fresh air billowed in as he opened the door. For an instant his head and shoulders were outlined against the night sky. Then he drew her outside. Standing a moment, they could hear men's voices and a hollow scraping sound.

"Loading furniture onto a wagon," East explained in a whisper.

He led her away from the direction of the great house along the uneven turf to a cluster of lilac bushes near the outside fence. Here he made her crowd herself into the midst of them. Then, thrusting a pistol into her hand, he hurried away. Ellen shivered. She was so far now from the great house that she could hear no sounds. Her eyes searched the sky for the flames they feared to see. Her mind flitted fearfully from the great house to her father, wondering, worrying. It might have been an hour later that there was the rumble of a wagon on the road. Soon East came and helped her out of the bush.

"They've gone, ma'am. Shall we go up and see what they've taken?"

"Not I, East. I'm going back to bed. Father is safe and they didn't burn the house. That's all I need to know."

The next morning Stone went up to the great house to see what had been taken. He returned to the cottage and took to his bed for the rest of the day, raging and moaning. Ellen and East both tried to persuade him to leave Stonehaven, but in vain.

Then East again urged Ellen to let him take her away, but she also refused. The past night's experience had proved that they could survive a raid, so she was more encouraged than otherwise. The loss of their possessions concerned her but little.

With the advance of spring, East began the yearly ritual of plowing, harrowing, and sowing grain. He also planted a vegetable garden. At first Ellen tried to dissuade him from all this labor.

"We may not stay here to harvest any of it," she said. "And besides, raiders will probably steal it as fast as it ripens."

"That's true, ma'am. But if we've got no food, we can't stay. And it might turn out we have to. Besides, wherever we go, we'll need to take as much food with us as we can. There's a shortage of it on both sides of the lines."

Ellen was so far persuaded of the common sense in this argument that at length she began helping East with the garden. Every morning she went across the fields to the secluded half acre that he had chosen for the garden plot and here she labored at hoeing, weeding, and cultivating.

It was soon evident that a woman's costume was poorly suited to work on the land. Ellen hunted out a pair of stout gray breeches and a white linen shirt of her father's. Wearing these, and with her hair clubbed back, she looked like a slender boy. Soon the effect was heightened by a smooth coat of tan upon her arms and face. At first this troubled her. The clothes she could take off at will and resume those of her rightful station. But the tan could not be removed. It branded her as a field hand. No true lady would ever allow her face to acquire this darkened hue.

But as the spring merged into summer and Ellen became increasingly engrossed in the work of the farm, she ceased to think of herself as lady of the manor or indeed to think of her position at all. She found this business of making things grow surprisingly rewarding. When the plants had matured and she carried home the vegetables to cook for the family table, her sense of accomplishment was keen. Her first mess of peas was a personal triumph. The most elaborate dishes that Aunt Lina had concocted had never tasted half so delicious. With East's help, she also learned how to milk the cows. Although she disliked this work and never became proficient at it, still it further increased her feeling of self-reliance.

And so, out of this toil that she had thought so debasing, Ellen Stone achieved a sense of fulfillment she had never before known. For the first time in her life she was truly useful. Despite the pervading atmosphere of fear and the worry over her father, she went about her tasks with a strange serenity.

Now in the rare moments when she had leisure to think of her past, she regarded the girl that she had been with something very close to scorn. What had she been good for, this spoiled, moody and idle "lady"? She thought upon the pale amusements that had filled her days — embroidery, music, reading, flower arrangement. Why had she thought herself a person of any importance? The humblest scullery maid in her household had been of more true value than she.

These thoughts were frightening. They threatened to overturn the very foundations of her world. Yet, if they were true, she must pursue them stoutly wherever they might lead. What then? If she had been born into the servant class, would she not feel the equal of any of these helpless aristocrats? Would she not actually be so in any of the ways that truly mattered?

Suddenly into her mind there flashed the memory of Dirk Hollenbeck's face, flushed and earnest, of his voice saying, "All men are created equal."

Within her there began to take shape the intensely disquieting conviction that these words were true.

☆ 14 ☆

BACK AT RIVERBRINK ONCE MORE, DIRK FOUND IT DIFFI-
cult to take up his former way of life. He went about his
duties mechanically, feeling as if he were moving in the
midst of a vast emptiness. His heart was back at Stonehaven
and he could not recall it. With the vestige of will power left
to him he fought against this bondage. He warned himself
that he must put Ellen out of his mind and out of his life.
Had she not told him herself, almost in so many words, that
she was betrothed to Gerit Van Wyck?

He tried to escape his thoughts by constant activity, undertaking enough farm work that spring for two men. And
twice a week he walked up to Peekskill in the evening to
drill with the militia. They practiced on the army parade
ground at the Oak Hill camp and there were always a few of
the regular army men looking on ready to make fun of the
yokels. Dirk, being conspicuously tall, came in for a large
share of the joking.

"Who's that one in the center that's a-horseback?" they
would ask, or, "Hey, Yellowtop, how's the weather up
there?"

Dirk took it good-naturedly and did not let it distract him from learning to follow the commands. He could not figure how all this drilling was going to make the militia better able to repel an enemy attack, but at least he would do his share.

A defense measure that met with his complete approval, however, was the building of a fort on the western end of Verplanck's Point half a mile from the manor house. A log blockhouse was first erected and then earthworks were thrown up around it. Dirk ran across the point at odd times to see how the work was progressing and at length fell into the habit of lending a hand with the digging. This led to friendly relations between him and the troops who were doing the work. They joked with him and, most of them being Yankees, called him Dutchy.

Dirk was allowed the freedom of the fort after its completion. The blockhouse was a two-story building lighted only by loopholes. Here the ammunition was stored and the garrison quartered. West of the blockhouse, facing toward the river, was a battery of three cannon — one eighteen pounder and two four pounders. A parapet of hard-packed dirt and stones screened them from enemy fire. On the landward side, the only fortification was a stockade. It was named Fort Lafayette.

Before the completion of this works another was begun across the river at the opposite terminal of the ferry — Stony Point. The intention was to put any enemy vessels that might venture up the river under a blistering crossfire and prevent their penetrating into the Highlands where the main body of the American army was stationed at another new fort called West Point.

These preparations gave confidence to the whole countryside. Farmers planted big crops with a good prospect of harvesting them. Along the King's Ferry Road every farm was under cultivation. Even Jedediah Pike had planted a large garden although Sam predicted gleefully that he would have no New York market this year. Where Pike had been during the invasion was not known. Many suspected he had stayed right on his farm. Determined not to ask his help at Riverbrink, Dirk must farm its broad acres singlehanded. He began mowing very early in the season intending to take a second crop later.

So on the last day of May he set to mowing the south piece, a lot near the King's Ferry Road. At noon Christina and Peter brought lunch and they sat under a small tree in a fence corner to eat it. It was a gorgeous day with blue sky and a light breeze. Dirk munched contentedly on the bread and cheese, washing it down with a mug of cider. Then he lay back a moment with his head on his folded arms, drowsing. Christina made a small clatter packing away the lunch things, and at a little distance Peter carried on a one-sided conversation with a chipmunk. At length Dirk arose, stretched himself, and began to whet his scythe. The rhythmic note rang out across the fields seeming to blend with the warm noon atmosphere. Suddenly another sound cut across it, a deep ominous boom.

"The cannon!" cried Dirk. He stood motionless, listening.

"It may be only target practice," said Christina hopefully.

"I'd best go see what it's about," Dirk decided.

He hung his scythe over a tree limb and jogged off across the fields. Before he had reached the fort, the cannon boomed again. It certainly was a signal gun, he figured. Meant enemy ships were coming up the river. Well, this would be a different story from last time.

The guard at the stockade gate did not know what was up. Inside there was a great hurrying about and shouting of commands. Dirk ran to the parapet and looked southward. A large fleet was approaching under full sail. It was an impressive sight, as it had been when he saw it before. He dropped back to the barbette and looked at the three cannon. A doubt began to flicker in his mind.

The crews at the cannon were swiveling them around to the southward. Dirk watched Gunpowder Joe directing operations at the nearest gun. This middle-aged trooper, dressed only in a pair of leather breeches and a gaudy kerchief about the head, was shouting commands and waving a ramrod for emphasis. The fleet refused to present a good target. The large ships dropped anchor at some distance and only a few galleys continued to move northward, keeping near the west shore. They were not yet within range of Fort Lafayette, nor had a shot been fired when smoke began to roll into the sky from Stony Point.

"They're abandoning the fort!" cried one soldier. "They're leaving us in the lurch, the traitors."

"What else can they do?" asked another more calmly. "They're just workmen with no artillery and the fort not half finished."

"Well, boys," cried Gunpowder Joe exultantly, "these three old girls" — and he patted one of the cannon — "are all that stand between the British fleet and the Highlands."

At that moment Captain Armstrong, commandant of the fort, appeared and looked out over the parapet with a spyglass.

"What say we let them have it, Cap'n?" urged Gunpowder Joe.

"I don't think they're in range yet," said Armstrong, "but they may not get any closer for a while. Try a round or two."

The three crews went eagerly into action but without success. All the afternoon they toiled at the guns but failed to deliver one really effective shot. The enemy did not retaliate. The galleys hovered in a little bay south of Stony Point where they were obviously covering a landing party. At dusk Captain Armstrong ordered the crews to cease firing.

"We'll get the varmints tomorrow when they try to run their boats upstream," the men assured each other while they mopped their faces.

Dirk, after watching the operation of the guns for a while, had found a number of ways to help the crews; he toted casks of powder from the blockhouse; he applied a shoulder to the carriage of a recalcitrant gun; he brought buckets of drinking water to the men. It was hard work. The acrid powder smoke stung his nostrils. The crash of the guns set his ears ringing. But he loved the excitement and best of all the sense of comradeship from working closely with other men. So it was with reluctance, after the cease-fire order, that he realized he must go home to the humdrum life of a farmer.

As he took his leave, one of the men called out, "Come again tomorrow, Dutchy. We'll show you some more sport."

"That I will," he promised heartily.

Near the rear stockade, Gunpowder Joe overtook him. He scowled at Dirk from a powder-stained face whose lashes and brows were singed away. "See here, Dutchy, you stay right to home after this," he said.

"Well, if you don't want me — " Dirk began.

" 'Tain't that, but you've got a farm and family. You'd best stay to home and tend them."

"But it's fun here at the fort," Dirk protested mildly.

"Certain it was fun today, shooting off the guns. Just a nice quiet target practice. But tomorrow, or whenever them Lobsterbacks get their cannon up to the top of Stony Point, 'tis going to be a different story. Then we'll be under fire."

"I understand that," said Dirk.

"Aye, you think you do. But their position on Stony Point will command ours. Do you understand *that*? Means they'll be placed higher. Can throw shells right into our works."

"Are you afraid?" asked Dirk in surprise.

The gunner stared a moment as if he did not understand the meaning of the words. "It's my life," he said simply, "but it isn't yours." As abruptly as he had accosted Dirk, he now turned and walked away.

All evening Dirk pondered what Gunpowder Joe had said and finally decided he was right. He went to sleep determined to stay away from the fort.

The next morning he had just finished milking when the guns started to pound again. Without pausing, he began to run across the fields toward the fort, telling himself that he was only going to see what was happening. When he had nearly reached the fort, there was a sudden swishing noise and the ground was jarred so violently that Dirk fell prone. He got up startled and shaken. Nearby a cannon ball had plunged into the earth. He stared down at it, his eagerness to go to the fort considerably diminished. Perhaps this had been sent by Providence to turn him back home. He took a few steps toward Riverbrink and halted. Was he going to let these men defend his home for him while he hid in the hayloft? With a set face he turned back once more toward the fort.

Here was the same organized frenzy that he had found the day before. Already a haze of smoke hung over the battery. Gunpowder Joe stared at Dirk and shook his head.

"Well," he remarked with a wry grin, "a whiff of powder smoke has made fools out of better men than you."

"What happened?" Dirk asked.

"They got some guns up onto Stony Point. Must have

worked like demons all night to do it. They're peltin' us from there." A whistling swish interrupted him as a ball passed overhead. "They're aiming wild," he remarked. "Ain't got our range yet."

The young lieutenant in charge of the battery overheard this. "We must get their range first," he said brightly.

"That's right, Lieutenant. I'm going after it right now."

Joe's sardonic tone did not escape the officer. "It can be done easily," he insisted. "According to the laws of ballistics — "

"I don't know nothing about them, Lieutenant. All I know is that when I get enough of an angle on my gun to reach up to their position, the ball goes right on over them."

"Try a lighter charge of powder," suggested the officer without conviction. Then, turning to Dirk, "We need a man to carry powder again."

The morning wore along. The cannonade continued unabated but neither side scored a decisive hit. Dirk, beginning to recover from the first excitement, realized he had had no breakfast. He gnawed a piece of hardtack from a soldier's knapsack.

Toward noon enemy shots began to reach their mark with shattering accuracy. Dirk was crossing the courtyard with an armload of cartridges when a sharp crack made him look toward the southern end of the parapet to see an infantryman reel backward from the firing platform and land sprawling on the ground. Several men sprang down to pick up their comrade and a shout was raised for the surgeon. Carrying the injured man among them, the group started on a half run toward the blockhouse. With the sinister swish that Dirk now recognized another shell plummeted into their very midst. Instantly, the group was transformed into a writhing, screaming, blood-drenched mass.

Dirk stood staring in a fascination of horror unable to stir a muscle. Others rushed forward and soon obscured the gruesome scene with their stooping bodies. At length, the voices of a gun crew roaring for more powder penetrated his consciousness. He stumbled forward, half-dazed, and delivered his burden. Still the shells screamed in. The men performed their duties mechanically, their powder-stained faces drawn with the strain.

"We can't take this. It's murder," they muttered.

At last a bugle call announced that the fort was to be evacuated. The cannon were dismantled and lowered from the platform onto carriages. Infantrymen scrambled about the blockhouse picking up all that they could carry of equipment and ammunition. In a surprisingly short time, the entire garrison was on the drill ground in marching formation. Dirk was placed near the front with a cask of powder under each arm. The stockade gate swung wide. It was a silent column that marched out, yet Dirk could sense a feeling of relief that they were to escape that unceasing bombardment.

They swung over the ditch and out onto the road that led around a shoulder of the hill to the ferry landing. From this bend they could see the whole rim of the bay with the highway curving up over a hill in the distance. And on that highway there approached a long column of soldiers in bright red coats.

"Halt!" Lieutenant Miles' voice cracked with excitement.

The order passed back to the rear of the column like a diminishing echo. Dirk stood and watched the red line advance along the road. His heart was pounding. How many were there? A thousand? Two thousand? Captain Armstrong rode up from the rear for a hasty word with the lieutenant. Then orders were bawled out to face about and march. Only the front ranks were held, to act now as a rear guard. Dirk stood hesitant between the two separating units.

"Get that powder back into the fort," roared Armstrong at him, so he followed the retreating column.

Again the captain galloped past. By the time Dirk reached the fort, he was calling orders, the bugle was blowing, and the men were resuming their battle stations with grim and despairing expressions. One boy wept openly. An older man muttered a rhythmic stream of curses.

As Dirk started toward the blockhouse with the powder casks, Armstrong called to him, "Don't put them away. Just set them inside the door. We've got to get rid of them."

He strode on past and a soldier in the blockhouse remarked, "That means he's going to surrender."

Surrender? Dirk tasted the word. "I can't be taken prisoner!" he exclaimed with sudden realization. "I've got to get back to my family."

A rasp of strained laughter went up from some men who were stripping off their equipment.

"Me too," cried one. "My mother needs me to home."

"Ye should have thought of that before, Dutchy," said another. "Ye're trapped now."

"I'll climb over the stockade," said Dirk.

"Aye, and be picked off as soon as you get your head above the top. By now the stockade is surrounded."

The door was darkened by the rangy figure of Lieutenant Miles. "Cap'n wants two volunteers to carry that powder down and dump it into the river," he announced.

There was a strained silence.

"You mean climb down the ramparts, Lieutenant," ventured one man, "and get through all them obstructions between the fort and the river?"

"That's the only way to the river now," snapped the officer.

"A body'd be exposed to cannon fire the whole time," someone remarked.

"Can't be done," muttered another.

"It can be and it's got to be," barked the lieutenant. "This powder mustn't fall into enemy hands. If you brave heroes won't volunteer anything but opinions, I'll look elsewhere."

He was turning away when Dirk said in his deliberate voice, "I guess I'd better do it. I could manage the two casks by myself and nobody else need go."

"You've got no call to take on this job for us," said Miles.

"I know," Dirk replied. "I want to do it for my own sake. If I can get to the river, I'll swim home."

"Come on, then."

207

Under Captain Armstrong's direction, they slung the casks over the parapet by ropes and let them down to the ditch. Just as Dirk prepared to mount the parapet, a soldier ran up to Armstrong and saluted.

"Cap'n, they's a party of the enemy at the rear stockade with a flag of truce," he announced. "They demand the surrender of the fort."

"I'll meet them," said Armstrong grimly. "It seems we're just in time with this." He grasped Dirk's hand. "Best of luck, soldier."

With a hatchet, Dirk chopped out several spikes in the top of the parapet, then hoisted himself to the space thus made. Here he perched briefly while he shoved the hatchet into his belt and looked over the obstacle course before him.

In front of the fort rows of sharp-pointed stakes had been driven into the ground at such an angle that anyone approaching the ramparts would be impaled on them. Between them and the river, fallen trees had been placed with branches outward as a further obstruction to a landing party. Dirk's task would be to chop his way through this maze to the river.

With a smile at the men who were watching him, Dirk began to descend the rampart. At first it was a sloping surface where he could brace his feet and walk down, holding to the rope. Then came the vertical face of the wall. He lowered himself hand over hand. The scream of an approaching shell halted him in midair. He clutched the rope, sick with fear, knowing what a target he must make dangling there against the wall of the fort. But the shell passed overhead and he reached the ditch.

Here he could pause in comparative safety, for on the outer side of the ditch there rose a high stockade. The two casks lay nearby. He piled one on the other, mounted them, and pulled himself to the top of the stockade. Then he hauled up the casks by their ropes and lowered them on the opposite side.

From this vantage he could see ahead a number of cannon balls, evidence that some gun in the enemy battery was dropping its shots in this area. Well, there was nothing for it but to get through as fast as possible. He climbed down the front of the stockade and began cutting a path through the forest of stakes with his hatchet. His position was fearfully exposed and every step took him nearer the enemy guns, but he worked away, not pausing to look up when the cannon roared.

At length he won through the stakes and into the fallen trees. The hatchet work was easier here but the footing more uncertain. He would walk forward along a limb only to have it give way beneath him and let him down to the armpits in a clinging, stabbing tangle of branches. The third time he fell through, one foot plunged into the river. Open water was only a few feet ahead. He turned back for the casks.

And now he could see that he was being watched from the fort. Heads were visible between the spikes on the parapet and voices were calling out encouragement.

"Bravo, Dutchy!"

"You'll win through."

He acknowledged this with a quick, left-handed wave before continuing.

With a cask under each arm, he returned through the path he had made. Only a few yards more now. He walked along a tree branch when, with a sharp crack, it gave way. He sprang outward toward open water but fell short of it into a tangle of twigs and branches that raked his face and tore painfully across one eye. Releasing the casks, which sank at once, he floundered desperately and at last fought his way into open water. Then he threw the hatchet from his belt, kicked off his shoes, and struck out upstream. As a final salute, a cannon ball plopped into the river behind him, sending out a few waves that pushed him gently forward. It seemed an anticlimax.

He arrived at the cottage barefooted, his shirt in rags, his face scratched and bruised, with a welt across one eye, which was swollen shut. Christina flung herself into his arms.

"Dirk, oh, what has happened to you?" she cried.

"I've been to war," he announced triumphantly.

Peter burst into howls of grief to see his adored brother so disfigured.

"Oh, Dirk, your poor eye!" Christina exclaimed. "Does it hurt badly? Let me bathe it."

But he set her aside. "The fort has surrendered," he said, the triumph gone from his voice. "And our boys are all prisoners."

"The fort surrendered, our fort? Oh no, Dirk!"

"I think so. They were fixing to parley when I left. I'll go over and see if they're moving out."

Against Christina's protest, Dirk jogged off again along the driveway. Near the brow of the slope that led down to the King's Ferry, he crept up behind a stone wall and looked over.

He was just in time. The red-coated troops stood at ease now along the road. As he watched, a bugle call sounded from the direction of the fort. At once there was a bawling of orders among the ranks which drew them up in lines each side of the road. Then drums sounded and after a time the American troops appeared marching between the lines of the enemy. There was a short halt beyond the ferryman's house while a score of British infantrymen left the main body and fell into formation as a guard for the prisoners, of whom there were some seventy. Thus escorted, they resumed their march and soon disappeared over the slope of the hill.

Long after the slam of drums had faded, Dirk sat motionless. In spirit he was marching with those defeated comrades. What would become of them now? There was little doubt they would be taken to New York. He had heard of the prisons there where men starved and festered with disease. Poor devils! And among them, but for the grace of God, he might himself have been.

He thought back on the struggle he had made to get out of the fort and to the river. All those obstructions set up with such effort (and he had himself driven some of the stakes) had not hindered the enemy one whit from capturing the fort but had only delayed one struggling patriot trying to get out.

Suddenly, it seemed to Dirk that the Americans were always doing the wrong thing. They had built the two forts in the wrong order. They had fortified Fort Lafayette on the wrong side. They were always the dupes, guessing wrong and being fooled, as they had done the previous fall. Was he risking all for a cause led by blunderers down a road of mistakes to final destruction? What would happen right now to the farm and his family? Must they flee again?

Another bugle call brought him out of these musings. The enemy troops were marching toward the fort. On the battlements the Union Jack flapped cockily. Looking at it and at the line of marching men, Dirk slowly clenched his hands. What kind of patriot was he anyhow that a few defeats could make him lose heart? He was free, wasn't he, free to fight again? He still believed in the Cause, didn't he? With his whole soul.

Arising from his crouched position, Dirk became acutely aware of his many bruises. Every part of his body was lame and scratched and sore. His tatters of clothes were soaked. His eye throbbed painfully. But he dragged one bare foot after the other down toward the barn and began his evening chores. This was where he had left off that morning. Between milkings he had gone to war.

☆ 15 ☆

STONEHAVEN WAS RAIDED HALF A DOZEN NIGHTS DURING that spring and summer. Each time East made Ellen hide in the lilac bushes. Sometimes her father did not awaken and they let him sleep, for they knew he would not leave the house anyhow. The cottage was never molested. There was sufficient loot at the manor house to occupy the marauders' attention.

On two occasions, none of the three heard the raiders and did not know they had been there until the next morning when Roderick Stone, on a visit to the great house, discovered fresh losses. At each such discovery he went into a violent rage.

"If I ever get a chance at those dastardly rebels when it will endanger no one but me," he would always say, "I'll shoot them. I'd die happy if I could take one of the thieving vermin with me."

It was always assumed by both Roderick Stone and East that the raiders were rebels, even though a few times East had recognized among them men he had thought to be Tories. These he labeled as renegades and condemned with special vehemence. Ellen accepted this judgment but wondered a little that rebels as a group should be such wretches when the few she knew personally were not that sort at all.

Whoever the thieves might be, they were doing a thorough job. The house was ransacked from cellar to attic. Everything of value was taken, even to the tiles around the parlor fireplace. On one occasion, two parties of marauders arrived the same night. After much shouting and an exchange of musket fire, one group was driven off.

Despite all these night alarms, the days were utterly calm. To see East and Ellen go about their work, one would have thought they lived the placid lives of normal farm dwellers. There was, in truth, seldom anyone to see them. The roads were deserted except for an occasional party of soldiers cantering past, or a lone traveler, urging his beast nervously. So the three at Stonehaven began to take for granted their safety by day.

One warm afternoon in August, Ellen was sweeping the cottage floor after clearing away the dinner dishes. The door stood open and her father had retreated outside to sit on a bench against the house wall. East had gone down to the woods with a sack of grain to try to lure some half-wild chickens he had noticed there the day before. He need no longer carry feed to the stock, for at this time of year they were turned into a pasture out of sight from the road.

Suddenly, a wild shouting and a pistol shot sounded in the distance. Ellen rushed to the door. Her father was on his feet staring down toward the lower pasture. The rapid thudding of hoofs approached.

"It's thieves! They've got our horses!" shouted Stone.

He bolted into the house and returned brandishing a musket just as two men appeared over the slope of the hill. They were riding bareback on Blodgett's horse and Star. Stone ran forward and stood on the roadway directly in their path.

"Stop, you thieving villains!" he roared.

The first rider swerved his mount off the lane and circled around Stone. As he passed, he aimed a pistol point blank at the crouching man but the hammer fell with a harmless click. Stone had dropped to one knee. He swung his musket barrel in a careful arc, training it upon the rider. The gun roared; the horseman clapped a hand to his arm with a howl of pain. Meantime, the second rider was bearing down directly on Stone. He leaned out of the saddle at the instant of passing and discharged his pistol into Stone's back. Without a sound, Stone slumped forward onto the road. The hoofbeats dwindled out into silence.

Ellen ran to the inert figure huddled in the lane. A red stain was spreading on the back of the blue coat. She slid to her knees and, seizing her father by the shoulders, turned him over. One side of his face was smeared with the dirt of the road. She fell to rubbing it with her handkerchief, all the while calling to him, whether audibly or in her mind she did not know. But her father did not respond and she knew that he was gone forever.

After a while she heard someone breathing heavily and Matthew East knelt beside her. Gently he edged her away and, after a brief examination, picked the frail body up in his arms. Ellen followed him to the house where he laid his burden on the bed. She would have flung herself down beside it, but East drew her into the main room.

"He's dead, you know, Miss Ellen."

She nodded.

"You mustn't feel too bad, ma'am. He couldn't have lasted much longer anyhow. This has saved him a deal of pain."

She nodded again. How could she tell East that she felt nothing except a numbed astonishment? In fact, she was ashamed to be showing so little grief.

East was looking at her, his bronzed face puckered with concern. "We can leave here now, Miss Ellen. There's nothing to keep us any more."

"Only that now we have no horses," Ellen reminded him.

"Yes, that's true." He paused, pondering. "We could walk, but we'd be too long on the road. It's dangerous on the road. If we were on foot and anything happened to me — " He left that possibility dangling. "With a horse you could make a run for it. Yes, we need horses. I must think of a way. Meanwhile — "

He broke off and looked toward the bedroom door. "Miss Ellen, will you hunt out some clothes to bury your father in? I'll get him ready."

Ellen climbed to the loft and began lifting from a chest

the clothes her father had worn in better days — white linen shirts and silk hose, bright-figured vests and broadcloth coats. As she handled them, vivid images flashed in her mind of her father as he had been when he wore these clothes, an active man, speaking in vigorous tones, moving briskly. She remembered how he smiled upon her, how he would cup his hand over her head in a characteristic caress. This was the father she had lost.

Suddenly, she was overwhelmed with a great wave of grief. Sobs caught at her throat, almost strangling her. She fought to control herself. There were things to do. She must not give up to sorrow. She choked back the sobs and forced herself to continue searching through the clothes.

East carried the body to the family burial plot in one corner of the grounds and dug the grave while Ellen stood looking on in a suspension of feeling. He worked furiously, contorting his face at each shovelful of dirt that he flung. And with this physical relief for his grief, there came upon him a mounting anger at the situation that had caused this death.

"Fine state of affairs! Man driven out of his own house by damned rebel raiders. Forced to live — no, to hide — in a cottage on his own property."

With a grunt, he tossed out another shovelful of dirt.

"And then to be shot by a thief on his own land in broad daylight! Your father used to say he had lived too long. I guess I have too, Miss Ellen. The world I knew is gone. We're back to the state of the beasts. And it's these damned rebels have done it. May they suffer as they have made us suffer. May they die by the score for every honest man of us they have murdered."

As he uttered these last words, East paused and raised a clenched fist in the air, his face twisted in an expression of ferocity that verged on madness. Looking upon him, Ellen felt a stab of fright cut across her mind's confusion. The vengeful words of this self-contained man shook her more than had all her father's ravings.

East had a coffin already prepared, as he had thought Mr. Stone might fall dead of his sickness at any moment. It was nearing sundown by the time he had finished the grave and put the body into it. Standing at the head, Ellen recited the Twenty-third Psalm in a tremulous voice. Then she and East said the Lord's Prayer together. After a moment of silence, East picked up his shovel.

"Now, ma'am," he said, "you'd best get us some supper while I fill this in."

Ellen walked obediently to the house. She could not think of eating, but East must have food. He had been doing hard work. She set out some jerked beef and some bread and butter. Then she thought of a pinch of tea leaves she had been saving until her father should especially need a hot brew. Now was the time to use it. When East came in, she poured him a cup of tea and replaced the pot on the trivet.

"You must eat too, ma'am," said the overseer.

"Oh, East, I can't."

"Drink some tea."

She poured another cup. The first swallow through her

constricted throat was an effort. But it relaxed the muscles and warmed her stomach. After a little, she was eating and feeling better.

East arose. "Now, ma'am, I am going out and get horses," he announced. "I am going to turn the tables on those devils and get their horses the same way they got ours from us."

"Oh, East, don't. It is too dangerous. You'll be killed."

"Not I, ma'am. If anyone dies tonight, it will be by my hand, a life for the one already taken."

East stepped to the fireplace and reached down his musket from over the mantel. The firelight showed his face twisted again with that expression of high anger. As he turned toward the door, she realized with a pang of fright that he had all but forgotten her and the chief purpose of his venture.

"But, East, what of me?" she cried after him. "What shall I do?"

He stopped but did not look around. "Why, go up to bed, ma'am. I'll be back before morning." He strode to the door and then, with his hand on the latch, added more gently, "If I should be — delayed, don't come looking for me. Wait here."

The door opened and closed. East was gone. In the silence the ticks of the clock on the mantel shelf surged forth. The room was nearly dark except for the flickering fire. And beyond the room there stretched on every side a dark wilderness in which roamed beasts and evil men, a dark wilderness with Ellen Stone at the center — alone. She leaped up with a stifled scream and flung open the door, her mouth shaped to call East.

But the summer night was reassuring. A balmy air touched her cheek. Crickets chirped as they had on a thousand other evenings. Ellen summoned her fading courage. After all, she told herself, East's undertaking was the one that called for real bravery. She need only wait. Surely she could do that much. If she should call him back now, his whole scheme for their escape would be ruined. She went into the house, bolted the door, and crept up to the loft. Here she cast herself fully dressed upon the bed.

Sleep was remote. Her eyes would not even close but fixed themselves on the open window in the roof peak. And her ears strained intently for the sound of East's voice outside calling her to let him in. But there was only the monotonous plaint of the crickets going on and on. Her mind whirled with images, impressions, and conjectures over which she had no control. She lay in the grip of a nightmare from which she could not escape by waking because she was awake already.

After interminable hours the window square lightened with the dawn. Her relief at this was sharply modified by her concern that East had not yet returned. At least for the moment, however, she felt safer. The tension of her nerves was eased. She drifted into sleep.

It seemed almost at once that she awakened with the sound of East's voice in her ears. She sprang from the bed and hurried down the ladder. But even as she crossed the room and laid her hand on the bolt, a suspicion arose that the voice had been only in her mind — a product of her wish.

And so it proved. No one awaited her opening of the door. Outside it was broad daylight in a hot and empty world. She stepped forth and walked up the lane to the entrance gate. The highway lay dusty and deserted. No one was in sight at the crossroads. She turned back toward the cottage.

There was no need to be alarmed yet. East had said he might be delayed. So she told herself. But underneath this surface assurance there lay a truer intuitive knowledge that he had gone to his death in a fanatical attempt to avenge her father. But this knowledge her conscious mind refused to recognize simply because the thought was unendurable. In order to keep on she must believe that East would come back.

So then, what now? He had said not to follow him on the road. She had no desire to do so; she feared the road. She would wait here. There was plenty of food. All she need do was keep out of sight of the road and she would be safe. At least when she put the situation in these terms, it was endurable.

When, on the other hand, she began thinking, "Here am I, a helpless girl, stark alone in the midst of a lawless land infested with marauders," at once her heart began to race, weakness flowed through all her veins, and her mind became paralyzed with a panic of fear. No, that way madness lay. She must hold a tight rein on her imagination and keep her body busy with the struggle to survive.

Just now she must attend to the chores that East would

be doing if he were there. The hardest one was milking the two cows. They were afraid of her and she of them, but somehow she accomplished it and, taking the milk to the cottage, made herself some breakfast. Then, after another fruitless trip to the gate, she began cultivating the garden. The *chock-chock* of the hoe in the soil seemed very loud amid the surrounding midday silence. So passed the morning.

As the afternoon waned, panic began to rise within her, for every moment brought darkness that much nearer. The first note of a cricket stabbed her heart with terror and her fear mounted with their swelling chorus. She stood at the gate for an hour or more, straining her gaze down the road, praying for a sight of East's stocky figure.

At dusk she locked herself into the cottage and climbed to the loft. But here she felt she would be trapped if raiders should come, so, picking up some blankets and her father's pistols, she went outside to find a safer spot. The corncrib caught her eye. This was a small outbuilding near the barn, now empty, which was used to dry and store corn. It stood on posts above the ground and its walls, sloping inward from the roof, were slatted to admit air. This seemed a good sleeping place; she would be sheltered, yet could see on all sides with a view of the cottage and the lane.

She spread her blankets on the floor, took off her shoes, and lay down in the shirt and breeches that had become her unvarying costume. Now darkness had come. There was no moon and a ground mist hid the stars. Whether her eyes were open or closed, all was black. With clenched fists she checked her trembling. She must control her mind and body think only hopeful thoughts, think of East's return and their escape from this place.

With an effort of the will, she imagined herself standing at the gate, looking down the road. But she could summon no image of Matthew East. There was only the empty highway as she had seen it all day. Whimpering in despair, she clenched her fists more tightly and tried again. It seemed vastly important that she should succeed, as though whatever she could imagine happening would come true.

For a long time, there was nothing. Then a rider appeared in the distance, a tall broad-shouldered man on a rangy horse. As he drew near, he pulled the knitted cap from his yellow hair and his teeth gleamed in a slow grin. With this image before her closed eyes, Ellen's body relaxed its tension. Her fists uncurled, her breathing deepened. The monotonous night sounds receded from her consciousness and she drifted into sleep.

For several days after the British seizure of Fort Lafayette the families living in that neighborhood did not know whether to go or to stay. There were excited conferences between the Hollenbecks and the Higginses, hurried packings and hesitant unpackings. But time passed and the enemy did not venture out of their fort on the landward side. Even to get firewood they put off in rowboats and went ashore elsewhere. Nor did the Continental forces show any intention of abandoning Peekskill.

Of course these circumstances, while encouraging, did not make it truly safe at Riverbrink. But where was it safe? Any place to which they might flee would be within range of enemy raiding parties from this base. Besides, their crops were now in the ground and needed care. If they left them, they would have no food supply for winter. So they decided to remain.

They came to this conclusion at a conference in the Higgins living room one evening. Dirk had brought his family along. Peter slept on the hearthstone, curled up against Pluck's side. Dirk and Christina sat in the Higgins family circle. Mrs. Higgins, with lips pursed, was knitting a stocking. Hannah worked at the family mending.

"Then 'tis settled we stay here," said Mr. Higgins.

"If there was some way the two families could be housed together," mused Sam, " 'twould be safer. We could fix it that one man should always be hard by to guard the womenfolk."

"But neither house is big enough," protested Mrs. Higgins.

"The great house would be." Dirk spoke musingly as though thinking aloud. "But it doesn't belong to us."

"Who does it belong to?" demanded Sam. "Not the Stones. They lost their right when they fled. You've the best claim on it, Dirk."

"Not me. I'm just a tenant. Who does own Riverbrink now, Mr. Higgins?"

The farmer drew a hand along the rough stubble of his chin. "Well, I should say the Colonial gov'ment does. After the war, if we win, they'll sell it off."

"But meanwhile, Pa, who'd object to our living there?" Sam asked.

"Nobody as I know of, unless 'twas Dirk." The farmer eyed his neighbor with quiet amusement.

Dirk looked up to find everyone gazing at him expectantly. "Well, sir, if it's the best thing, and I guess it is, I'll try to get used to the idea. But the great house has always been where the master lived, not a place for me even to think of."

"Oh, it would be fine!" broke in Christina. "We could cook and eat together. We'd eat in the dining room."

"Food would get cold, lugging it off to another room," Mrs. Higgins objected. But her eye gleamed with interest.

"And we needn't use the servants' wing at all," Christina continued. "Mr. and Mrs. Higgins can have Mr. Stone's room and Hannah can have Miss Ellen's room, and — "

Into Dirk's mind there flashed a picture of Hannah moving familiarly about in Ellen Stone's room, her work-reddened hands touching the dainty fittings on Ellen's dressing table.

"No!" He did not realize how loudly he had spoken until he saw the circle of startled eyes. "There's no need to use those rooms," he added, more gently.

"But why shouldn't we, Dirk?" asked Christina.

"Because — because — "

Hannah broke through his stammerings. "Dirk thinks I'm not enough of a lady to have Miss Ellen's room."

Dirk felt the hot color sweep into his face. He began an embarrassed denial.

"Well, now, I think Dirk's right," declared Mr. Higgins. "We don't need those rooms and it's only decent to leave them empty — if we do move in, which we haven't decided yet."

But they did decide that night and began moving in the very next day. A week later they were comfortably installed. The men continued to work the two farms and Sam kept on in his occasional capacity as guide. Although the Higgins family had moved nearer the enemy, they did not feel that they had increased their danger, for the manor house was off from the main road and not in sight of the fort. And the double household was surprisingly happy. Christina, having lived with the Higginses while Dirk was at Stonehaven, had become like a member of their family. Hannah treated her as a younger sister although Sam jokingly made it clear that he had no desire to be a brother to her.

At first it gave Dirk an odd feeling to be living at the great house. Moving about the spacious rooms, he would gaze with a guilty start at the high ceilings and handsome furniture. But familiarity gradually melted away the vestiges of his childhood awe. It was only a house like any other, he realized, though an exceptionally beautiful one. And a man became no whit different from living in it.

Being at the manor house made him think of the Stones even more frequently than before. He was now virtually in Roderick Stone's position, lord of the manor. It was not a wholly enviable post, he discovered, and he often wished for Mr. Stone's advice. But most of all, of course, he missed Ellen and worried about her safety. He would have made a trip to Stonehaven to see how she was faring, but the situation at Riverbrink was too precarious for him to leave.

There were a few days in mid-July when it seemed that the danger of the enemy fort might be removed. The Americans recaptured Stony Point in a bold night attack and planned to besiege the British fort the following day, but the latter scheme misfired, leaving the situation unchanged at Riverbrink.

Dirk's only possible contact with Stonehaven was Sam, whose journeys as guide to the army sometimes took him into that neighborhood. He inquired about the Stones on every possible occasion and finally, one morning in August, he returned from a three-day scouting expedition with news. Dirk and Hannah were picking beans. The flower beds behind the great house had been planted to vegetables this year and it was here that Sam found them. He dismounted, his face drawn with fatigue.

"News at last about Stonehaven, Dirk," he said. "The place has been burned to the ground."

"What of the Stones?" Dirk demanded at once. "Are they safe?"

"I heard nothing of them. They must have moved to New York."

"But East would have let me know."

"How?" asked Sam. "There's no way a Tory could get news to anybody on our side."

"I suppose not, but I feel something is very much amiss. I'd better go see what has happened."

"What d'ye mean 'go see'?" Sam's tone was disgusted. "Go to Stonehaven? There's nothing to see there but some burnt timbers."

"Why, Dirk Hollenbeck!" Hannah cried. "I never heard

such a fool idea. You're needed right here. You shouldn't think of chasing off after those Tories."

Dirk fell silent and finally began picking beans again. But his mind was greatly troubled. All day he speculated on what could have happened to the Stones. By night he knew that, however foolish it might seem, he had to go and see for himself.

When he found that Dirk was determined to make the trip and was, in fact, preparing to start on foot that night, Sam offered his horse.

"But wait till early morning," he urged. "Then go down and back the same day. Highboy can do it."

Dirk started before dawn. It developed into a hot sultry day. He allowed the horse to take an easy pace, in view of the long trip ahead. It was a depressing journey over the deserted countryside. Weeds and brush grew along the ditches. Hay stood in the fields, dried brown and swamped down by rains. Most of the houses looked abandoned. Some were only a heap of ashes in a black cellar hole.

There were few people to be seen and those few only in quick glimpses. A man was driving a hog across a field. At sight of Dirk he scrambled over a fence. A woman appeared from behind a house with a pitcher in her hand. Seeing Dirk, she turned with a flirt of her skirts and fled to the shelter of the house. So it went. Fear was in the very air. Human beings skulked like animals. Dirk felt a strong revulsion of spirit against it all. To think that he had left Ellen Stone in the midst of such a land!

He reached Stonehaven before noon. As he rode through the gate, the stench of the charred timbers rolled upon him in a strangling wave. For the first time he felt a sense of futility. So this was what he had ridden twenty miles to see. What, indeed, had he expected? The house was burned and the Stones had gone. Why linger in this reeking atmosphere? But a stubborn Dutch persistence held him. Since he had come, he would at least take a thorough look.

He dismounted and unsaddled Highboy. The horse jogged off to where the grass had not been seared by the fire and fell to grazing. Walking to the site of the manor house, Dirk stared down into the ruins. If he had thought to learn anything from this experience, he was disappointed. The heat beat down from the sky and shimmered up from the rubble making him slightly giddy. He turned away and started down the lane toward the barn. This at least had not been burned. Nor the cottage. There it stood among the lilac bushes.

Suddenly he halted, stared, and gripped his gun more tightly. The door of the cottage stood open. Was some marauder inside? He waited, tense, for a time, but there was no sound from within. He moved to the door. The place had been occupied recently. It had a lived-in look. The air was sweet, not musty.

Raising his gun, he stepped across the threshold. On the table a candle had guttered out in a pool of grease. A water pitcher and mug stood side by side, both empty. As he came opposite the bedroom door, he glanced in. Someone lay on the bed, seemingly asleep. It appeared to be a boy dressed in a dirt-streaked white shirt and brown breeches. The delicate features, deeply tanned, were smudged with ashes. Some familiar look about the face drew him nearer. A floorboard squeaked and the eyes flashed open. For an instant he looked into their unguarded depth.

"Ellen!" he whispered, unbelieving.

With horror he noted that her expression changed instantly to one of fright. She sprang up and scuttled to a corner of the room, where she cowered, trembling visibly. For a moment he could only stare in astonishment. Then he thought that it must indeed have been frightening for her to open her eyes upon the sight of a man standing over her with a musket. He put aside the gun but her aspect did not change.

"Ellen, don't you know me? It's Dirk."

Still the fear stood in her eyes. She fell to coughing, a heavy sound from deep in the chest. Impulsively, Dirk stepped toward her but she shrank away. So he waited helplessly until the paroxysm was spent.

"Please, Ellen, lie back on the bed," he begged. "I won't come near you if you don't want me to."

Panting from the exertion of coughing, she studied Dirk. For the first time there was recognition in her eyes. He smiled reassuringly. She turned to the bed and lay down.

"Ellen, tell me what has happened," Dirk urged. "Where is your father? Where is Matthew East?"

But she lay with closed eyes. Her face was flushed. Strands

231

of disordered hair clung damply against her neck and fore-head. "Water!" she croaked out suddenly.

Dirk caught up the pitcher from the table and ran for the barn, glad at last of something he could do. The water ran from a wooden pipe into a tub, making a monotonous music. Here he had dipped buckets for the stock during the previous winter. Now the stalls were all empty. At least he need not worry about what to do with the animals when he took Ellen away.

His great concern was how and even whether he could take her away. She was ill, how gravely ill he did not know. She had a fever and so should be put directly to bed, not started on a long journey. But he did not know how to nurse her. She needed a woman's care, possibly a doctor's, too. Here there was no medicine, not even food, so far as he knew.

Nor was her state of health the only difficult factor. There was also the fear she had of him which might well make a journey together impossible. He wondered what had caused it. Was it only the delirium of fever? He thought not. She had been through a tragic experience. By some hideous mis-chance she had apparently lost both the men who might have protected her and had been left alone in this desolation for Heaven knew how long. It was no wonder her mind seemed unhinged.

But beneath all his thoughts ran an irrepressible undercur-rent of exultation. He had found Ellen Stone and she was in his care. Surely all lesser problems could be solved since this one had been.

He hurried back to the cottage, struck with a sudden fear that she might have run away. But she still lay on the bed. After taking a deep drink, she thanked him huskily. Her eyes had lost the look of panic. Dirk was encouraged.

"Ellen, do you think you are strong enough to ride back to Riverbrink?" he asked.

She nodded.

"Good. Could you leave today, right now?"

Another nod.

"Are there any horses in the pasture?"

A shake of the head.

"Too bad. It would be much easier, but we'll get along with one. Now, Ellen, before we go, I must be sure of one thing. Do you expect your father or East to come back here?"

The answer was long in coming. She lay with eyes fixed ahead. Dirk wondered helplessly what past horror she was seeing. Perhaps his question would throw her mind out of balance once more. Nevertheless he had to ask it.

"Should we wait for them, Ellen?"

Slowly she shook her head.

"Then let us go. I'll saddle the horse." He strode to the door, then turned. She was sitting up, looking bewildered. "When you're ready, come outside," he added.

Highboy had wandered some distance. It took time to find and saddle him. Dirk sprang on his back and rode pelting down the hillside to where Ellen waited before the cottage door. At his noisy approach, she took fright once more and fled inside. Dirk found her prone on the bed, face buried in a pillow.

"Ellen! Ellen!" he exclaimed. "What are we to do? You must conquer this foolish fear of me."

She lay rigid. Only a pitiful whimper came from the depth of the pillow. The sound touched him, made him ashamed of his impatience.

"I'm sorry, Ellen," he said more gently. "You can't help it, I know. Let's fight this thing together. Shall we? Let's pretend we're back at Riverbrink and it's two years ago. Your horse is outside. Wouldn't you like to take a ride?"

He seemed to have struck the right note, for she got up in the most natural manner and walked to the door.

"Where is your cloak?" he asked.

"In the loft. Please get it."

Despite the croaking tone, there was much of the former "lady of the manor" air about this request. Dirk grinned to himself as he climbed the ladder. Returning with the cloak, he took a quick glance around the cottage, then ushered Ellen out and closed the door.

As he helped her mount, she protested, "This is not my saddle."

"No, but you're a boy now. You must learn to ride like one. Straddle his back."

She complied, looking puzzled. Dirk adjusted the stirrups and handed her the bridle reins. She sat erect and guided the horse out to the lane. Dirk walked behind, his gun slung across his arm. Perhaps this was going to be easier than he had feared. She seemed strong. But it was not long before her shoulders began to droop and her grip on the reins slackened. So Dirk took up a position at the horse's head where he could guide him.

From here he glanced back frequently at Ellen. Her expression was somber, preoccupied, and her face was greatly changed, thinner, sadder, the youthful contours subtly sharpened. Dirk's heart was twisted with pity. Suddenly another fit of coughing seized her. She swayed in the saddle and caught at Highboy's mane for support. Dirk stopped the horse. Springing to her side, he held her firmly about the waist. When the attack had passed, she slumped forward in exhaustion.

"I can't go any farther," she whispered. "I'm too weak."

Dirk hardened his voice. "Do you want to go back?"

"No, not that, please!"

"Then you must go farther, Ellen, much farther. I'll help you but I can't carry you twenty miles and the horse can't carry both of us so far either. Perhaps some food would strengthen you."

"I don't want any."

"Well, I do."

He rummaged in a saddlebag and drew forth a chunk of cornbread wrapped in a napkin that Hannah had given him. Ellen continued to refuse the food but she straightened her shoulders and took the reins. Dirk returned to the horse's head, munching on the cornbread, and they resumed the journey.

Shortly afterward they met the only other travelers that they saw that afternoon. It was apparently a scouting party from the Peekskill camp. The men stared at Dirk and Ellen but did not stop them. Ellen managed to pull herself erect until they had passed.

Somewhat later Dirk looked around to see her clinging to the horse's mane, her face beaded with perspiration. Again he sprang to help her and found that her whole body was quivering with the effort to hold herself in the saddle. He slung the musket across his back, gently released her grip on Highboy's mane and slid her arm over his own shoulders. Then taking the reins and supporting her around the waist, he clucked to the horse. So they could start forward once more.

It was late afternoon when they reached Pine's Bridge. Highboy and Dirk thumped across in interfering rhythms. As they gained the far end, Ellen pitched sidewise against Dirk and he dragged her, unconscious, from the horse's back. Lowering her to a grassy bank, he chafed her wrists and wiped her face with water from a canteen. She soon opened her eyes and looked up listlessly. When he put the canteen to her lips, she drank with eagerness.

"How much farther?" she asked.

"We're nearly there," he lied, smiling. "And I'm going to ride, too, the rest of the way."

Highboy was cropping the dusty grass in the ditch. Dirk lengthened the stirrups and led him to where Ellen was lying.

Then he lifted her to the horse's back, sprang into the saddle and drew her back against him, holding her with his right arm. It was a heavy load for the tired horse. Dirk did not force him but let him take his own pace which at first was slow. But as he came into familiar territory and realized that he was headed toward home, his gait quickened.

Dirk and Ellen rode silently through the gathering twilight. In Dirk's heart there was peace and fulfillment. If he remembered that this could be only an interlude in their lives, that she was betrothed to another man, that a short while ago she had run from him in fear — if he remembered these things, he did not think of them. He did not even worry any more about her illness. They would soon be where she could receive proper care. For the moment it was enough that she was in his arms, leaning her weight back against him — safe, sheltered, cherished. He drew her cape around her as the night air freshened.

By the time they reached Riverbrink, it was dark. As the weary horse plodded up the final slope, the roofs and chimneys of the great house came into sight. From Ellen there was a choked exclamation. Sam appeared out of the gloom beside the door and helped Dirk dismount with his burden. Then he led the horse away.

Inside, Christina was waiting. Her eyes were full of questions but without a word she hurried upstairs and opened the door of Ellen's room. Dirk put Ellen down upon the bed. She lay quiet, her dark eyes moving slowly about the room.

"Well, Ellen, here you are," said Dirk briskly. "You're back home safe in your own room."

Suddenly, and for the first time that day, her eyes suffused with tears. "I never thought," she whispered, then choked, "I never thought to see my home again."

☆ 17 ☆

ELLEN WAS IN BED FOR MORE THAN A WEEK AND CHRIS-
tina took care of her. She slept a great deal, awakening at intervals to eat a little. Gradually, her fever went down. But
even when she was well enough to get about in her room,
Christina reported that she did not speak at all except to express thanks; she asked no questions nor showed an interest
in anything. Even when, at length, she could get downstairs
and out of doors, she took no part in conversations at table and
spoke only when directly addressed. She was eager to work,
however, and as soon as her strength permitted, she helped
in the kitchen and garden.

Summer faded and harvest time came around, a busy
season on a farm. Ellen entered into this work with a will
and seemed to be making an effort to resume a normal life.
Still she never laughed aloud and her rare smiles appeared
forced. There came occasional black days when she kept to
her room and, according to Christina, lay on the bed, crying. On one such day the household fell to discussing her
queer conduct as they sat at dinner.

"She's just got a fit of pride is all that ails her," sniffed

Hannah. "She thinks she's still lady of the manor and too good to sit at table with us common trash."

But the rest disagreed.

"No, I've got to say she's not a bit like that," protested Mrs. Higgins. "She never tries to set herself up as better than us."

"Land o' goodness!" Sam exclaimed. "It's a wonder she's as sane as she is after all she must have gone through."

"What did happen when she was down there alone?" asked Mrs. Higgins.

"She never speaks of it," said Christina, "and I don't ask. She just wants to forget it all and the sooner she can, the better."

Dirk took no part in the conversation. His thoughts about Ellen Stone he kept to himself but in this case they did not agree with Christina's. It was no doubt true that Ellen wanted to forget but he did not think she would succeed by keeping it all to herself. These memories, it seemed to him, were like a hidden, festering wound. They must be brought into the light and air before healing could take place. How this could be done he had little idea but he was determined to try it if an opportunity arose.

He had his chance one rainy afternoon in late September when he was working in the barn with Christina and Ellen. He sat on an upended cask carding wool and watching Christina teach Ellen to spin. They had set out their work on the threshing floor with the haymows looming up on either side.

The two girls and the spinning wheel were framed by the open doors with the rain falling gently behind them. Christina would set the wheel in motion and take two or three smooth backward steps, drawing out the long strand of fiber as the wheel twisted it into a thread. Then she would move gracefully forward letting the thread wind back upon the spindle. Next Ellen would try to imitate the process. Sometimes the wool would snap, at other times snarl upon the spindle. Still she persisted, with flushed face.

"It looks so easy when you do it," she wailed.

"It is, truly. There's just a little knack to it," Christina said.

"You speak like an old hand," remarked Ellen. "How long ago did you learn to spin?"

"When I was six. My mother taught me. Weaving is harder. I must have been ten or eleven before I mastered that."

Ellen shook her head with a wry smile. "And to think that I was growing up on this same estate so ignorant and helpless."

Christina and Dirk both gaped in astonishment at this unexpected point of view.

"Do you truly feel that way about your life before the war?" Christina asked. "Wouldn't you have those days back if you could?"

Ellen hesitated. "Of course if it would mean having my father alive and Gerit safe from the war — "

At Ellen's tone in mentioning Van Wyck, Dirk was

seized with an emotion so violent that it threatened to choke him. He had been cherishing a foolish hope that she had forgotten this Tory. Now it was proved groundless. The memory flashed through his mind of the mocking laughter with which, long before, Van Wyck had greeted his statement that all men were created equal. His air of superiority over Dirk had been provoking at the time but what cut deep now was that he had proved it true in the only area that mattered to Dirk — the heart of Ellen Stone. Dirk wished intently that this man would be killed — and that he might be the one to kill him.

As soon as this wish had shaped itself in his mind, he was brought up short with horror. In all his life he had never had such a savage, evil thought. He felt his face reddening with shame. He forced his attention back upon the conversation.

Christina was saying, "But at least you learned how to do some useful things."

"Yes," Ellen agreed, "there was that much good amidst a great deal of bad."

Dirk saw his opportunity. Gently he said, "Ellen, suppose you tell us some of the bad things that happened to you."

Ellen stood rigid. A mask of withdrawal settled upon her face.

Christina flew upon her brother like a little fury. "Dirk Hollenbeck, you leave Ellen alone. Can't you see how you're making her suffer? She needn't tell anything she doesn't want to — not ever." And she pummeled his chest with her fists.

"But she does want to tell us, Tina," Dirk persisted. "That's why she's so unhappy, keeping it bottled up in her own mind. Isn't that true, Ellen?"

He put Christina gently aside and walked over to face Ellen.

"Yes, I suppose it's true," she admitted in a breathless voice, with lowered eyes. "I must tell you all about it some time — but not yet. I — I can't yet. I can't."

She would have turned and fled but Dirk had both her hands. "No, Ellen, that won't do and you know it. It's never going to be a bit easier than it is right now. Ellen, how did your father die? Was he killed? Tell me."

Her fingers twisted in his grasp. "Yes, he was killed." Her voice was tense. "He was killed by rebels."

"And East?"

"Rebels killed him, too." Suddenly emotion surged into her voice. "And if my father could know that now I am living with rebels, letting them support me, as if I had forgotten what he thought of them, what they did to him, he would — he would —"

Dirk was completely taken aback by this outburst. He himself had come so far from the rebel-and-Tory attitude in relation to Ellen that it was hard for him to imagine her feelings. Yet he should have realized, he thought now, that she could not help absorbing some of her father's bitterness.

"Ellen, are you sure it was rebels who killed your father and East?" he asked quietly.

"But of course. Who else would attack and rob loyalists?"

"Who would? Why, cutthroats and thieves. You see, Ellen, there are really no politics in the Neutral Ground. There are only people who have property and people who want it. Do you think rebels would rob Colonel Van Cortlandt? And yet his house on the Croton River has been totally dismantled by raiders."

Ellen gazed up earnestly into Dirk's face. "Oh, if I can only think my father and East were mistaken! Then I need not feel guilty about liking all of you."

"Do believe it, Ellen," urged Dirk. "It is true."

Christina rushed forward. "Why, Ellen, you know we are the best friends you have in the world," she cried, almost with reproach.

"Yes, dear, I do know."

Ellen turned to her and suddenly was sobbing in her arms. Dirk and Christina led her to a bench where Christina sat down beside her. For a time she cried unrestrainedly. Then she began to talk. Gradually, as she gained control of her thoughts and voice, the story of that tragic summer emerged. Dirk resumed his wool carding so as to make the atmosphere seem more casual. He and Christina prompted her with occasional questions. She told of her father's death, of East's departure, of the long days and nights alone on the manor, of how two thieves had stolen her cows.

"Were they the raiders who burned the great house?" asked Dirk.

"No, that was a large group, about a score of men. That was the most frightful night of all." She paused, remembering.

"Tell us about it," said Dirk.

Ellen reached for Christina's hand. "Well, it was a sultry night with a storm threatening. I was lying in the corncrib watching lightning wink on the horizon when I heard hoofbeats and drunken shouts on the road. The lights of their torches moved from the gate toward the great house. Watching them, I clutched the slats of the corncrib and my whole body was limp with fear."

"Didn't you run away?" asked Christina.

"No. I could have then and I should have but, terrified though I was, I had to see what they were doing to my house. I ran up the hill and hid behind some bushes to watch them. They broke into the house and tossed their torches inside. They threw flaming brands on the roof. Soon the place was ablaze. They drew back from the heat and looked on, passing a bottle among them.

"It was then that I should have run away. But I thought I could slip off any time in the darkness. I didn't realize that the fire was lighting the whole countryside like broad day.

"Well, after they had rested for a time, they got posts and fence rails and made themselves new torches by lighting them in the flames. Then they started toward their horses and I thought they were going away to fire some other house,

245

so I drew back out of the bushes and ran down the hill. As I reached the lane, I looked back, and what was my horror to see them all coming behind me, some on foot and some mounted, flourishing their torches and yelling. They were coming down to fire the barn. And I was in plain sight just a few yards ahead of them. It was like the most impossible nightmare. In my frenzy to get away, I tried to run faster and fell. A man overtook me before I could get up.

"He said, 'I'll be dummed if you ain't the drunkest of us all.'

"So for the moment at least I was saved. My masculine clothes had led him to take me for one of their number. He had two torches and handed one to me. Then he ran on ahead. By this time, others had overtaken me. I moved along slowly in hopes they would all pass me and I could slip away unnoticed. But one man, who may have been their leader, came up on horseback and looked me over keenly.

" 'I don't remember seeing you before,' he said. 'When did you join us?'

"I muttered an answer, trying to make my voice gruff, but I thought discovery was close at hand. Then it began to rain. When the first drops fell hissing on our torches, the man spurred his horse and shouted to the others not to fire the barn as they would need it for shelter. But some beams were already ablaze and they all began desperately trying to put out the flames they had just succeeded in lighting. It was easy for me to drop my torch and slip away across lots to the woods."

Ellen paused and drew a deep, shivering breath.

"Then you stayed down there in the woods all night!" exclaimed Christina. "You must have gotten wet."

"Wet! I was soaked, drenched, all but drowned. It rained torrents."

"I should think such a downpour would have put out the fire at the great house," said Dirk.

"No, but it raised a great white cloud of steam. When the rain stopped, which it did soon, the fire blazed up again as strong as ever. I longed to get near it, near enough to dry my clothes."

"That was the cause of your sickness, that night's soaking," Christina declared.

"Without doubt. I tried to warm myself with exercise but it was little use. I couldn't stop shivering."

"When did the raiders leave?" Dirk asked.

"They must have gone during the night. The barn was empty in the morning and the cottage had not been touched. I think they never noticed it."

"And how long were you lying sick before Dirk found you?" asked Christina.

"I don't know. From that day I lost count of time. I remember going to the cottage and changing into dry clothes and eating. Then I fell into a heavy sleep and when I woke, I was feverish and my chest ached. From then on my mind was confused. At intervals it would clear for a few hours at a time but I never knew how much time had passed between those intervals."

"There's one thing I'd like to ask," said Dirk. "Why were you afraid when you first saw me?"

Ellen looked at Dirk, then abruptly away. A slow red crept up her neck.

"Of course if you'd rather not — " he began.

"It was just the effect of her fever," Christina interrupted. "Her mind was clouded."

"No, there was a reason," said Ellen quietly. "I want to tell you about it. On the afternoon of the day I was taken with the fever, I roused up feeling thirsty and there was no water, so I took a pail and went to the well at the great house. I couldn't have been right in my mind then, for I had forgotten about the fire and was momentarily shocked to find the place in ashes. I stood looking at the frightful ruin, still smoldering in places, and suddenly I remembered how I had hesitated that night last winter to let Dirk's horse into the house for fear he might damage it. In my feverish condition, this thought seemed very funny and I laughed aloud. At least, I meant to laugh, but the sound that came from my throat was more of a croak.

"Just then I heard a noise, the click of a horseshoe against a stone. I threw myself prone in the ashes, then cautiously raised up until I could look over the slope of the lawn. Near the entrance gate a man sat his horse. He was tall and broad-shouldered with yellow hair. Dirk, I thought it was you. I ran toward him, calling your name."

Ellen's voice faltered a moment. The wool cards clattered

to the floor as Dirk sprang up to stand looking down at her intently.

"Blinded as I was with tears, I had nearly reached the man before I realized it was not you.

"He stared at me and exclaimed, 'Blast me, if it ain't a woman!' Then he started to dismount.

"I ran back toward the ruins with his feet pounding behind me. I plunged into the cellar hole and floundered across it over the debris, raising a cloud of ashes that swirled up like smoke. The man started to circle the ruins to come at me but the smoke from a smoldering heap beside me billowed straight into his face. Whatever way he turned, the smoke followed him. Finally he stopped to cough and rub his eyes, muttering that it was bewitched. Then with a sudden thought, he stared at me.

" 'You're a witch!' he said.

"His eyes popped and his jaw hung down. Both he and the idea were so ridiculous that I gave a sudden croak of laughter.

" 'Yes, and I heered ye cacklin' like that all by yerself when I first come along,' he said. 'Ye can walk through fire. Ye can make smoke do yer biddin'. A witch! A witch as I ever seed!'

"Again I laughed and with that he ran back to his horse and galloped away. I threw myself down in the ashes still laughing, or crying — it's hard to say which — until a spasm of coughing ended it."

"Oh, Ellen," cried Christina, wiping her own eyes. "I see now why you've acted as you have since Dirk brought you back. With all that hidden in your memory, how could you be happy?"

"And he was right to make me tell about it," said Ellen. "I feel much better now."

Dirk dropped to one knee before her and covered her two hands with one of his. "Now you have told it and you can forget it," he said. "Just remember this, Ellen. It never can happen again. You're safe now here with us, utterly safe."

☆ 18 ☆

DIRK WAS ALL TOO WELL AWARE JUST HOW FAR FROM THE truth his words of assurance to Ellen had been. Safe — with an enemy fort half a mile away! But he was determined to give her an illusion of security because she needed it so badly. She must never be frightened again. It would not be enough that he should repel any attack upon the house. There must be no attack made, for such a threat to her safety might destroy her peace of mind that had been so precariously restored.

For a time the enemy seemed to be cooperating in Dirk's attempt to make Ellen feel safe. September spun itself out in a succession of warm, hazy days and the vicinity of River-brink remained utterly quiet. Except for the boom of the sunset guns and occasional bugle notes drifting on the wind, the existence of the British fort could easily have been forgotten, for there were never any soldiers to be seen.

But they were active elsewhere with midnight raids, one of which burned the church at Crompond where the Committee of Safety had its headquarters. They always left the fort by boat, thus avoiding the danger of an ambush on the landward side, came ashore at some unguarded point, made their raid, and returned by the same route. These attacks, many of which were not upon military objectives but upon private houses, terrorized the countryside. Since the army was unable adequately to patrol all roads and the shoreline, they called on the militia for help. So on the nights when he was not on guard at Riverbrink, Dirk sometimes patrolled the nearby roads, trying to do his share of militia duty without straying too far from the manor house.

One night Sam was with him and they were walking down the post road below where the King's Ferry Road joined it. Sam had been in the Neutral Ground the night before and planned to keep Dirk company for only an hour or so, then return to Riverbrink and sleep.

"I think I've found what happened to this man East," he said. "He was killed by a couple of Continental soldiers."

"How did you hear about it?"

"One of the soldiers that did it was telling. We were riding along the road not far from Stonehaven last night, and he said that was where it happened. Said this man challenged them from behind a tree. Told them to dismount and leave their horses."

"Sounds like East. It was horses he was after."

"Well, one of them fired on him and with that he came from cover and shot that man in the shoulder and then the other one shot him dead and they rode away."

Dirk was touched with sadness. "So Matthew East ended his life in a roadside ditch. He deserved better than that."

"We aren't sure it was East," Sam reminded him.

"More than likely it was. As soon as it's safe to leave here, I'll go down and look for his body and give it a decent burial."

"Listen!"

The two halted and in the silence could hear the shuffle of feet on the road ahead.

"They're coming this way. Must be half a dozen," said Sam. "Too many for us to tackle."

"We'd better get over the fence." Dirk moved toward the ditch.

"No, let's turn around and keep ahead of them. That way we'll have time to stop and rout out some help while they're coming up and passing."

The boys began to hurry northward.

"Maybe it's only an army patrol of our own," Dirk suggested.

"No, they'd be mounted and making more racket."

The two paused an instant to stare back at the oncoming party. But the starlight gave them only the sight of a dark moving mass. They hurried on.

"Where can we get help?" Sam pondered.

"Well, we could turn off at the King's Ferry Road and get the Cartwrights. They live near enough the corner so that we might have time to rout them out and then follow these raiders up toward Peekskill, wherever 'tis they're going."

At the intersection of the two highways, Dirk stayed to

watch the enemy party pass up the post road while Sam ran to the Cartwrights' house. What was Dirk's astonishment to see the shadowy group swing around the corner onto the King's Ferry Road and march directly toward him. He could have slipped into the ditch and let them pass but he must warn Sam or the boy might run right into their arms. So, stooping almost double, Dirk sprinted down the road.

"Ho, there!" called a voice behind him and a shot buzzed over his head.

But he ran on.

Sam was just coming out of Cartwright's lane. "I can't rouse —" he began, but Dirk seized his shoulder.

"They're coming down *this* road," he said in a harsh undertone. "They must be going to Riverbrink."

"Couldn't be anywhere else," Sam agreed. "What'll we do?"

"We've got to stop them. We've got to."

They were hurrying down the road at a lope to keep ahead of the raiders.

"Maybe we can get the women out before they get to the house," Sam panted.

"They mustn't get to the house," said Dirk grimly.

"How you going to stop them?"

They stumbled along in silence. "Ambush," said Dirk.

"The two of us ambush all them?"

"They don't need to know how many of us there are. Here, let's get over this stone wall."

The boys threw themselves over the wall and, crouching

254

down, trained their muskets back on the road. They were panting heavily. Very soon the scuffing tread of the invaders became audible. Dirk waited until they were nearly opposite him.

Then he said in a gruff voice, "Halt! Drop your weapons. We've got our guns on you."

The footsteps stopped abruptly and there was an instant's silence.

"It's an ambush!" someone hissed.

Then a musket cracked and a bullet ticked against the stone wall.

"Hold your fire, men," commanded Sam to an imaginary squad of soldiers. With that, he discharged his gun into the midst of the raiders. "I said hold your fire," he roared.

The lid of his powder horn clicked. "Don't fire till I've reloaded," he warned Dirk.

Meanwhile a groan and a scuffling on the road showed that Sam's bullet had found a mark.

"Get him to the rear," muttered a voice.

"Hold, you bloody cowards! Charge that wall!" cried another voice.

But the diminishing sound of boots on the road told that some, at least, of the enemy were in retreat.

Dirk gripped his musket more tightly. There was something familiar about that officer's voice, most disagreeably familiar.

"Charge that wall!" it repeated, and by the sound Dirk could tell the man was approaching.

Suddenly, like a shell exploding in his face, came the realization of whose voice this was — Gerit Van Wyck's. Hatred welled up stranglingly in his throat. He trembled all over at this dazzling opportunity to kill.

A dark figure loomed before him upon the wall. In his too great eagerness, he pressed the musket trigger without taking aim and the gun discharged into the air. Suddenly the dark mass catapulted down upon him. As he was borne backward, he felt a sharp streak of pain sear his arm. He crashed heavily to the ground and the weight of the man upon him knocked out his breath. For an instant he lay helpless, pinned down by his assailant. Fingers groped at his throat and tightened suddenly, throttling him. With a strangled growl he put all of his might into a lunge that flung the man off. Another heave put Dirk atop him. Snarling, he seized his opponent's throat in the vise of his fingers. The man writhed and gasped horribly but Dirk held on, probing through the silken stock for the windpipe.

"Dirk! Help! Dirk!"

Sam's voice finally penetrated the welter of rage surging through his brain. Sam in trouble! Dirk staggered to his feet and stood an instant, panting. There was the sound of a scuffle nearby. He moved toward it until he could see two figures weaving in a violent embrace. But which one was Sam? Then he glimpsed the flash of a knife held outstretched by two rigidly struggling arms. Sam had had no knife. With a powerful grip, Dirk seized the hand that held it. He gave

256

the wrist a sharp turn. There was a howl of pain and the knife thudded to the ground.

"Whew, that was a close one," panted Sam. "Hang onto him till I can tie his arms back."

Their prisoner secured, Sam inquired, "Where's the officer?"

"I killed him," said Dirk. He stood bemused, repeating, "I killed him."

And now his jealous hatred was gone, purged away by the violent act he had committed. In its place was a cold emptiness that was yet full of the realization of his deed. He had killed a man because he hated him. Deliberately, with a mad abandoned pleasure, he had done this thing that could never be undone to the end of time. He groaned aloud.

Sam was standing over the spot where Van Wyck lay. "He doesn't act very dead," he remarked.

Dirk sprang to his side. Van Wyck was writhing on the ground while labored rasping breaths were sucked into his lungs. Dirk fell to his knees.

"What can we do to help him?" he asked eagerly.

"He'll come around without help." Sam's tone was disgusted. "What's the matter with you? He's just another Tory."

But Dirk was murmuring, "Thank God! Thank God!"

As Sam had predicted, in a quarter of an hour, Van Wyck was on his feet and the boys had started marching their prisoners toward Peekskill. The journey seemed interminable.

Dirk became aware of a stinging pain along his left arm and of blood dripping slowly from his hand. He guessed that Van Wyck's sword had grazed him. Well, it would have to wait.

In the dimly lighted corridor of the jail, the boys had the first good look at their prisoners. They were wearing the green uniforms of their loyalist military unit.

"Here's a couple of raiders we caught," Sam announced to the jailer.

"Raiders, is it!" demanded Van Wyck in a husky voice. "And what, may I ask, did you 'catch' us raiding?"

"Why, you were on your way to Riverbrink!" Dirk exclaimed.

"We were on the way to our fort," Van Wyck retorted.

"You mean to say," demanded Sam, "that you left your fort, got into boats, landed a mile or so downstream and were marching back to your fort. What in thunder was the object of that?"

"No object," Van Wyck replied. "Just a routine scouting trip."

"Come, come!" cried the jailer impatiently. "That doesn't have to be settled tonight." And he cut off further debate by thrusting the two prisoners into a cell.

As the boys turned to leave, Sam noticed Dirk's blood-spattered clothing. Dirk protested that it was nothing, just a sword scratch.

"Nothing, eh? Let's have a look."

Sam shucked him out of his jerkin and tore the sleeve

from his smock, revealing a long, shallow cut along his forearm. He tore the tail from his own smock and bandaged it.

As they set forth for home, a faint light was streaking the east. They trudged along for some time in silence.

Then Sam said, "We'd ought to have let them get to Riverbrink. The way it is now they can claim they were just a scouting party and be treated like honorable prisoners of war."

Dirk set his teeth. "I'm still glad we didn't let them get there," he said.

Again they walked in silence.

"I can't figure how those Tories knew their way around here," Sam remarked, "unless maybe their guide was one of the men that got away."

" 'Twas Van Wyck, their officer, that knew his way," Dirk explained.

"Van Wyck! Wasn't he the man that refused to help you when you were captured?"

"Yes."

"Too bad you didn't kill him."

Dirk clenched his fists until pain stabbed his wounded arm. "If I had, it would have been murder."

"Nonsense. He's your enemy, isn't he? Would have killed you if he could, wouldn't he? You had every reason."

"The way I felt, it would have been murder," Dirk repeated.

His mind gave him back that moment when he thought he had slain Van Wyck. It was like a dank draft out of a pit into which he had nearly fallen. Suppose now he were walking home with the knowledge that he had killed the man Ellen Stone wanted to marry!

He drew a long, quiet breath. "I thank God I didn't."

Sam shook his head. "You beat me," he declared. "You certain do beat me."

19

In the Riverbrink kitchen next morning the air was heavy with the odor of spices and vinegar. All the womenfolk were making pickles. Mrs. Higgins and Hannah measured sweet with sour into stone crocks. Ellen and Christina were peeling pears.

Ellen felt serenely content. It was pleasant here with the September sun falling through the small-paned windows. She savored fully the joy of being surrounded by friends, of making herself truly useful, and most of all, of feeling secure. This she hugged about her like a cozy blanket. She was safe.

Thus fortified, she could even dare think back upon her dream of the night before when once again she was alone at Stonehaven, running from some pursuer — running, running. These nightmares were the only traces now of all the mental tortures she had suffered. And these were growing infrequent.

But with last night's dream there was mingled a touch of reality. She had awakened abruptly, as always, and lain trembling. But she felt her dream had not reached its climax, that something external had roused her. A gun shot? She tossed for hours. Suppose it was not safe even at Riverbrink! Suppose that raiders might storm into the house, up the stairs, seize her. The thought was almost insupportable.

Shortly after dawn, there were footsteps downstairs and the mutter of conversation. Ellen recognized Dirk's voice, its slow, placid tones reassuring as always. At once she fell into a heavy sleep.

This morning Sam and Dirk had lain abed. This was not unusual, especially for Sam. Mr. Higgins was doing the chores. It was a day like any other, Ellen told herself, and nothing had happened the night before.

Suddenly Hannah, who was standing near a window, exclaimed, "A man on horseback is coming up the drive! It's — yes, it's Colonel Van Cortlandt."

A great flutter ensued.

"Where's Dirk? Wake him up." That was everyone's first thought.

But then it was evident that Dirk needed time to dress. Someone else must let the colonel in. All eyes turned to Ellen.

"Oh, no!" she cried. "It isn't fitting for me to go. I'm not the mistress here any more."

But Christina slipped off Ellen's apron. "Yes, it is fitting," she insisted. "The colonel is your kinsman. It is you who should receive him."

While Ellen washed her hands, Christina scurried upstairs for a fresh white kerchief which she arranged around Ellen's neck. A moment later Ellen found herself walking dazedly through the front hallway, smoothing down her blue linsey woolsey dress. At the door she paused and drew herself up. Something of her old proud manner came back to her as she admitted the colonel. He gazed upon her in pleased surprise, swept off his hat, and bowed deeply.

"A distinct honor, madam!" he exclaimed. "I am glad to see you so well."

Ellen led him to the parlor where they took chairs.

"Permit me to express my deep sympathy, madam, at your father's passing," said the colonel. "Although we held opposite political views, I always respected Roderick Stone as a man of courage and integrity."

Van Cortlandt spoke with a sincerity that Ellen could not but believe. She felt the tears spring to her eyes.

"I have heard, too, something of what you endured afterward alone," continued the colonel, "of the courage and resourcefulness you displayed. Believe me, madam, it made me proud to call you my kinswoman."

Ellen glowed with pleasure at this praise. "You are kind to say that, Colonel," she replied. "I must confess, though, that my own resources were not sufficient. If Dirk hadn't brought me out, I should have died there."

Van Cortlandt smiled. "A man in a thousand!" he exclaimed. "Has he told you that he has been commissioned a lieutenant of the militia? By the way, where is Lieutenant Hollenbeck this morning?"

"I think he will be down shortly. Ah, here he is now."

Dirk paused an instant in the doorway, bowed in greeting to Ellen, and then strode across the floor toward the colonel.

"This is a great honor, sir," he said.

Van Cortlandt arose and the two men shook hands. Ellen, looking on at this meeting, saw in Dirk's manner the dignity and simplicity of a true gentleman. It seemed only fitting that the colonel should treat him as an equal.

She noticed now that Dirk carried his left arm stiffly. Under his sleeve was the bulk of a bandage. Then something had actually happened last night; it had not all been a dream.

Ellen took her leave, guessing that the colonel's business was with Dirk. She went back to the kitchen and quietly resumed her work. A few moments later, Dirk looked in.

"Ellen, can you come back a moment?" he asked. "The colonel's errand concerns you."

He conducted her back to the parlor where Van Cortlandt explained the situation.

"You see, madam, last night there was a little skirmish on the King's Ferry Road not far from here."

"And Dirk was wounded," Ellen put in impulsively.

"Indeed? I had not noticed," said the colonel. "Ah, yes, your left arm."

"It is only a scratch," Dirk muttered in embarrassment.

"A scratch, eh? Then it must have been an officer's sword that did it. This makes your present attitude even more astonishing, sir." The colonel turned to Ellen. "Madam, during this skirmish some Tory prisoners were taken, including their commanding officer, Lieutenant Gerit Van Wyck."

Ellen uttered a little gasp and leaned forward.

"Lieutenant Van Wyck has requested that he be paroled here at Riverbrink in the custody of Lieutenant Hollenbeck. Just now I asked Lieutenant Hollenbeck whether he was willing to take this enemy into his household. He says it is to be as you wish."

"You mean Gerit would live here?"

"For a limited time until an exchange of prisoners is effected. Frankly, madam, I had little thought that Lieutenant Hollenbeck would agree to the proposal but it was my duty to make it. He favors it because he thinks it will please you. Is that the case, madam?"

"Of course I would very much like to see Gerit but — "

A long pause followed while Ellen felt a blush suffuse her face. Her thoughts were in a turmoil. If she said yes, Gerit would come and Dirk would soon see that they were not betrothed as she had claimed. Yet, pretending this bond with Gerit, how could she say no? Aside from this whole problem, she would truly like to see Gerit again to find out once and for all what was her real feeling for him.

"But what, Ellen?" Dirk prompted gently.

She seized upon a handy pretext. "Gerit is a British officer and for all you know, I may still be a loyalist. Aren't you afraid we will plot against your cause?"

"Not at all, madam," said the colonel. "Van Wyck will be under oath as an officer and a gentleman. And as for you, madam, you inherit no taint of dishonor from either the Van Cortlandts or the Stones. No, this arrangement is somewhat irregular in that the Riverbrink property abuts directly upon an enemy fortress but I would go bond that there is no danger of secret dealings."

"Do you want him to come, Ellen?" asked Dirk and his blue eyes were intent upon her face.

"Why, yes, of course, I — " she began.

"Then that is settled," said Dirk.

The colonel rose. "I shall notify headquarters," he said.

When he had made his farewell to Ellen, Dirk accompanied him out. She could hear Van Cortlandt's voice in the hallway.

"May I say, sir, that seldom have I seen such a magnanimous spirit as you are displaying?"

"No, Colonel, that's not the way it is," came Dirk's voice. "This is something I have to do — for myself as much as for Ellen."

Their further conversation was cut off by the closing of the outside door.

Ellen sat motionless. She should have been delighted at the prospect of seeing Gerit, but instead she found her mind puzzling upon Dirk's motives in allowing him to come. What did it indicate about his feeling toward her? She had always thought that Dirk was more than a little in love with her. In fact, why else had she pretended betrothal to Gerit except to keep Dirk at his distance? Yet here was Dirk allowing his successful rival free access to her company. It could mean only one thing, that Dirk did not care for her. She found the possibility most disturbing.

And now she remembered a conversation she had held with Christina not long before. She had asked Christina why Hannah Higgins always treated her so coolly. And Christina had replied that it was a touch of jealousy.

"Of course she has no right to feel so," Christina had added.

Ellen had taken this to mean that Dirk had never given Hannah any reason to feel a claim to him. But perhaps she had meant instead that Hannah should have been confident she had no rival in Ellen. Well, what did it matter, she asked herself. Surely she had never intended to marry Dirk Hollenbeck. However, she had assumed that he would always be available and very much at her service. A world without Dirk anywhere in it suddenly looked very bleak. But she would have Gerit. She must concentrate on that.

He arrived at Riverbrink that afternoon escorted by a Continental soldier, who delivered him into Dirk's hands. From the front porch she watched them mounting the steps. Gerit was as handsome as she had remembered, with the sleek, alert look of a highly bred dog. His green uniform coat was perfectly tailored and brightly colored. This in itself was something Ellen had not seen in months. Everyone's clothes, including her own, were drab and rusty. She had forgotten there were any new things in the world.

Dirk walked at his side looking rather uncomfortable. An unknowing observer would have picked the wrong man for prisoner, as Dirk had no weapon while Van Wyck still carried his sword swinging within inches of Dirk's wounded arm.

At sight of Ellen, Gerit swept off his green cocked hat and sprang up the steps. She extended her hand, painfully conscious that it was work-scarred and calloused. The pear juice had added a final dark stain. It was far from being the hand of a lady any more. Gerit stooped over it. She could see his shocked start. He looked up at her sun-darkened face.

"My dear girl, what have they done to you?" he asked. The implication was unmistakable. "They" could be only rebels.

At this, her shame gave way to indignation. "Oh, Gerit, you don't understand at all," she protested. "My hands may not look as well but they are far more useful and that is what matters."

He stood staring at her, completely incredulous.

"Do you want to go to your room?" asked Dirk gruffly and led him away.

At supper that night it was arranged that Ellen and Gerit should be seated alone in the dining room while the rest of the household ate in the kitchen. At her own insistence, Ellen carried in the food. The first time she brought a dish from the kitchen, Gerit leaped to his feet.

"Where are the servants who should be attending us?" he demanded. "This is an outrage!"

"There are no servants in this house," said Ellen. "There are only my friends."

"What nonsense is this? Do you mean to tell me you are no longer mistress in your own house?"

"Need I remind you, Gerit, that I am the daughter of an avowed Tory, who has very kindly been given refuge in a household of — of American patriots?"

For an instant Gerit looked puzzled. Then, with a wink and lowered voice, he said, "I see. You mean that circumstances have forced you to accept this situation."

Ellen found no words to answer. Why, they were worlds apart! She did not know where to begin to tell him what she meant.

"Remember that song we used to sing, Gerit?" she said at length. " 'The World Turned Upside Down.' "

"Yes, of course. It is still popular in New York."

"I have thought of that song often lately. But, do you know, I believe it is wrong. I think the world is being turned right side up instead."

Gerit leaned across the table, his eyes dark with horror. "Great heavens, Ellen, that is pure rebel doctrine if I ever heard it! They must have been filling you full of this nonsense. It is fortunate that I have come to set you straight."

Ellen flushed with annoyance and began an angry retort but checked herself. She had changed and Gerit could never understand why. Of what use to argue?

"Let's eat our omelet before it falls," she suggested.

After supper, the two went out to stroll on the bluff be-

269

fore the house. Twilight was falling and there was a cool breeze off the river. Gerit adjusted Ellen's cloak about her shoulders.

"Now that we cannot be overheard, I'll tell you," he said in a low tone. "Last night when we were captured, we were on our way here to rescue you."

Ellen drew back in astonishment. "But — but — how did you know I was here?"

"One of our guides told me, a man named Pike. He used to be your father's overseer."

"You were going to attack Riverbrink, raid it?"

"Only to rescue you, my dearest. Would you have come away with me? Will you come — and marry me?"

Gerit bent his head close to Ellen's. His arm pressed her side. But she felt no tremor of response. She could only think that after all she had suffered from raids, it was shockingly ironic to find Gerit taking part in them, and the more so that he had thought thereby to rescue her.

But he was still urging. "Come to New York with me, Ellen. It's gay in the city. All the gentry we used to know are there. They have balls and theatricals every night."

Still she made no answer. This gaiety ought to sound tempting; she liked to dance. But somehow the whole picture of a life in New York with Gerit struck her as sterile and purposeless — dancing while you waited the war out, twirling your fan, making small talk. And after the war? It would depend upon who won. At best it would be a tiresome idleness. At worst? She tried to imagine a life of poverty with Gerit, but failed.

With Dirk it would be different. They would not be dependent upon anything outside of themselves to make their life together a success. Working together, they could create a home and happiness out of nothing. She checked these thoughts sharply. It seemed Dirk did not want to make a home with her.

"How could you get me to New York?" she asked as they resumed their stroll.

"Easily. After I get exchanged, of course. We can arrange a method now by which we could come here and signal you. Then you would come down and let us in."

"Gerit Van Wyck!" Ellen halted abruptly and drew her arm out of his grasp. "You have given your word of honor that you would not take advantage of this release — "

"Hush, Ellen!" Gerit tried to take her arm but she drew back. "I promised not to try to escape and that I have not done. Besides, a gentleman's word of honor can be truly given only to his equal, whereas the rebels who demanded it of me were poor farmers, in no sense gentlemen or even soldiers."

"In short, the oath you gave was worthless." Ellen spat out the accusation. "I had always thought an oath had value only according to the integrity of the man who gave it. Now it seems it depends instead on the person who receives it. That puts the Colonials at a great disadvantage. Since they consider all men to be equal, they must always have to stand by their word."

"Very well, Ellen. If you insist on quibbling over the propriety of our arranging a raid, I'll have to think of some other means. I have it! We can marry while I am here. Then the rebels will probably let me take you along when I am exchanged. No doubt they'd be willing to stretch a point in order to get rid of you."

"To get rid of me! You think they want to?"

"Of course. No matter what nonsense they may tell themselves about confiscation of loyalist property, it must be embarrassing to have the rightful owner in residence. Why else do you think they allowed me to come here if it wasn't to take you away?"

"But — but Dirk went down to Stonehaven and brought me back. If he didn't want me here, why did he do that?"

"Your homespun hero, my dear, has a strong sense of duty."

This was so true that Ellen was brought up short in the face of it. So that was the answer, Dirk's sense of duty. That could account for everything he had done. But this was un-endurable — that he, that all of them had not truly wanted her here. She struggled against the realization.

"But they were all so wholeheartedly kind. They never made me feel like an enemy."

"Oh, they have been clever," Gerit agreed. "The next best thing to getting rid of you was to make you a thorough-going rebel and that they have very nearly done. You've been talking like a damned rebel all evening. It's another reason I must get you away — before you're entirely corrupted. Come, Ellen, will you go with me?"

Ellen's eyes dwelt a moment on Gerit's figure outlined against the darkening sky, then swung out across the river.

"I don't know. Perhaps. I must think about it. Please take me indoors now."

20

EARLY THE NEXT MORNING DIRK AND SAM SET TO WORK IN the cider mill, down by the shore. They were washing and adjusting the wooden machinery that would crush the apples.

Dirk's mind was not half on his work. It carried too vivid a picture of Ellen as she had walked the bluff the night before, on Van Wyck's arm. Knowing he had only himself to thank for that picture added to his torture. And yet, his conscience would never have felt right if he hadn't done it. This chance to make up to Ellen for so nearly killing her betrothed seemed to have been sent him by Providence. He just had to take it.

But he did wish the reunited couple would stay indoors and not parade their happiness around outside where he couldn't help seeing it. He gave an impatient yank on a wooden bolt, which promptly fell to the ground and split in two.

"Rats!" he growled, kicking it into a corner.

Sam's astonishment showed how unusual this conduct was for Dirk.

Suddenly Peter bounced in at the door. "Fort's on fire!" he squealed.

Behind him Christina repeated the message. "It truly seems to be. Come and look."

Sam and Dirk bolted out of the door and up over the hill. From here they could see in the sky a black billow of smoke shot through with red flames.

"Must be the blockhouse," panted Sam.

The boys ran across lots toward the fort until they came up with a group of American scouts standing beside their horses, watching the fire. Several of the men knew Sam, including their officer, Major Waldbridge. They told the boys that the enemy was abandoning the fort, that several boatloads had already put off down the river.

"Place'll be deserted by nightfall," added the major.

Sam leaped into the air with a wild whoop of glee. Dirk grinned.

"Easiest victory we ever won," boasted one of the men. "Didn't fire a shot."

"Why did they leave the fort, sir?" Sam asked the major.

"Well, it just wasn't worth what it cost them to hold it, a thousand men in deserters and prisoners — for nothing."

"Do you think they'll ever come back here, sir?" Dirk asked. "It means a lot to us folks that live so near the Point."

The major shook his head. "I doubt if they ever do. Your families can live in safety from now on. The enemy will never have a better chance to take the Highlands than they

275

had this past summer. If they couldn't do it then, they never can. And they know it."

The boys soon hurried home to tell their families the news. In the kitchen at Riverbrink there was wild rejoicing. The women hugged each other and laughed and cried. Peter darted about squealing with all his might until he collided with an andiron and the squeals changed to howls. Ellen looked into the kitchen to find out the cause of the excitement. When they told her, she smiled and expressed pleasure but soon went out again.

Work was put aside and everybody went to the garden at the back of the house where they could watch the fire and talk. The Higginses began making plans to go back to their own house although the Hollenbecks urged them to stay all winter.

"You come home with us, Tina," Sam said banteringly, yet in earnest. "Just a simple ceremony and you'll make the most beautiful Higgins that ever stepped in shoes."

"Oh, Sam, hush your nonsense!" exclaimed Christina, but a telltale rush of color swept her face.

By noontime the fire had died down to a lazy column of smoke. They all trooped back to the kitchen, suddenly conscious of hunger. What followed was more of a raid on the larder than a routine meal — cold chicken, pitchers of milk, cheese, some apple tarts, bread and butter, cider. All were set out on the table and everyone grabbed.

With a tart in each hand, Sam started for the fort. "Soon

as the enemy's out, we'll go in. Come on, Dirk," he called.

"Not me. I've been in there," said Dirk grimly.

The women decided to walk over to the Higgins farm and prepare to move back. Mr. Higgins began by warning them not to act too hastily and ended by offering to take a load of goods back for them in the oxcart. As everyone prepared to depart, it occurred to Christina to ask who was going to stay on the place.

"I will," said Dirk. "Got to carve a new bolt for the cider mill."

So by midafternoon all was quiet on the manor. Dirk was in the carpenter shop, a small room at one side of the carriage house. From his place at the workbench he could look out over the garden behind the great house. At this late season it was just a tangle of yellowing vines. He could hear Peter in the adjoining carriage house playing around an old farm cart and humming softly to himself.

Dirk began sorting over pieces of wood to find the most suitable one for his bolt. He heard footsteps scamper across the floor and looked out of the window to see Peter running toward the garden where Ellen and Van Wyck were strolling along the path. Dirk hurried to the door and called Peter back. Those two would not want a small boy around. Peter came into the shop now and squatted down to play in a pile of shavings. Dirk took his work to another bench away from the window.

They were both surprised when there was a light step at

the door and they turned to see Ellen Stone standing before them. She looked around timidly as if she was not quite sure of her welcome. Peter left her in no doubt of that as he sprang up with a shout and flung himself against the skirt of her red dress.

"See what I'm doing, Ellen," he demanded. "Look, Ellen. Look!"

And running back to the shavings, he began fitting a curl over each stubby finger. Ellen stooped to admire the effect and then turned to Dirk.

"I saw you were alone here," she began, "and, well, there's something I want to ask you."

Dirk could only look at her with his heart pounding violently.

She swallowed. "You see, Gerit wants me to go to New York — to go with him when he leaves here, and I don't know. Perhaps it would be best. I wondered if — " Her voice tapered off into silence.

"What do you want me to do, Ellen?" Dirk was surprised at the calmness of his tone over the tumult of emotion within.

"I wondered what you would think, whether you think it would be best — for everybody — if I should go." Again her voice stopped as if she had run out of breath.

"Why, Ellen, it's not for me to say. You must do as you wish. Of course, I — we would miss you."

"Then, I wonder if you would want to ask Colonel Van Cortlandt, or whoever is the proper authority, whether Gerit could take me with him when he is exchanged, whether it would be allowed if — if Gerit and I were married."

Well, there it was, and he must face it. Her eyes were leveled upon him as if she expected to find her answer in his face. He took a desperate grip on the piece of wood in his hands and even managed a faint smile.

"Of course, Ellen, I'll ask him."

She lowered her eyes and turned toward the door. "Well, then — thank you," she murmured vaguely. "Good-by."

Peter stood up in the midst of his pile of shavings and looked from one to the other. Their words meant nothing to him, but he sensed the emotional tension and was troubled by it.

"Is Ellen going away?" he demanded. "Don't let her go, Dirk. Stop her."

As Dirk made no move, Peter ran forward, intercepting Ellen at the door. "Don't go away, Ellen," he cried, tugging at her skirt.

With a choked exclamation, she stooped down and kissed the little boy. Then she was gone.

Peter rubbed his cheek. "Wet," he said. "Her face was wet."

Dirk gazed at the child abstractedly. A faint light was dawning across his black world. Her faltering tone, her subdued manner, and now her tears — were they to be expected in a woman making the arrangements to go away with the man she loved?

"Ellen!"

He plunged across the room and out of the door. She was already returning.

"I forgot to tell you a thing you ought to know," she said, not looking at him. "The man Pike is not to be trusted. He has been guiding parties of — of Tory raiders."

Dirk paid no heed to her words. He propelled her by the shoulders back into the workshop and seated her on a bench. Peter promptly scrambled into her lap.

"Look here, Ellen," said Dirk, "we mustn't lose you through some foolish misunderstanding."

She tried to smile but tears welled from her eyes. Dirk dropped to one knee before her, studying her face.

"Ellen, you couldn't have thought for a minute that *I* wanted you to go. Why, you know how I feel about you, have felt all these years, hopeless though it was."

Ellen put out a hand and rested it on Dirk's shoulder. "I thought I did, but when you seemed so eager to get Gerit here, I decided you must want to be rid of me."

"Why, Ellen, I was only doing what I thought you wanted. You told me yourself you were promised to Van Wyck. After all, it would be only natural and fitting, he being a gentleman, while I — "

"Don't let me hear the word gentleman!" Ellen tossed her head. "You're ten times the gentleman he is, Dirk. But I'm glad you brought him here again. Otherwise I would never have been so sure I didn't want him. Dirk, would you ask the colonel if he could have him quartered somewhere else?"

"*That* I will gladly ask him."

Peter squirmed around until he could look into Ellen's face. "Are you going to stay here?" he demanded.

"If you're sure you want me," she said with a smile.

"She's going to stay forever," Dirk exulted.

Ellen leaned toward him, her dark eyes glowing with happiness. He clasped her in a hungry embrace and their lips met over the little boy's head.

"Let me out!" piped a shrill voice. "It's too crowded here."

Peter scrambled to the floor and resumed his play.

"Look, Dirk! Look, Ellen!" he cried, with a shaving balanced over each ear.

But he could not attract their attention.